Hawaiian Rebellions

BOOK 3 OF THE *JOHN TANA* TRILOGY

A Novel

Bill Fernandez

This is a work of fiction and the product of the author's imagination except for actual events involving these historical figures: King David Kalakaua, Queen Liliuokalani, Princess Kaiulani, Dr. William Hildebrand, Walter Murray Gibson, British Commissioner Wodehouse, William Seward, Claus Spreckles, Robert William Wilcox, Robert Louis Stevenson

Front Cover: Iolani Palace, 1890s.

The quotation in Chapter 44, "…to die, to sleep, perchance to dream…" is from *Hamlet* by William Shakespeare.

ISBN 099903264
ISBN 9780999032664
LOC
Makani Kai Media Publisher
Printed in the United States of America, 2018

www.kauaibillfernandez.com fcb: Bill Fernandez Hawaiian Author
An Approved Kauai Made Product

Dedication

—

I lovingly dedicate this book to

my wife,

Judith Fernandez

Acknowledgment

—

The Hawaiian ethic of family, *ohana*, means no one accomplishes alone. We are who we are today because of who came before us and who are with us along our path of life. I particularly want to say *mahalo,* thank you, to my teachers, especially those at Kamehameha Schools who turned this barefoot boy into a serious student. Vernon Trimble, my sophomore class advisor, stands out in my memories as a strong influence on me urging me to attend college.

My editor and friend, Bill Bernhardt, taught me about commas and tries to mold me into a good writer.

Many others have helped me in many ways, encouraging me to continue writing. Mahalo to the Kauai Historical Society, Kauai Museum, and Kauai libraries for honoring me by including my books in their publication sales and collections and inviting me to give book talks. Bill Buley of *the Garden Island Newspaper* and his wife, Marianne, encourage me in many ways. Several readers who enjoyed *John Tana, An Adventure Novel of Old Hawaii,* and *Gods, Ghosts, and Kahuna on Kauai,* Book Two of the trilogy, urged me to continue the story about my Hawaiian hero, John Tana, as he struggles to adapt to Western business interests and religion consuming the native people of the islands. Thank you to Hanapepe Bookstore for invaluable advice, carrying my books, and inviting me to do book signings.

Without the encouragement, support and hard work of editing, design, photography, and sketches, publication, and promotion of my writings and book talks by my loving and devoted wife, Judith, I could not have written my books. All the credit for what I have written goes to her.

Reviews of Author Bill Fernandez

Kirkus Reviews:

John Tana: An Adventure Novel of Old Hawaii
(Book One of the *John Tana* novel trilogy)

"Set in **19th-century Hawaii**,…<u>historical novel</u> stars a **handsome young hero**… the story chronicles a **hatefully racist time and place**…Fernandez (*Cult of Ku, a Hawaiian Murder Mystery…*) a **native Hawaiian**, is an **authentic voice** for John and the Pacific archipelago's turbulent history. **Plot twists** come thick and fast…the seductive undercurrent of John's **love** for Leinani…**vivid and intriguing details of Hawaiian daily life in the 19th century ring true**…the striking ending is not tidy, a plus…For the setting and era alone, this **ripping adventure yarn**…" (Emphasis added.)

—

Gods, Ghosts and Kahuna on Kauai
(Book Two of *John Tana* trilogy)

"…**resourceful Hawaiian John Tana is back**…Hawaii is at a **political tipping point**…is this the beginning of the end for the Kingdom of Hawaii…**racial tensions…gods and superstition**…a festering wound on the marriage…As a Hawaiian, **he wants the respect that he feels he deserves**…introduces readers to **Hawaiian history and culture including the mysteries and terrors of the…**"old religion"…sketches by **Judith Fernandez**…effectively **primitive charm** to the story and bring to mind Antoine de Saint-Exupéry's sketches for *The Little Prince.*" (Emphasis added.)

Cult of Ku, A Hawaiian Murder Mystery

(A *Grant Kingsley* novel)

"Hawaiian history, folklore, and labor struggles…a 1920-set mystery packed with violence and murder…Grant Kingsley…returns to his home in Honolulu…only to find that his **status in his wealthy family…is in question**… **A deathbed confession by his mother**…grandmother…wants to **disinherit** him…found dead…charges Grant with the murder…Four more…The **depth** of the author's **historical knowledge** is evident…many **fascinating insights** into the era…explores **cultural conflicts** in Hawaii…" (Emphasis added.)

—

Crime & Punishment in Hawaii

(A *Grant Kingsley* novel)

"**An attorney finds trouble** in paradise…**novel set in Hawaii**…**skin diving** with his friend…come under fire. Keoki is killed, and Kingsley is left with an enemy who vows to **harm his family**…local news …**a different case**…**the Massie Affair**…**racial unrest**…story combines the factual and the fictional and seasons them with…**gunfire and Hawaiian history**…a **vivid** picture of discord…" (Emphasis added.)

MEMOIRS

Kauai Kids in Peace and WW Two

"1930s and 1940s **Hawaii**...**childhood**...Kauai...isolated... **multiracial**... poor families share...large Japanese population ...gives **marine life glorious** coverage...does his best to avoid **sharks**...**Part II: War**...**Pearl Harbor and its after-math**...overt **racism**...engaging **tales of innocence and worldly wisdom**... father opens the **Roxy Theater**..." (Emphasis added.)

—

Hawaii in War and Peace

"...**military school in Honolulu**...**1944**...**war**...once the war was over, **Hawaii remained at unrest**...**worker's strike, tsunami**...**toured the mainland** U.S. with his family and found a **nation with unbridled prejudices**...**riveting** account of...a world in disarray...the **grandest impression is the more personal side**...mistake him for a **Mexican**, mistreating him...which of the segregated restrooms he could use...**Engrossing** and identifiable." (Emphasis added.)

Other Reviews

Other Works by
Bill Fernandez

Non-Fiction Memoirs
Rainbows Over Kapaa
Kauai Kids in Peace and WW Two
Hawaii in War and Peace

Fiction
The Grant Kingsley Series:
Cult of Ku, A Hawaiian Murder Mystery
Crime & Punishment in Hawaii

John Tana Trilogy
John Tana, An Adventure Novel of Old Hawaii
Gods, Ghosts and Kahuna on Kauai
Hawaiian Rebellions

Glossary

—

alii	Chief, ruler, royal	**aikane**	Friend
aina	Land	**ana ana**	Death dealer
ahupuaa	Land from mountains to sea	**amakua**	Personal god
aue	Gosh, wow!	**awa**	Potion
da kine	Many meanings	**ha**	Breath
haole	Caucasian	**heiau**	Religious temple
hele mai	Go	**huakai po**	Night Marchers
hui	Organization, group	**kahuna**	Priest, expert
kanaka	Man	**kapa**	Barkcloth
ki'i pepe	Voodoo doll	**kokua**	Helper
kuuipo	My beloved sweetheart	**leiomano**	Shark tooth weapon
limu	Seaweed	**loi**	Taro field
lua	Military arts	**mai pake**	Leprosy
mano	Shark	**makaainana**	Commoner

me ke aloha pumehana		May you be surrounded by love	
ohana	Family	**pake**	Chinese
pilikia	Trouble	**uhane**	Ghost, spirit

(Note: Diacritical marks in Hawaiian are omitted for ease of reading.)

Prologue

THE JOHN TANA novel trilogy sweeps the reader along the turbulent history of the remote Pacific Hawaiian Kingdom as it emerges from its centuries of isolation in the 19th century. The impact of the Western world on the communal society of native Hawaiians is told through the experiences of a commoner native Hawaiian, John Tana. The story begins on the island of Maui when the seventeen-year-old orphan is thrown off his farmland. John sets out on a long struggle trying to stay alive and make his way in the ashes of the destruction of his culture.

It was 1778 before the Western world learned of the existence of these islands when Captain James Cook stumbled upon them. He found a well-organized society free of Western diseases. The isolation of the islands ended because they stood in the path of expansion of Western capitalism inspired by the American Doctrine of Manifest Destiny. Whalers, missionaries, disease, and the rapacious sugar industry crushed the sharing agricultural and fishing lifestyle of the native people who believed land was a living thing. Ownership of it was a foreign concept. John tries to learn new skills and adapt but sees his native Hawaiian people weakened by Western disease flounder as they lose their communal way of living and religious beliefs. Western private property ownership was destroying their ability to survive on the land and sea. This clash of cultures continues to impact Hawaiians in modern times.

John Tana, An Adventure Novel of Old Hawaii
Book One

The trilogy begins in 1867 when sugar baron Robert Grant kicks John Tana off his inherited farmland on the island of Maui. Unbeknownst to John, Western business interests had begun to seize control of communal lands to establish sugar plantations. He sails his canoe to the town of Lahaina seeking family and encounters whaling ships and sailors who torment him. He finds Aunt Malia and two cousins: David, a young man succumbing to liquor and women, and Leinani, a beautiful, young fourteen-year-old. John learns that liquor and a Christian-forbidden romance with Leinani will lead to trouble. He befriends Ah Sam, a Chinese merchant and former laborer for a plantation, who is threatened when he opens a competitive business. John interrupts an attempted shanghai and rescues kidnapped Leinani. When he learns the sugar baron hired a killer (Gonzales) to find him, John escapes in his canoe with family and friends for the island of Oahu.

Life on Oahu and in the new city Honolulu is more complicated. He works in taro fields and Ah Sam opens a restaurant. But David continues his risky life in bars where he meets new friends who attack the family. Leinani is sent to a private girl's school for safety, and John joins a secret martial arts (*lua*) group in the mountains. A future king (Kalakaua) invites him to join the militia. When a Chinese man is accused of killing his white employer, the city erupts into racial violence. John finds him a Hawaiian lawyer (Joshua). Leinani introduces him to an attractive French classmate, Maria, who falls in love with John.

When Leinani's true ancestry is revealed, John realizes his love for her is not forbidden. But before he can act, she is persuaded to marry rich, white, James Kingsley. John is bereft but realizes Aunt Malia is right: "A Hawaiian man has nothing to offer a woman but poverty, while a rich white man can give her and a future family a comfortable life". John knows he must escape in his canoe once again when he faces a rape claim and learns that the killer Gonzales has found him. He sails to the island of Kauai to find a peaceful life. Leinani remains in Honolulu.

Gods, Ghosts and Kahuna on Kauai
(Book Two)

Christian missionaries help John and his friends settle in on the north shore of Kauai. The sugar plantations are expanding, and missionaries impose strict rules. John finds work providing security for a plantation, marries Mahealani, and seeks acceptance by the Western business world.

Kauai is a mysterious island of swirling clouds, plunging waterfalls, and kahuna (priests) practicing black magic. Strange happenings occur: an octopus attempts to drown a relative, mysterious illnesses strike. His wife's stubborn reliance on the old religion threatens John's marriage because he accepts Christianity, she does not. A shark encounter shakes his beliefs.

Meanwhile, he begins to worry that Western businessmen will overthrow the monarchy. Joe Still, newly arrived from Europe, teaches him about the American Doctrine of Manifest Destiny and the potential seizure of the Hawaiian Kingdom by America. He learns about the disease of leprosy which is disrupting the lives of Hawaiians. Despite the turmoil, John and Mahealani settle into a comfortable life on a farm with their two young children.

Hawaiian Rebellions
(Book Three)

In the final novel of the *John Tana* trilogy, John and other native Hawaiians realize they must resist the increasing power of the colonizers who seek to limit the power of the monarchs in the late 19th Century. The feared disease, leprosy, strikes on Kauai. Many Hawaiians are forced into isolation on the remote peninsula of Molokai Island. Resistance builds when some Hawaiians seek their own refuge on the north shore of Kauai and fight for their lives. Political intrigue by Western businessmen leads to the eventual overthrow of Queen Liliuokalani and the Hawaiian Kingdom just as Joe Still predicted. But many Hawaiians refuse to accept it.

Iolani Palace, Honolulu

The trilogy of *John Tana* is destined to become classic literature depicting the turbulent events in the 19th century clash of cultures in the Hawaiian Kingdom. The author, half-Hawaiian, weaves the history into a dramatic story filled with strong characters and the tropical beauty of the mountains and ocean. There are many examples in literature of colonization of indigenous cultures by the West; this one stands out for the depth of the author's research, beautiful story-telling, and personal experiences woven into the story of how the indigenous, communal-living Hawaiians were swept aside by Western commercial interests and religion which still impact Hawaiians to this day.

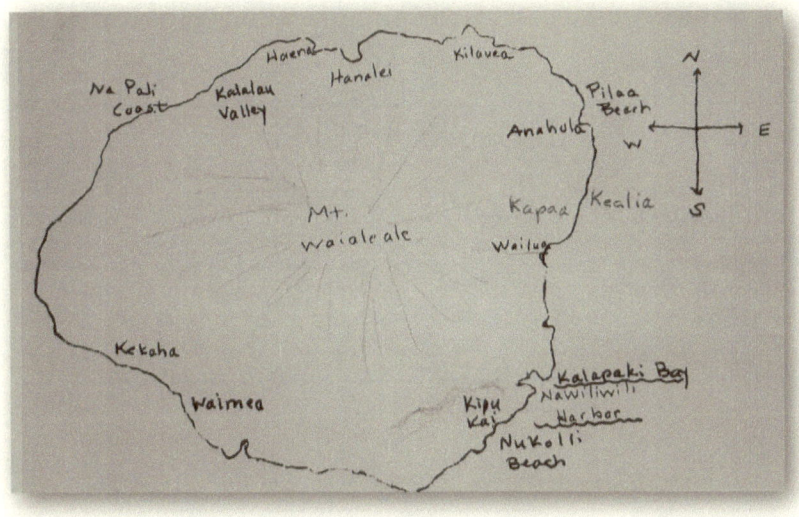

CHAPTER 1

———

John Tana heard his wife's piercing cry. He chucked his horse to a gallop and raced into the family compound. Her scream had aroused other family members. John brought his horse to a rearing halt at the veranda steps. Mahealani sat weeping on an outdoor couch, her hands waving frantically. She kept saying, "Kahuna, kahuna, kahuna."

John dismounted and raced up the stairs, soon joined by his two children and grandmother Anuhai Alapai. "Are you hurt?" he asked, anxiety in his voice.

"Don't you see it?"

The elderly woman followed her daughter's pointing finger.

"Oh my God!"

"Just a doll," John said.

Mahealani recovered herself. "It's not a doll. It's a *ki' i pepe*, a symbol of evil. Our name is on it. Red color, like blood, covers it—"

"And it hangs from the rafters by the neck," Grandmother moaned. "It's a warning from a kahuna. It means death will come to one or all of us."

"Oh, we are in trouble," Mahealani cried. "Call Haku. Have him get a kahuna to fight the *ana*."

"This is nonsense," John interjected. "We have been through this many times. All this black magic stuff is bogus. Someone may be planning to do us harm, but it is not by using mystic arts."

"You don't believe. You have never believed. But think of the children."

"I think of them always. But I know that this shaman, or whoever has made this doll, is trying to get into your head. These devil worshippers use fear to control you. They place doubt in your mind until you sicken and die."

A grumpy Haku Alapai came up the stairs. "You sent for me?"

"Yes, I want a kahuna, now," Mahealani demanded. "I don't," John said.

Haku Alapi paused, scratched his head, thought for some moments, then answered, "Don't know of any. Last one who helped grandma, died. Maybe ask Al Akaka."

"This is pure nonsense," John said.

"Don't know about that," Haku answered. "Didn't you see the stick with the white tapa on top when you rode in?"

"I noticed something, but what of it?"

"That's a *kapu* pole. Used in the temples before a sacrifice to Ku. Didn't you tell us that Hawae cursed you and called on his god Ku to destroy you?"

"Yes. In fact, the kahuna cursed Al too. Maybe we should invite him over as you suggest and help us get to the bottom of what's going on."

By mid-day Akaka arrived and saw the ki'i and kapu pole. "When I heard of what is troubling the family, I came right over. Strange things have been happening over the last few days. You have heard of the Night Marchers?"

"Yes, dead warriors and chiefs who stomp the earth after sunset," John answered.

"You don't mess with *huakai po*," Haku said. "If they see you they drag you with them to hell or wherever they are going."

"So, you know about them."

Mahealani and Anuhai nodded. The children remained silent.

"You recall the temple at Kalihiwai near my home?" Without waiting for an answer Akaka continued, "It was there during the 1824 rebellion that more than a hundred tattooed Kauai chiefs were slaughtered. They had fled to those rocks believing that god Ku would save them. Last night as the moon shone over those stones, I heard the drums, then chanting, followed by the blowing of the conch shell. Feet pounded on the ground. I could hear them pass by my door heading to the temple of Ku. I made my family go to the floor, shift our eyes from whatever could be happening outside.

The sounds passed away. This morning I found at my door this tiki doll that Mahealani calls a ki'i pepe."

"It is the same kind of doll that was hanging on our veranda," John said. "In the past you have not believed in ghosts, kahuna, or evil spirits."

Akaka sighed. "That is true. But just three days ago I received word about Karlov."

"I remember him. Called himself Brudda. He helped me hunt down the wild pig."

"Yes. He is dead, strangled to death. A ki'i pepe was in his pocket."

CHAPTER 2

———

Light along the horizon slowly pushed away the night. At the government roadway John saw the dim outline of a horseman. Anxious, he removed the sling cord from his forehead, retrieved three stones from a bag at his side, and stood with his left foot advanced, ready to fling his missiles.

The rider guided his mount onto the dirt pathway leading into the compound. As he approached, John's tension increased, and he inserted a stone into the sling's pouch. "Who are you?" he challenged.

"Joe Still. Is that you John? It's hard to make you out."

"It is. When did you get here?"

"A week ago, I told you I'd be coming someday. I didn't know exactly when, but then I met this fellow Charles Rogers. He took a fancy to my cooking. With our friendship growing he told me he had an interest in Kilauea Plantation and would be coming here for three months. I got an invitation, a job as a supervisor, plus being a cook for Mr. Rogers. He took care of everything."

"How did you find me?"

"You're well known. I have some bad news for you."

"I've had nothing but unwanted news in the last two days. What's it this time?"

"A man in your office at the plantation has been badly beaten."

"Oh my god, it must be Eleu! I sent him to the mill to do security work while I guarded my family."

"Very interesting. What's going on?"

John explained the dolls, the death of Karlov, and the threat to his life. "Whoever hurt Eleu must have thought it was me."

"You're making this sound like voodoo stuff. But who on this island would want to kill you?"

"I can think of only one person. A kahuna named Haewa. He practiced the dark arts, prayed people to death, made little tiki to puncture or mutilate. An awful old man who I thought was dead."

"It wasn't an old guy who beat up your worker, but two big men."

"Why do you say that?"

"Last night, after dinner, Rogers and I strolled the plantation. I had learned the location of your office and came to visit. We heard crashing sounds. I raised my lantern and saw a big fight going on. One guy hit Eleu on his head and another one wrapped a cord around his neck. Lucky for him that Rogers and I began to yell and charged forward to help. The two men ran away. We let them go and took Eleu to the plantation dispensary."

"Could you tell who they were?"

"Too dark."

"It looks like an attempt at a ritual execution like in ancient times. One man bashes the victim, and another puts a choke cord around his neck."

"So those who attacked Eleu are Hawaiians?"

"Probably. I think there must be a connection between them and Haewa."

"A man you thought to be dead is resurrected and controls Night Marchers and stranglers?"

John sighed. "I have no other explanation for Karlov's death, the attack on Eleu, and rag dolls being passed out as warnings of coming doom. I never told you about the ki'i I found in Haewa's hut and the stillborn birth of my son. It's the same kind of doll. That's why I connect what is happening to Haewa."

"What did you do to this guy?"

"I tried to stop him from using his black magic tricks to hurt my family. It's a long story. But the bottom line is I threatened him, and he cursed me."

"You think him dead, but maybe not. If he's alive do you know where he might be?"

"No. His shack near the mountains is gone. What I don't understand is why two men wanted to kill Eleu?"

"It was dark when Rogers and I walked near your office. Maybe the attackers meant to kill you and made a mistake."

"Yeah, that makes sense. Haewa has no reason to strike down Eleu."

"It means the thugs will come after you again." Still was silent for some moments. "I think you need the protection I can give you and your family."

"I don't want you to get hurt. I can deal with it."

"Nonsense, your team is one man down. You need me. I'm off to work. I'll be back before sunset. I'll check on Eleu for you. Keep a watch out for trouble."

CHAPTER 3

—

John checked his weapons. He set aside his piikoi and chose a baton. Around his waist he wrapped a sling and pushed a knife between his belt and pants. He thought to load his shotgun but set it aside. At night you might not be able to tell friend from foe. He would challenge intruders eyeball to eyeball. Mahealani sat nearby, weaving a mat. "You are preparing for war."

"I'm just making sure the family is protected."

She shook her head. "The ana can strike you from afar. Your weapons are useless against his prayers."

"I have to hear him say death words first before I could be harmed. Besides, it was not a kahuna who attacked Eleu, but real men."

"You do not believe in the power of a priest like Haewa. He can conjure up the Night Marchers and send forth the gods to destroy those who do not believe. I'm going to sleep with my mother tonight. We will have ti leaves covering every opening and entrance to ward off the evil spirits."

John sighed. "You are taking the children with you?"

"Yes."

"It is for the best. Whoever is out there wants to get me and not the rest of the family. Go and I will make sure that Haku is well armed. Moana and I will be on watch while you sleep."

Mahealani's face took on a grim aspect with downturned eyes and lips. "I am not abandoning you. But you do not believe in the old ways to deal with evil spirits. Haku and Anuhai have ancient knowledge and we have read the books on prayers combating the death dealer. We will spend the evening invoking the help of the gods. We do not want an unbeliever to break the spell we are casting. *E aumakua e. E aumakua e...*"

His thoughts immersed in the chant his wife was reciting, he did not hear the loud rapping at the door until a booming voice shouted, "Hey, you deaf Hawaiian, open up."

Startled, John rose from his squat and rushed to the door. Joe Still stood on the veranda. "What took you so long? Some watchman you are. An enemy could sneak up on you and bash your head in and you'd never know it." Still uttered this ominous opinion while his lips wreathed into a smile.

"Sorry old friend, I was listening to my wife, and you know how important that is. What's that silver tube attached to your side?"

With a rasping of metal on metal, Still drew from a scabbard a gleaming sword of highly burnished steel. He waved the three-foot-long weapon in a rhythmic circle, abruptly stopped its movement, raised the hilt to his nose, and ended his salute with a flourish.

John clapped. "Very good. What are you going to do with that thing, split breadfruit?"

"You make fun of this weapon. In the right hands it will do great damage."

"Where did you get it?"

"I told you that in 1870 I fought in the battle of St. Privat. We were ordered to retreat despite destroying the flower of the Prussian Imperial Guard with our rifles. I was protecting the wounded during the withdrawal. Those cursed cuirassiers chose to strike us in the rear. I was sabered by a horseman but managed to shoot him from the saddle. This is the weapon he used."

"You brought this all the way from Alsace?"

"Yes. It is a very effective close combat weapon. I have been practicing with it."

"Don't you want another killing tool? Maybe have a big stick or spear?"

"This will do just fine."

"Stop comparing weapons of war. Haku has roasted pig and fish. Lots of poi. Dinner is ready," Mahealani interrupted.

A three-quarter moon rose from the sea, spreading its light across the water. Thin clouds occasionally drifted by, making it seem like smoke in the sky. John watched the peaceful movement from his guard post on the veranda. Several dozen feet away his family slumbered in Haku's home. On a bed inside his house, he could hear the steady snoring of his Alsatian friend. Despite Moana's revelation that this was the cursed moon of Kanaloa, the night remained peaceful. He did not hear chanting or marching feet.

John's eyes slowly closed. In the stillness drifted a pleasant sound like soft wind sighing through leaves. The music changed to light tremors of water flowing in a stream. John felt hypnotized by the changing sounds. There was nothing shrill, the melodies were very soothing.

Then he heard the crushing of leaves and a stifled cry. Startled awake, John looked toward the sound. In the slight light of the moon riding high in the sky, he saw a woman being pulled into a coco tree.

"Stop!" John yelled, released the club tethered to his side, and charged toward the macabre scene of his wife being garroted.

Before he could get to Mahealani, the haft of a spear struck his head. He fell to his knees and heard chanting:

Oh Uli, mother of the gods;
Bite his throat;
Wrench out his jawbone;
Speed his death by the ana ana;
It is the fire of Ku that destroys him.

Dazed, John felt a cord wrap around his neck. Pulled onto his back, he tried to rise, but the slim rope tightened around his throat, and his attacker dragged him along the ground. He reached his hands to try to ease the strangling, but his enemy drew the binding tighter. Breath no longer escaped his lungs. He gagged, tried to cough, but nothing could break through the constriction that starved him of air.

Death approached. He mourned. He would no longer be able to protect his family. He had no aumakua to turn to. Could the Christian God help?

Sudden noise erupted behind him. A cry shattered the quiet of the night. John felt breath returning as the pressure on his throat vanished. He lay on his back and saw Still thrust his sword into the side of a man.

Another attacker came at his friend with a spear. They fenced for some moments, Still easily parrying his opponent's thrusts. With a loud "hiyah" he moved to the left and swung his sword in an axe-like sweep onto the shaft of his enemy's spear.

The weapon shattered. The attacker stared at the nub of what remained of his weapon, dropped it, and fled.

"Behind you," John croaked, his throat aching and his chest moving like bellows as he sucked in air. He tried to rise but could not as the second assailant attacked Still with a *leiomano*. The shark's teeth shredded Joe's shirt, drawing blood from his side. With a slash of the sword, he sliced into the attacker's arm. As the man tried to move his weapon to his other hand, Joe shifted his parallel to the ground and thrust his blade into the man's chest. The attacker collapsed moaning.

The turmoil drew family members from Haku's house. They rushed to Mahealani who appeared to be all right, her strangling not serious. John stood and stumbled to the assassin.

"Hear me. You're dying, tell me why you attacked."

The man coughed blood. His eyes shifted from side to side. "Haewa our teacher." More blood erupted from the wounded attacker's lips. "He wanted you dead."

CHAPTER 4

———

With the panic of the family calmed and a search of the compound proved that intruders were no longer on the Tana property, Joe Still called for a war council. "The attacker is dead. I didn't think he would survive the sword thrust into the belly. Did you get any more information from him before he died?"

"His name is Honua, the turtle. The other man is Pueo, the owl. They are the only two disciples of Haewa. There are no others who will fulfill his curse," John answered.

"That's important information. At least we know that there is only one man left who might do you harm. Did he tell you where that survivor might be?"

"No. The man was delirious most of the time I tried to speak with him. He did say one thing several times before he slipped away: 'Take me to Kapuna'."

"Where is that?"

"I have no idea, but the way he said it I didn't think it was his home."

"Any way we can find out the location?"

"We can visit with Al Akaka, he knows the north shore."

"Let's go see him. We got to get that last man before he gets you."

At Kalihiwai, with Kaipo and Kunani at his side, Akaka listened to John relate the events of the last several days. He stroked his chin when the word 'kapuna' was mentioned. He said, "I'm not familiar with that place. You sure he wasn't saying kupuna, meaning elder person?"

"He said the word several times and it was not kupuna."

"Maybe we should approach this whole problem from another angle," Still said. "I brought over pieces of the strangling cord. Never saw fiber like this. It doesn't stretch or kink and is thicker than cords I'm used to. Who sells this?"

"What you have is called olona," Akaka answered. "It is one of the only inedible plants the early voyagers brought with them to these islands. It's a tall, reed-like plant that is pounded for its white fiber. These strands are wound together to make the strongest rope. It was used to bind parts of a canoe together and anything else that needed to withstand the power of the sea. Today, it is cheaper to buy rope from the plantation store. No longer is olona pounded and fibers twisted together to make cords."

"Then we are dealing with two men who live in the old ways, making rope and using ancient methods of killing people."

"What you have just said jogs my memory," John interjected. "At the time I was being choked I heard a death prayer. There was never a pause in its reciting. If the ana ana pauses, it has no effect."

"Interesting, but where does it get us?" Still asked.

John brushed the objection aside saying, "What drew Mahealani out of her home was pleasant sounds. Music she had not heard since she was a child in Kau. I found a nose flute after the fight."

"I'm beginning to get the picture," Akaka said. "These men live in the past. The curse of Haewa is really a kapu. And in ancient times the punishment for breaking kapu was death by strangulation. One warrior bashed your head and another one put olona cords around your neck."

"Okay, we are dealing with Hawaiians living in the Stone Age, but how do we find the surviving attacker?"

"Patience my friend," Akaka answered. "Often those killed who breached kapu were taken to the burial place of a chief or kahuna, there to be used as a sacrificial offering to the deceased."

"You're saying those two guys were going to kill me and take me somewhere sacred? Doesn't make sense, I'm too big for them to carry."

"You remember the story of Captain Cook coming to Kauai," Akaka answered. "From his ship he saw many white towers. When he landed in Waimea he asked to inspect them. When he did, he found that at each tower there were human skulls and he was told a great man was buried nearby. Still, you were cut by a leiomano. That's a convenient knife to slice off John's head and take it to a white tower."

"That makes a lot of sense," Still said. "You don't need a whole body to rot at a burial spot. A head would do as a symbol of fulfilling the curse."

"Exactly."

"What you're saying is there's a white tower called Kapuna that these guys would have taken my skull to."

"Maybe, or maybe it's a temple close to the tower," Akaka answered.

"How do we find this white thing, fly like a bird until we spot it?" Still laughed.

"It may not be that difficult. Olona grows in marshy hilly terrain, places like Wainiha, the far end of Hanalei, and a remote area along the shoreline called Pilaa, not far from John's home."

"Yeah, and that place has an old *heiau*," Kaipo said.

"Then let's investigate," Still said.

CHAPTER 5

Akaka, Still, and John rode onto a dirt pathway leading from the main roadway to Pilaa Beach. The terrain was rough and sloped toward the sea. Dense, low bushes bordered the path obscuring the way ahead. To John's left a fast-flowing stream knifed through a ravine, its water churning over dark, round rocks.

After a half-mile of travel, the three men stopped where the ridge they were on took a steep drop to red dirt and then a yellow sand beach. From his vantage point John saw *loi*, a taro field, a white tower with wooden shelves adjacent to it, and, close to the ocean, a shack.

"A rocky beach, the only clear spot to enter the ocean is ahead of us," Akaka observed. "The stream below flows into a channel where the waters move rapidly out to sea. It can create a very dangerous rip tide."

"Tie up the horses, and we'll slide down the trail to investigate," Still said.

When they reached relatively level ground John commented, "Taro field has been worked on. Plants are lush. Is that stalks of olona bordering the hill?"

"Yes, whoever is tending this loi is a good farmer," Akaka said. "Let's check out the tower."

When they arrived at the structure, they saw a rack with four skulls on it. "Guess you would have been number five." Still laughed, slapping John on the shoulder.

"I don't think that's funny. Akaka, do you believe these four heads represent men who Haewa cursed?"

"Possibly, or maybe battle trophies. This could have been a spot for the burial of a chief although I doubt that, most Kauai chiefs were wiped out in the 1824 rebellion."

"Maybe there was a survivor who came here to live in this and died in this place. What was the rebellion about?" Still asked.

"Kauai's king surrendered this island to Kamehameha. After both died, Oahu chiefs took over and were going to divide the land among themselves. Kauai royalty didn't like that, and they revolted but lost. The slaughter was huge. I never heard of any survivors."

"It's getting to be late afternoon," John said. "You two check out the beach and the shack. I thought I saw a structure around the bend. I'll take a look."

"Don't know if we should split up. Safety in numbers," Still objected.

"Go, go, I can take care of myself."

Still shrugged and headed with Akaka to the shore. John went around the ridge searching. He found a hut nestled against the side of a hill and above it a stone mound like a small heiau. He moved briskly to investigate. Something came hurtling from above. It struck the side of his head, dazing him. A brown, nearly-naked body detached from the hill and smashed closed fingers into John's navel.

He had a second to tense his abdomen muscles to blunt the full impact of the lua strike. His opponent put his hands against John shoulders, bent his face, and tried to fasten his teeth on John's larynx.

John twitched the side of his face into his enemy's nose while driving a clenched fist into his abdomen. The attacker stepped back. John followed up with a right cross which his opponent blocked and moved his hands to John's throat, squeezing.

Pain erupted up and down his body, his neck tender from the garroting of the previous night. With a supreme effort John pushed up his forearms between his enemy's arms and slammed his hands onto his opponent's ears. The attacker immediately released the choke hold and moved backward.

Every breath John took caused severe pain. He assumed a defensive stance waiting for Haewa's disciple to make an offensive move. The man feinted with his left hand. John almost threw a right-handed punch but held back when he realized his opponent would make a two-finger strike at his eyes. He danced to the side. The enemy's attack missed his face.

His sudden movement dislodged rocks and John lost his balance and fell. His attacker removed a club from his side and swung downward. John barely avoided the blow. The man kept swinging and scored a glancing hit on a shoulder. The overreaching of the attacker gave John a chance to plant a foot between his enemy's legs and kick. The attacker's arms fell as he reached for his crotch.

John had time to roll, regain his feet, and face his enemy. He decided to reason with him. "Pueo, why are you doing this? Honua is dead. You have nothing to gain by killing me."

"Wrong, I promise Haewa to revenge him." The killer paused. "I no like you. You take haole money. You jail Hawaiians. You traitor to *makaainana*."

"You are wrong. I help our people, give them jobs, feed—"

"Enough, friggin' *kaka*. Prepare to die." Pueo moved forward and swung his club at John's neck.

John blocked the strike with his left arm, pivoted, and brought a stinging blow with his right fist onto his opponent's bicep. The club fell weakly on John's shoulder.

"My arm is numb," Pueo screamed.

John followed his advantage with a crushing left hook to the stomach.

Pueo head-butted then turned and ran for the beach, his right arm limp at his side.

Pausing for some moments to recover his senses, John started in pursuit. He heard Akaka yell, "Hey you, stop!"

Breaking through the sea-side shrubbery, John saw Pueo uncover a small canoe and drag it to a channel. It was the only way to pass through the crescent of fringing reef that circled the shallow bay of Pilaa.

John pushed through the soft sand. Pueo dragged his craft to the sea. Before he could launch it, John leaped at him.

"Hey, we are coming to help," Akaka yelled.

John wouldn't stop his attack. Though stung by Pueo's accusation, the man had killed his friend, Karlov, and harmed his wife. Any humanity or compassion that he might have had evaporated.

The tackle toppled the assassin onto the canoe and his head struck an edge. His flailing foot smashed into John's face and both men fell into a roiling sea. A rip tide swept the shore water and rushed into the ocean. An inert Pueo went with it.

With a supreme effort, John tried to fight the tide and grasp the unconscious man. But he floundered onto his face as the rushing water swept him off his feet and pulled him towards the deep.

He felt someone grasp his foot, stopping momentarily the overpowering tug of the current. He felt a slow drag of his body onto sand. John saw the human chain of Akaka and Still that saved him.

From the shore the three friends watched Pueo's body sweep out to sea. "When you see death occur, you realize that revenge has bitter results and none that are good." Still shook his head. "The desire to kill caused three to die and left a family shattered because of it."

John shrugged. "It's not revenge. Our island is still trapped in the old beliefs. I don't know why or how to escape it."

"It is getting dark. We are not going to solve anything standing here. Let's go home." Akaka said.

CHAPTER 6

—

Robert Grant waved his cigar like a band conductor. "Jones, you are right. Kalakaua is running wild. Spend is all he does. A Versailles-like palace, an elaborate coronation, and now a failed attempt to make Samoa and Fiji part of a Hawaiian empire. It's a wonder that we are not at war with Germany."

Bruce Jones nodded in agreement. "Gentlemen, it's time to put this monarchy to sleep. What do you think about that idea, Cartwright?"

"Humph, I don't believe we want a revolution, at least not yet. The monarchy still has friends among the older generation, but if Prime Minister Gibson keeps talking about 'Hawaii for the Hawaiians' then I guarantee you that the recalcitrants will come over to our way of thinking. Just one more misstep and Kalakaua will be reduced to the status of a puppet."

"Whenever we decide to make our move, the Honolulu Rifles will be ready," Jones said. Then turning to Grant, he asked, "How is the immigration of new foreign laborers progressing? I've been hearing some disturbing reports about the Chinese government's reaction to it."

"I wouldn't put much store in rumors," Grant sneered. "The Chinamen need to be squeezed. They come. They finish their four-year contracts then go into business competing with white merchants. Without families, they undersell legitimate businesses. We will stop our dependency on those people. We have Portuguese workers from Madera, Germans from Bremen, Fijians, and a trickle of Japanese coming in."

"Very good, with this new wave of immigration we are following our usual policy of divide and rule, playing one race against another. But in the short term we have an immediate problem, too many Chinese workers and they are striking."

"Jones, they're a disorganized bunch, just like children, without any real leaders. The crackdowns will come. I've got armed men near various camps ready to act if there is any hint of labor trouble."

"Capitol," Cartwright said. "With the Honolulu Rifles poised for action and your strikebreakers ready to end labor strife, the new year could be a significant one for the sugar industry."

"You invested in that Kilauea sugar plantation?" Jones asked. "Have you gained control of it?"

"Not yet," Grant answered. "The two Scots and Brit who have the biggest interest don't like Americans. It's been an uphill push, but everyone needs money to operate and my son-in-law is their primary financier. It is only a question of time before I am in."

"I understand that many of these imported workers have been sent to Kauai. I'm sure some of them have gone to Kilauea Plantation."

"That is true." Grant rubbed his hands together and smiled. "From rumors reaching me they are an unhappy lot and causing the plantation trouble. Labor unrest will be my wedge to take control."

"That's an interesting ploy, using troublemaking workers to take over. How will you do this?"

Grant laughed, slamming his palm against the room's wall. "That is my little secret, but I will give you a clue: the sheriff who makes arrests on Kauai gets a cut of the criminal fine."

"Very intriguing," Jones said. "You find an advantage in corruption."

"Yes, and, my friends, that is how we will bring down our king. It's his greed for money."

CHAPTER 7

———

John and Still rode their horses onto a black rock-covered roadway heading to an imposing mansion. A wall of ferns, coconut trees, royal palms, and flowers circled the plantation manager's property like a multi-colored necklace. A manicured green lawn surrounded the home, giving it a sumptuous splendor. Through the enclosing foliage the two men could see the dark blue mass of Makaleha Mountain, shadowed in the early morning light.

As they dismounted, the men paused to listen to the sweet song of a Eurasian Skylark, its melody drifting to them in the stillness of the air. "That is a peaceful sound," Joe said.

"I agree. Let us hope that our meeting with McKnight is as pleasant as that music. I have been hearing stories of labor unrest. I suspect that is the reason for our meeting."

They tethered their horses to a hitching pole. Still began cleaning his boots on a scrub brush fixed to the bottom step of the manager's home. "You best do the same. Don't want to dirty the owner's carpets."

"Don't you take off your shoes before entering?"

"At your place I do, but I'm not sure the boss likes to see naked feet."

"You're saying we would look like natives if we went in without boots on," John answered as he also used the scrub brush on his leather footwear.

"You get my thinking. Take a deep breath before we go in. Smell the gardenias that grow along the veranda of this house. It will make you feel better before we face whatever storm is coming. I hear rumors that the plantation people don't like your friend Kalakaua."

"Not much I can do about him," John said as he and Still mounted the steps and knocked on the dark koa entry doors of the mansion.

A servant let them in and led them to a well-furnished living room and to another door. He knocked and announced, "Mr. Still and Mr. Tana are here."

"Come in," McKnight answered. The two friends were ushered into a richly furnished den. Early light peeping through partially curtained windows fell on dark red wine-colored koa wood. The furniture, walls, and floor reflected the sunbeams, adding a golden-brown color. An intricately patterned Persian rug covering the floor matched the redness of the soft chair cushions. McKnight took a seat behind a heavy wooden desk and directed the two men to chairs in front of him.

Behind the manager a mahogany carving decorated the wall. In its center the head and body of a bronzed man rose above a field of taro leaves. Bordering the figure and above his head were blades of sugar cane. Oil rubbed into the koa wood gave the central figure a rich glow.

"You admire the art?" McKnight said. "It's the god Lono. Legend tells us he planted himself into the earth to make things grow. The sprouting taro you see feeds the people, while the sugar cane enriches them. Upon his countenance the sun smiles, giving life to man and his plants. A Chinese made this for me. It's very valuable."

"Stunning," Still said.

John sat silent, studying the manager. He was white, reflecting his British heritage. Neatly trimmed, light brown hair descended into mutton-chop side-burns along the side of his face. His eyebrows were thick and bushy. His eyes glinted blue beneath them. His hawk nose pointed to thick lips discolored brown by tobacco.

He reached into a humidor on his desk and drew out a cigar, clipping off an end. He lit his cheroot and inhaled deeply then blew from his lips a small cloud of pungent smoke.

"I am sure that you are wondering why I asked you to come here." Without waiting for a reply, the manager continued, "I have an assignment for both of you. John tells me that you, Still, speak German?"

"Yes, I do."

"Good. Then this is your task: I want you to visit our German laborers from Bremen. They are complaining, even threatening to strike. Make friends with them. Find out why the trouble. Visit the Portuguese, Chinese, and Fijians. I don't want labor unrest. Give me a report in a few days."

Leaning across his desk, the manager's voice became strident. "Your friend in Honolulu, Mr. Tana, is acting like Napoleon. He has a fancy coronation party crowning himself King and his wife Queen. Then he comes up with the grandiose idea of being Emperor of the Pacific! He sends emissaries to the island nations proposing unity with Hawaii and him as the leader of the empire. What a waste of money! What foolishness.

"Ever since he traveled around the world, he has developed grandiose ideas of how to spend our money. Is he trying to compete with Queen Victoria?"

Still removed his hands resting on his chest and inquired, "Are you saying that John has something to do with the King's spending?"

"No, I am not. But, Mr. Tana, you should know that if your friend continues with his extravagance and pagan ways that the people who put him into power can just as easily remove him. Maybe the King's work to secure the Reciprocity Treaty with the United States saved the monarchy for a while, but his wild spending will quickly end it."

John straightened himself in his chair and answered, "I recognize that you and other business men are upset, but I have little influence over the king and his habits."

"Proceed with your assignment."

McKnight turned his chair to face the carving of Lono as he blew a halo of smoke around the god's head.

CHAPTER 8

———

As John galloped away from the mansion, the rhythmic canter of the horses soothed the turmoil welling within him. *Why the lecture on Kalakaua's habits? What's the reason for the abrupt dismissal? Am I in trouble? That could not be. There was not a hint in the conversation that I am failing in his security work. What the manager said at the end is sedition. Could that be why he abruptly ended the conversation? What did the sugar people have to worry about? They held all the cards in the economic and political games being played in the monarchy of Hawaii.*

The two men trotted their horses across the county road as they passed several two-room cottages. These were the residences of the supervisors, the second tier of plantation management. The attractive homes were painted dark green with white trim. Each had an outside kitchen, a toilet placed downwind, and land sufficient for a vegetable garden.

After passing the supervisors' homes they entered a narrow path bordering the Kilauea River. Water rolling over jagged rocks cascaded in sheets across a wide lip of hardened stone into a pool, the falling water frothing the pools' surface like boiling steam. They rode north passing buildings where sugar cane is processed, cooked into molasses, granulated into brown crystals, bagged, and shipped off to market.

A narrow alley bordered the plantation complex. A low hedge of hau wood grew along one side. Opposite lay a hodgepodge of ramshackle buildings, some showing raw wood. It was a jumbled mix of cottages, barracks, and grass shacks.

Still and John trotted to the first shanty along the path. It had a tired, neglected look, its sides needed paint and patching. They reigned in the horses and dismounted. As they did, a pair of half-naked urchins with grimy faces and open sores on their legs charged at them.

One child wiped his runny nose with the back of his hand, and then opened it begging for money. Joe gave each of the children a small coin. A broad-faced peasant woman appeared in the door of the shabby cottage and called: "*Hier kommt!*" The children immediately ran to her.

Still and John walked to the steps of the shanty and removed their hats. In German, Still said, "Good morning. I am a plantation supervisor. May I speak with your husband?"

With a start the fat woman called into the home, "Kurt! Come quickly! We have a German speaker to see you." She wiped her hands on her apron and said, "Please come in. Would you like water, maybe some cheese?"

As he pulled on suspenders over a sleeveless sweatshirt, Kurt walked into the parlor of the sparsely-furnished shanty. "Hail to the Kaiser," he saluted, then introduced himself and his wife. "I am Kurt Himmelsbach, and this is my wife Sarah."

After he offered John and Still the only comfortable chairs in the room, Kurt went to a rough-hewn bench. He sighed loudly as he settled onto it and twirled the ends of his moustache that pointed upward like the horns of a devil. "We are from Bremen, and you?"

Joe munched on the sour cheese Sarah had brought, and coughed, the acrid taste of the curdled milk stinging his throat. "Alsace."

Himmelsbach slapped his knee with delight. "Ah, so you are from the German provinces that Bismarck forced France to return to the fatherland. Alsace and Lorraine were always German territory. Chancellor Bismarck he is very smart, I read a lot about him in the newspapers."

John watched Still suppress his anger. He knew his friend had fought the German ogre to keep Alsace for France.

Word spread through the camp that a German plantation supervisor had come to visit. In a short time, neighbors arrived at the Himmelsbach home. They had many complaints about conditions at the plantation.

Himmelsbach broke though the jumble of words and said, "May I speak for all of us? Correct me if I say something that you disagree upon."

People were slow to end their complaining. A murmur of agreement with Kurt's request gave him sullen permission to speak for the German community in Kilauea.

"We are farmers from Bremen," Himmelsbach said. "We did not own the land we farmed in the old country. We leased it from a rich man in the city. Hard times came upon us. We ran low on food and had very little money. Some of us noticed this sign in a shop. It said something like: 'Come to Hawaii'."

Still drank some water. "That is interesting. A few years ago, I was in Bremen. There was a sign in the window that said something like: 'Good Workers wanted...opportunities in Hawaii'. Is that the sign?"

Kurt's eyebrows furrowed, through tight lips he hissed, "That is the devil sign." Agreement with his words flowed through the room.

He begged for silence, then with less vehemence, "Several of us sought out the owner of the sign. We met this friendly man. He was a good talker. Said Hawaii had opportunities for families. Sign a labor contract with him and we would get free transportation and work in Hawaii."

"Lie," a voice yelled, "the labor contract said we had to pay for transport from our wages." Many heads nodded, agreeing with the man's words.

"Please, my friends, let me continue. Mr. Still will not know our story if you stop me on every word."

As they quieted, Kurt continued, "We were told it would be four years of farm work in a climate blessed with sunshine. We would get good pay, a clean house with a yard—" A chorus of angry voices drowned his words.

"My friends, let me finish," Kurt begged. Although grumbling continued there was moderation in its tone.

"We were promised free medical care—" The roof nearly blew from the shanty as Kurt's words aroused an eruption of hostile voices.

John stood. He realized that many promises had been made to cause these people to travel eight thousand miles. But these oral promises were all lies. He wondered if the Germans had read their labor contracts.

"Your neighbors keep mentioning your trip to the islands as being deadly. What happened?" Still asked.

An agitated Kurt seized his arm. "It was a nightmare. Everyone became seasick. It was hot. We stank. Bugs, rats ate into us. The food, what there was of it, was spoiled. Then the measles struck. Every day we buried someone at sea. Children, grown-ups, all died." Kurt sobbed, he could not continue, others in the room joined in his mourning.

It proved useless to remain. The room became frigid with sorrow. Still stood and said to Kurt, "Pick two of your neighbors. Come to my cottage tonight for a good German meal. I have some pork sausage and homemade sauerkraut. There will be fine beer and a special desert."

There were thanks all around and the two men left.

Out of the hearing of the Germans, Still said, "These people are in pain. Their homes and yards are shabby, not like the Germans I know who are always clean and neat. They are dispirited. I will find out tonight what ails them."

A dog raced beside the horses, barking and seeking to nip the trotting legs. Still kicked at the cur, the dog stopped his harassment and stood howling in the roadway, a warning not to intrude on his territory again.

They cantered beyond the German buildings and found themselves in the Portuguese compound. A bevy of wood-framed structures spread before him, each painted green with white trim, and flowers blooming along the borders of grass-covered yards. From within the encampment hammers pounded. North of it, cattle lowing filled the air. The sounds and sights were a picture of organization, prosperity and permanence.

They reined in at a pretty cottage. A woman in an apron opened the front door, a clean two-year-old boy clinging to her legs. From inside the house a male voice called, "Who is there, Mama?"

The comely woman surveyed the men. "A white man and a Hawaiian. Come in." John and Still stepped into the cottage. A clean-shaven, medium-sized man joined the woman and child at the door. Still stuck out a calloused hand and said,

"I am supervisor Joe Still. This is John Tana, and you are?"

In a tone of respect, the Portuguese answered, "Frank Silva, wife Renee, and Frank Jr. You come for?"

Inclining his head to Renee, Still reached to tousle the hair of the young boy. The child dodged Joe's hand and buried himself into his mother. Joe gave up his attempt to pet the young Frank, and answered his father, "Manager asked me to see how you folks are doing. Plantation wants to be sure everything is going well." Silva smiled broadly as his wife was pulled away from the door by the vigorous tugging of her two-year-old son. "Everything good. Come."

The living room was clean and neat. Curtained windows let light flood onto white cream walls that gave an air of freshness to the interior. Art pictures hung on the walls. Flowers set in vases gave off sweet scents disguising any unpleasant odors. Sparse furniture sat on dried-leaf mats covering the floor. On a wall stood a small altar with a statue of Jesus giving a blessing.

"Hawaii like Madeira," Frank said. "Rocks same as Kauai rocks. Volcano make island. Our side plenty rain like Kilauea. Sugar cane, bananas, mangoes, flowers same. Sea around us, we eat plenty fish."

Renee, who had been pulled by her son into the kitchen called, "Like some honey cake, malasadas, and chorizo?"

"Bring all."

"Don't bother," Still protested.

"No bother, in Madeira like Hawaii we eat before talk."

John broke off a piece of honey cake that Renee offered him and savored its sweetness. "Outstanding. You must give me your recipe, Mrs. Silva."

Renee's heart-shaped lips broke into a smile. From a platter in her hand she offered sugared donuts. "Best malasadas ever," Still said, then asked, "What brought you and your family to Hawaii? Did many Portuguese bring wives and children?"

"Only rich or poor live in Madeira. Poor like Renee and me have nothing. No school for children. Work hard for what?

"Town doctor, Hillebrand, lived in Hawaii. He talked of the plantations and the land, just like Madeira. He say, 'Go Hawaii. Start a new life.' Why we came."

"It is such a long way to come. Weren't you afraid?"

Silva threw his hands into the air, "Ayah, you should hear what our friends said. You crazy. Wild people, cannibals will eat you. I tell them, better to live with wild people where I chance to be rich than live in Madeira where I no have chance."

"What was the trip like? I understand Germans lost 50, maybe 60, people on the way. They say it was a terrible voyage."

"Five months trip, only one lost. All on ship knew each other. We work together. Help each other. No trouble."

Silva leaned toward Still and, with a confidential tone, said, "Our plan is finish labor contracts then go into business in Hawaii. No go back to Madeira."

Still nodded. "I understand that Portuguese men are skilled in many things, mechanics, carpenters, stone masons, dairy farmers, bookkeepers. The plantation can make good use of your skills."

"Yes. Women and children work too." Silva called his wife, "Renee, how many rat tails did you sell this week?"

"Twenty."

"At twenty-five cents a tail, five dollars for the family. Renee does laundry, household work, cleans stables, shops. We do well in Kilauea."

"Good. Thank you, Frank, thank you, Renee." Still and John left.

Riding toward Kahili Ridge, the only portion of a dead caldera that had not surrendered to the sea, John said, "Those are good people. Once they finish their contracts the Portuguese will build communities, schools, everything needed to make Hawaii a better place."

"Yes, there's a huge difference between them and the Germans who are ready to go home. Maybe it's the many deaths on the way here that have made them unhappy. I'll know tonight."

Chucking their horses, the two friends loped up the roadway toward the Chinese compound.

CHAPTER 9

A roadway crossed their path and John and Still turned right toward the river. Wooden fencing bordered the road and, with other fences, created an enclosure. Cattle chewing on grass within the corral stared at them with large, sad eyes. Several switched their tails ridding themselves of flies. Within moments the animals returned to eating.

Beyond the rectangular corral there were unpainted barracks. On a slight rise near them stood thatched buildings with bamboo poles protruding from them. Laundry strung on ropes between the poles flapped in the wind. A Chinese man sat on a tub outside one of the shacks smoking a pipe. He watched intently as the two riders approached the compound.

Along the river embankment bordering the settlement there were pigpens, a roofed cooking shed, and a three-sided outhouse. Several Chinese in black, padded clothing chatted with each other as they worked at cooking, cleaning, and tending to the pigs. Activity halted as the riders reached the entryway of the Chinese camp.

John and Still dismounted and walked into the compound. "You know these folks better than I do," Still said. "This time you do the talking for us."

Suspicious eyes watched them. John felt it was not hostility that motivated the stares but fear that some wrongdoing would be discovered. He knew that opium smoking, gambling, the making of moonshine were prohibited by law. From time to time, sheriffs had raided Chinese camps of the sugar mills. Workers had been seized, jailed, and fined. John knew it was a corrupt practice since half the fine would be given to the arresting officers.

"Aloha, you know me. Who speak *da kine*?" John asked, using the common language of Hawaii, pidgin.

"Ayah, I spik da kine. Dis one stay Hawaii long time. You big shot da kine police?" a pigtailed Chinese man answered.

"Me no da kine big shot. Me da kine small shot. You da kine big shot *pake*." John pointed to the Chinese who laughed, enjoying this acknowledgment of his superiority.

"I come stay your house?" John asked, seeking an invitation into the barracks. "Eh, wat kine guy you? Luna, makai, *aikane*?" the Chinese asked, checking out John's credentials: field supervisor, policeman, or friend.

"Me no da kine police, me aikane, friend. Like make da kine talk." Satisfied, the Chinese said, "Me Chang Low. I know you. Who this?"

"Name Joe. We like see where you live."

"Come look. Why you come? Spy?"

Stepping into one of the barracks, John squinted, his eyes gradually adjusting to the unlighted interior. "We not spy. Manager sent us to see how you are getting along."

Kang reared back as if cold water had been thrown on him. "Manager want know how we are! First time. Nobody care for Chinese. We rubbish."

His vehemence made both men pause at the threshold of the building. "I wonder if the manager wanted us to go this far?" Still said.

John shrugged. "To make a full report we have to see how people live."

"But look at this hell hole."

"If manager want to know, look. Plenty *pilikia*. Chinamen live like *kela moku*."

"What did he say?"

"The Chinese have big trouble. They live like sailors on a ship."

"I can see that, there are rows of bunk beds stacked from floor to ceiling. There must be more than a hundred people sleeping here."

"Maybe a hundred-fifty, look on the floor."

Rolled blankets covered the surface of the barrack floor.

Still took a deep breath and gagged. "This place reeks of dried sweat and human waste, let's get outside."

Breathing deeply of the noontime breezes, the two friends looked at the clean sky. "I would rather sleep under the stars and in the rain than in that hellish building," John said, barely controlling the nausea that threatened to erupt.

"The only light and air comes though this door?" Still asked. Kang nodded.

"Go other house?"

They walked up and into the second building.

This barracks was the same as the first building. Except on the far wall there were single bunks against it. Motioning to follow him, Kang showed a comfort pot under each bed and several small tables, each holding a basin and water pitcher.

"Dis kine for da kine headman, for da kine sick," Kang said. "Good, huh?"

John shook his head. The air smelled stale although the evil smells were not as bad as in the other building. "Let's get outside."

In the fresh air blowing from Kahili ridge, John studied an old Chinese steadily smoking his pipe on the rise above him. "From that vantage point, that guy can see for a great distance."

"A lookout?" Still asked.

"With the enclosing fence surrounding the shacks and what looks like locked doors into them, he's a watchman. See the bell close to him?"

"Yeah, and I can hear lots of laughing and shouting. Gambling is going on and maybe some weed smoking."

Still turned to Kang and said, "I know this is Sunday, where are all the Chinese?"

Kang shrugged and waved vaguely about him. "Look for food, fishing, at river do laundry."

A light rain fell as they left the Chinese compound. John looked up to the shacks on the low rise. The old man continued to sit smoking his pipe. "Tell grandfather to get out of the rain. We are not the police."

The two friends mounted their horses and galloped west.

——

CHAPTER 10

As the men rode past the cattle corral, Still said, "At least half of the plantation labor is Chinese. I've been here for just a short time. What I hear the sugar people saying is the Chinese are intent on crippling the plantations by strikes, rebellions, raising havoc and committing arson, thievery, and property damage."

"I think if they had better pay and living conditions like the Portuguese there would be no trouble." John answered.

"I got to agree with you. But you can't make money by spending it. The reason plantations are profitable is cheap land and labor. If the Chinese cause trouble, then the sugar mills will keep bringing in different races to counter them."

"Why are the Portuguese doing so well?"

"They're pseudo-white and have skills the imported Chinese don't have. Plus, they brought families with them. I also think they have made themselves indispensable to management."

"But aren't the Germans white? Why aren't they doing better?"

"I haven't got an answer yet. I know in the old country they were neat and orderly. The people we met are depressed. Maybe it's the many deaths they experienced in transit."

"I don't know everything, but I don't think it's wise to play one race off against another to make sure labor is cheap."

Still nodded. "I agree with you. Right now, the business people are telling the Hawaiian government to end Chinese immigration. They are urging the bringing in of Japanese. I don't think that suppression by racial dilution of Hawaii can be the right answer to labor unrest."

"Look, there's a funeral service going on."

At the Fijian encampment men were standing in front of three mounds of dirt singing a hymn.

John and Still dismounted and strode toward the gathering. The hymnal singing stopped. A Hawaiian dressed in vestments of black standing by three rectangular holes in the ground stared at them, then asked, "Are you here from the sugar plantation to pay respect to the Fijians who are dead?"

Startled by the minister's question John asked, "Are you saying that there are three Fijians dead?"

"Yes, and many more there, there, there," the minister said, pointing to mounds lying low upon the earth.

"What's happening here?" Still asked.

"I am Kahu Kaluna. Are you telling me that the plantation does not know what's happening to these South Sea Islanders they brought here? They are dying."

"Look, minister and you men, I am not responsible for bringing people here. Not my idea."

"Maybe you are not responsible. Who is? In just one year, one-third of the Fijians brought here are dead. The rest need to go home before they all die."

John shook his head. "The plantations are sticklers for observing the contracts. Every person brought here must pay for their transportation out of wages. Can they pay?"

"No, but I'm willing to take up a collection from my congregation. It may not be much. But will the owners let them go?"

"We will present the problem to management. We will help as much as we can."

Still and John began to shovel dirt into the graves. As he worked John asked, "I see a bunch of grass shacks. How are living conditions for these people?"

"In a rain the roofs leak all over the bunks where the men sleep," Kaluna answered. "The toilets are open to the air. Drinking water must be boiled then strained to get rid of the dirt and animals in them. It's terrible to live here."

The two friends left the Fijians, disturbed by what they had heard. "I don't know for sure what we can do for these people, but we'll try," Still said.

John nodded his agreement.

The two men mounted their horses and rode away from the sorrow-filled encampment. "What a horrible situation," John said. "The Fijians are in a state of total demoralization and Chinese have every reason to strike, rebel, and raise havoc. Were you prepared for those disgusting living conditions?" he asked.

"No, I was not."

"When I first took this security job, the Chinese population's primary form of retaliation for bad treatment was arson. That only made things worse. Their repression is severe. Now, it appears the bosses want to get rid of them and continue to bring in other races. Mark my words, there will be trouble."

"I agree, but from what we've seen, the Chinese have few options. What can they do? When they rebel or strike, they get thrown in jail. Run away, and they're hunted down like dogs and imprisoned."

"No surprise there's such a big alcohol and opium problem in the camps. At least in the dream world of drugs, they can fantasize about a better life. It will be interesting to hear what the Germans tell you tonight."

CHAPTER 11

—

"This is good food," Kurt Himmelsbach declared as he ate pork sausage and homemade sauerkraut. "Yes, yes, very good," Hans Gruber and Johann Steinmetz, neighbors of Kurt echoed. Joe Still bustled about his cottage serving dishes and pouring beer for his guests.

In the twilight, four satisfied men finished sugar-coated apple strudel. They loosened their pants, stepped onto the porch of the home, and lit pipes.

"Labor contractor lied to me," Gruber said. "The man tells me I would get a good home, enough land to farm, medical care, and school for my children. All lies."

"You be right about what you say," Steinmetz agreed. "Instead of good homes we have wooden shacks with broken siding, cracked floors, and leaking roofs. There is no land to farm like we had in Bremen."

Smoke exploded from his lungs as Himmelsbach said, "The work hours are long. My frau wakes me at 4:30 in the morning. I must be in the fields by 5:30. Work is hard, and I must do it for ten hours in the sun and rain. On irrigation days, I must work twelve hours. Sundays are an off day and except for an occasional Saturday, all the men work twenty-six days a month."

Hitching his legs onto the porch railing and emphasizing his point by waving his pipe as the wad of tobacco fumed in the air, Gruber swore. "Damn it, the pay is only $12.00 per month. Without a plot of land to grow food, a man's earnings cannot cover what a family needs. My wife and child have to work for us to survive."

Steinmetz looked at Hans with mock astonishment. "You swore, a terrible sin. Too bad there is no Lutheran church in Kilauea to cleanse your soul." Turning towards Still he said, "That is a huge problem that German families have. In this plantation town, there is not a proper place to worship God."

Himmelsbach leaned forward, his pipe thrusting out between his lips. He scratched his head then took out his pipe, pointing at each of his friends. "I think we are all sad to have left Germany. The newspapers we get report that there are huge changes in the new Reich. Chancellor Bismarck supports health and disability insurance, pensions, regulated working hours. German factories are booming. There is plenty of work in industry and the farmlands of Deutschland."

"Das Reich will soon be the greatest nation on earth!" Steinmetz declared. The other two Germans nodded in agreement.

Still sat quietly smoking, such world power can only come through war. He left Alsace and the new Germany to end forever his role in fighting other men for the powerful few.

"If you plan to go back to Germany be sure to finish your labor contracts before you do. Don't run away. Hawaiian courts are on the side of the sugar planters. Workers who escape from the plantations, when caught, are put in jail."

The next day John and Still reported to the manager. Still recommended that money be spent on better housing for the Germans, providing them with land to farm, and the building of a Lutheran Church.

"Bringing in South Sea Islanders is a huge mistake," John continued the joint report. "The same diseases killing Hawaiians are wiping out the Fijians. From a work force of a hundred and ten, you have only seventy left and they continue to die. Send them home."

"Ridiculous. They haven't paid for their transportation costs to get here. And now you're asking the plantation to pay to send them back! No! No!"

"Church people and others are raising money to pay the cost. What we need is your okay and an amount."

"And you expect the plantation to feed and house them while you raise the money," McKnight said.

"If you agree to let them go, we can work something out."

"I want the money first before any deal is made. I'll check with the business office to see how much is owed for transportation costs of a hundred-and-ten Fijians. What else do you men have in mind?"

"The Chinese live in horrible conditions. Overcrowded, filthy housing, non-existent sanitation, it's a breeding ground for strikes and trouble. If the plantation provides better housing, and allow them to have wives and raise families, it will add stability to their lives and improve their work output."

McKnight answered, "I didn't send you to become social workers or labor representatives. Enough of this, I'll consider your reports. Get out."

John was relieved that he hadn't been asked about his suspicions. "At least he didn't want to know about crime. In the shacks on the hill, opium smoking and gambling activities are going on."

"He didn't even ask us what the community is willing to do, just got angry with the recommendations. We must do something for those workers. You've got a big hall maybe we can use it for a Lutheran Church for the Germans."

"I'll have members of the Alapai family reach out to the Fijians. Try to see what we can do to help them. Once McKnight gives us a figure we can raise the money."

"Chinese are a special problem. It is beyond our means to help them. Let's hope McKnight will do something for them. Let's keep pressing him."

The two friends galloped home. McKnight did not act before tragedy struck.

—

CHAPTER 12

John stood by a long brick barbeque. A dozen fish lay on a metal grate frying, their oily aroma drifting under a low roof that protected the outdoor wooden stove from rain.

Still cantered into the compound and rode up to the open-air stove, dismounted, and asked, "What are you doing?"

"Can't you see, you blind Frenchman? I'm cooking for a party."

"Oh yeah, is that why you asked me to come over here to be part of a party you are giving? What kind of party?"

"An engagement party."

"Who's getting married?"

John shuffled cooked fish over to a cooler side of the grill. He plopped new scad onto the hot irons and slathered oil on them. A wall of fire leaped through the iron grates and fish hissed and sizzled.

"You!" John answered.

Still laughed and reached his arm out to ruffle John's hair. "You're joking."

"No, I am not. Your friend Rogers believes it is time for you to marry. I agreed with him. There are thirty young ladies coming here. You're to pick one for a bride."

"This is crazy, besides no young lady would want to marry a grizzled old guy like me."

John sighed. "Rogers explained this to me. You don't have a chance with plantation daughters. There are few of them and their choices are within their own circle. But Hawaiian families want their young girls to marry white men."

"Why is that?"

"You have status and money," John said with bitterness in his voice. "I haven't agreed with that in the past, but for you at this point in time there are no other choices."

John dug up a vessel of home brew, poured beer into two cups and, taking a plate of fried scad, invited Joe to join him at a table. "In the past the only Hawaiian women who married whites were of royal blood. Those marriages were all about land and status. The common Hawaiian woman was viewed as having nothing to offer except sex. Her choice for a husband was either a Hawaiian or a Chinese. But, as I said, it's the desire of many Hawaiian parents to have their daughters marry a white man."

"So, you invited me here to discuss the lack of marriage prospects for the Hawaiian woman and I am to fulfill this need whether there is love or there isn't?"

"Rogers says love will come. The most important decision is to choose. Look, here is your friend escorting families with eligible girls."

Rogers came trooping into the compound followed by scores of Hawaiians. The Alapai family stood at the door of the common house and invited people in. Tables of food were set out in the large building. Moana came to the outdoor fireplace and took sizzling fish into the feast.

Rogers came to the two men. "I'm sure you recall my admonition that it is time to get married."

"You did, but I thought that there is always a courtship beforehand?"

"I'm sure John explained that your options are few. I felt before I left Kilauea the process of selection should be hastened."

"How do you propose to do this?"

"After lunch, we will clear the tables and thirty young girls will be around you. Pick one."

Still sat in the center of the room, surrounded by young women in their finest clothes. Along the walls of the building parents stood. Some wandered outside complaining of heat. At the door Rodgers had a benign look on his face and with his hands waving, he mouthed the word, "Decide."

Still stood, stroking his beard. He took a slow spin around the room. He cast his eyes down stroking his forehead wondering how he ever agreed to this event.

He had thought of marriage, realizing that his youth and vigor were passing. He had agreed with Rogers that the time had come, but he never thought the choice would be made like this. What about love? John had assured him the girls were eager to marry. Love would come later.

Rogers waved his hands almost shouting out the word, "Decide." Still heard laughter. He stared at a corner of the room and saw a furtive movement behind a young girl. He looked away, then heard a high, quick laugh. Turning swiftly, he saw a pretty girl in the middle of a giggle. Their eyes met, and the young lady ducked behind another. Still took two quick strides to the corner, pointed his finger, and said, "I pick you."

"Not me! Why me? Many others to choose from."

"Why were you laughing?"

"You looked so funny standing there. Not knowing what to do."

"And that's why I pick you. You're bright enough to figure out my dilemma. Your pixie laughter made the choice for me."

John came to the young girl, took her hand and placed it into Still's. "This is my daughter Nani. She is our pride and joy. She cooks, works hard, and is a delight to be with. If she is your choice, we welcome you into our family."

Smoke soared from an open pit of hot rocks and two well-cooked pigs added a rich aroma to the grey vapors. Beyond the oven, Akaka served drinks at a long bar. Standing nearby were people of all races including plantation supervisors drinking, swapping jokes, and enjoying the marriage feast.

For music, there was the booming sound of a pole-stringed tub accompanied by the strum of guitars and the plunking of a ukulele. When a sign was given, everyone moved to where white chairs were placed in long, neat rows. Women in colorful gowns draped a fragrant lei around the neck of each guest. A rich baritone voice sang of the discovery of love, asking if his chosen one loved him. A woman joined in a duet, her lovely soprano voice affirming that he was her heart's choice.

Two women appeared on a flower-strewn path and behind them walked John with Nani clinging to him. Father and daughter moved gracefully to a flowered arbor crowned by the leaves of a towering hala tree. Under the tree, a minister stood with Joseph Still. Beyond them, the sun cast rays of gold, yellow, and red, the fiery arches of color slowly disappearing behind Makalena Mountain. As darkness covered the land, Joseph Still and Nani Tana exchanged vows.

The wedding ceremony took only minutes. The festivities continued for three days. John built a home on his seven acres of land and gave it to Nani and Joe Still.

CHAPTER 13

———

Out of breath, Bruce Jones pounded on Grant's office door.

"What in tarnation are you trying to do, knock the building down?" an irritated Robert Grant said as he opened the entryway.

"You must come to the armory. There's a big meeting brewing. Everyone of importance will be there. It's about Kalakaua."

"It's about time the business community did something about that buffoon."
"I believe they are ready to act. My Honolulu Rifles have been asked to guard the assembly and be prepared for action. This time we will force the king to abdicate."

"I doubt if it will go that far. There are still some missionary folks who want to keep the monarchy. But let's see how we can turn these events to our advantage."

When they arrived at the armory a large crowd had already assembled. Speakers had taken to the podium and complained about the King's spending on a world trip, expensive palace, and coronation.

Grant got his chance to gain the podium. He waited until the crowd of more than two thousand men became silent. "That is not the worst of his expensive spending, he has sent out emissaries to Fiji, the Gilbert Islands, and Samoa, all aimed at creating a Hawaiian Empire. This plan has failed and made us the laughing stock of the Pacific. It almost pushed this country into a war with Germany. Where has the money come from to foster this foolishness? From bribes and corruption. The Legislature passes an opium monopoly bill with a price of $30,000 for it. Kalakaua sells it for $80,000 to one Chinese and takes $71,000 from another! He won't pay it back. He's spent the money. It's time to end this monarchy and create a Republic."

"Congratulations," Jones said. "You gave a great speech. Too bad the assembly didn't act on your recommendation."

"At least they will force a new Constitution upon him and make the man a puppet. Thank you for making the motion to give me the authority to rid the country of that pest Gibson."

"Yes, and I am making you a major in the militia. One of the best decisions the assembly made is to have the legislature repeal the Opium Monopoly Act. Legalized sale of that drug ruins our work force."

"It was all Kalakaua's doing that the bill got passed in the first place. He needed the money and sold the license multiple times. His corruption brought him down. With the rescinding of the bill, we can attack the opium problem head on."

"How do you propose doing this?"

"As a major in the militia, I'll have special officers raiding Chinese camps. We'll catch those gooks red-handed. Off to prison with them. Then large fines to get out which will pay for the cost of enforcement."

"Are you going to hire that fellow, John Tana?" Jones laughed, slapping Grant on his back.

"You're crazy. Once I'm through with Gibson, Tana's Kauai security job is my next target. After that, who knows what will happen? I'm off to the harbor."

"To hang Kalakaua's Prime Minister?"

"Yes."

CHAPTER 14

———

"You can't lynch this man," British Commissioner Wodehouse protested.

"Why not?" Robert Grant demanded. A dozen members of his voluntary militia watched the discussion between the two men. They had built a temporary scaffold at the Honolulu docks. A looped rope hung over its projecting bar and Walter Murray Gibson stood below it, his hands tied behind him.

"Isn't there an anti-lynch law in Hawaii? Does King Kalakaua approve of such summary action on your part?" Wodehouse asked.

"The Hawaiian League has revoked the law. A new Constitution will be signed by the king. It vests control of the Hawaiian Monarchy in the Cabinet of Ministers. Your government should not oppose us. You know that this man is the architect of the Polynesian Confederation between Kalakaua and King Malietoa of Samoa. War between Germany and Hawaii almost occurred, and your country was ready to fight us as well. The League intervened before a disastrous engagement occurred. Britain may not know this, but Gibson imported weapons to foster an armed takeover and return control of the Hawaiian Kingdom to the Hawaiians. The armaments have been seized. For these and many other reasons, you should support the hanging."

"Yeah, lynch the Hawaiian lover," a militia man yelled as he settled the noose over Gibson's neck, tightening the knot so it snubbed into the prime minister's throat. Other militia men prepared to haul on the rope.

"Major, shall we tie his legs or let the bastard kick in the wind?" a militia man asked.

"I'm surprised that talk of political change in Honolulu has gone this far," the British Commissioner said. "And what you reveal about Gibson may be true. But

Her Majesty's government is opposed to summary action against any Minister of State. Your constitution provides for a trial before a man is condemned to die. My government insists upon it."

Grant scowled. He looked at the harbor with its British, French, and American warships riding at anchor. He noted that behind the Commissioner stood a squad of armed Marines. He knew the American Secretary of State supported action against Kalakaua who had turned against United States interests and the planter-missionary elite that dominated the government. These anti-American, anti-business feelings of the king were fueled by Gibson's rhetoric and his espousal of Hawaiian nationalism. But the white community needed all the foreign support it could get. "Let Gibson go," Grant ordered. "Place him under house arrest until he can be tried."

Grant dismissed the militia and trudged back to the Honolulu Club. He had wanted a revolution. Seize full control of the government backed by U.S. marines and the militia. But there were still those in the community opposed to totally ending the monarchy.

He met Cartwright at the club. "How did it go with the king?" he asked.

Cartwright laughed. "The man has no courage. He saw armed men with bayonets and he folded. He signed a new Constitution. Executive power will be with the king and his cabinet, but the cabinet has veto power over any of his actions. The League will appoint the Cabinet and the members of the House of Nobles. The military will be under our control. Asiatic foreigners can't vote. Only men of property with money can."

"Then we have won. All we need to do is maneuver the political situation so that America annexes Hawaii. Once that occurs we need worry no more about sugar profits. Tell me of the opium bill."

"The king confessed that he had taken money from two different Chinamen and couldn't pay it back. He agreed to repeal the law immediately."

Grant rubbed his hands and smiled. "Now I can begin the crackdown of the trade. Kauai will be the first island to be dealt with."

CHAPTER 15

———

Horses' hooves disturbed the quiet of the night. John glanced toward the direction of the sounds. A three-quarter moon shone through banks of clouds, its weak light outlining dark-clad horsemen galloping toward the Chinese compound.

John stopped his arson patrol at the sugar mill, studying the fast-disappearing riders. The horsemen were not stealthy, their passage past the workers cottages marked by hounds barking. They were moving with great speed toward their destination.

John was in turmoil. The dark riders meant trouble for someone. Should he remain at his security job, protecting the sugar mill or pursue the raiders? Even if he caught up with them, what could he do? Other than a nightstick and a knife, he had no weapons. But the Chinese were his friends. He would do what he could to help them. John left his job, running after the horsemen.

Weak light from newly-lit kerosene lanterns shone onto the alleyway aiding John in his pursuit. Excited voices yelled out questions, but John had no answers, and he did not return the calls. Dogs barked, with one cur charging him as he raced past the cottage the hound protected. He thrust his fingers at the face of the snarling animal who shied away howling in anger.

Far ahead John could see torchlight glinting, loud voices yelling commands in Chinese. A rifle shot whined. A sharp cry pierced the night. John stumbled, catching his balance before he sprawled on the dirt. A mixture of voices crackled in the dark: screaming Chinese, angry English commands all melded together in a cacophony of noise.

Sounds of splintering glass were followed by the pop, pop of pistol fire. A battle was underway at the Chinese compound, and John feared for the poor men who were under attack. Heedless of the dangers, John wiggled through a fence and rushed along a grass field. Great shapes loomed in the darkness as he dodged among the cows resting in the field, praying that he would not run into a bull.

Ahead John saw a major fire lighting the low hill where the Chinese shacks had stood. There a string of men tied together were being led to level ground. In the compound he could see a face-off between a thin line of dark-clothed raiders and a crowd of Chinese. He raced to a fence bordering the dirt roadway parallel-ing the compound. Towering above the crowd was a man on horseback issuing orders.

"Hey," John yelled at the horseman, "what's going on here? This is private property."

Swinging to the sound of John's voice the horseman peered at him. "Who are you?"

"I'm Chief Security Officer of Kilauea Plantation and I want to know who you are."

"I'm special police and we are rounding up criminals. You're a pretty lousy security officer letting illegal gambling, opium smoking, and prostitution exist right under your nose. Now you get out of here while we do our work, or I'll run you into jail with the rest of these chinks."

John thought for a moment to vault the fence and challenge the officer. As if sensing John's intention, the lawman pulled out a revolver pointing it at John. "Get out of here now, or you're a dead security man."

The day following the raid, McKnight faced John Tana. "Didn't you report that there was no opium at the Chinese encampment?"

"I never said that. Did I know about it? I had my suspicions, but no one asked."

"It's because of your incompetence that we have a king-sized mess. Nineteen Chinese are in jail, with more injured and unable to work. And let's not forget the dozen or so deserters."

The manager leaned toward John. "As for the rest of them, they're refusing to work. It's on you to make things right. One of our prime investors, Robert Grant, sent the special police here to clean up the opium problem. He has strikebreakers ready to wade into the Chinese and end their hold out. You will help break them. "Once that happens, you will hunt down deserters and bring them back. If you have to do it forcefully, do it. Mr. Grant wants an example made of them, so no one will ever run away again. As for the ones who refuse to work...well, they'll find out fast what's in store for them."

John's face darkened as he glowered at the manager. "You didn't listen when I reported on the terrible living conditions. You wouldn't even consider letting the Chinese have wives and families. In truth," he added, the edge in his voice nearly clipping his words, "all you wanted to do was squeeze every ounce of work out of them. Well, you did it, and now you're paying the price. If it's repression and inhumanity you're after, you're on your own. I refuse to hunt down deserters. And when they're found, I'll have nothing to do with beating them or humiliating them in any way!" By the time he was finished, his throat was painful and his voice hoarse. Never in his life had John Tana stood up to authority with such conviction.

McNight was silent for a long moment. "If you won't co-operate Tana, you're fired!"

"You're out of a job? I was with you in the investigation. He didn't mention me?" Still asked.

"No, he didn't. I had the impression he needed an excuse to end my work at the plantation."

"And you fell into his trap?"

"I think it's Grant who set me up to lose my job. He needed an event to make me vulnerable. He knows that Chinese without families gamble and use drugs."

"And he counted on you being Hawaiian not to report the criminal activity going on."

"Possibly, but I think it's the assignment we were given. McKnight was very vague as to what we were to do. But when I saw him, his first words were: 'Didn't you report there was no opium at the Chinese camp?'"

"You're right, he never asked us to check on criminal activity. It seemed he wanted to know about worker morale, and today he called you to his office and not both of us. You were going to be fired no matter what you agreed to do."

"Why did he need an excuse? He hired me, and he can fire me."

"I think it's an investor thing. Rogers is my friend, there are other partners in the enterprise. There may be some sympathy among them for the plight of the worker. He had to come up with a legitimate excuse to dismiss you. Whatever the reasons, shall I resign?"

"No. You need the job. Most important, you're an insider. As long as you're with the plantation we can find ways to help the workers. Are you with me?"

"Of course, together we will seek ways to make things better at the Kilauea plantation."

CHAPTER 16

—

Chinese men bustled about the compound, washing clothes in the river, cooking in an outdoor stove, tending to animals and growing taro. John stepped from the porch of his home, listening to the happy chatter of the Chinese as they went about their morning chores. At the stove, Ah Lok left his cooking, and with exaggerated bowing and mincing steps, came up to him. "Aroha Mista Tana, tank you for help us."

Smiling, John bowed in return. "You men have had your freedom from the sugar plantation for only a few days, yet you work like slaves. Relax, enjoy a little rest."

"No can. Much worry. What we do?"

"I have made arrangements with Chinese friends to give you jobs in the rice fields. After you get some money you can go home to China or stay in Hawaii and enter business."

"Ayah, no can believe why do dis?"

"Let's just say that I'm a friend of the Chinese and…Well, I wonder what those men want?" John said, pointing at six horsemen trotting into the farm.

Ah Lok squinted at the riders, "Dat big guy, he strike-breaker. Attack six months ago, many injured. He bad."

Frightened Chinese quit their work and rushed over to where John stood, jabbering.

"Scatter and arm yourselves," John yelled. He scowled when he saw the coiled whip tied to the saddle of the lead rider and the long sticks that each of the six horsemen were armed with. He whispered to Ah Lok, "Get Moana. Tell him to bring his rifle."

Anger mounted within him as the riders halted a few yards away and the leader pointed his whip at John. "Who owns this place?"

"Who's asking and what do you men want?"

"Name is Larsen. Sven Larsen and I'm head of security for Robert Grant. Do you own this place?"

"Yeah, I do. Name is John Tana. This is private property and I'll thank you to state your business and get out."

"You got a bad attitude, Mr. Tana, maybe somebody should teach you some manners, but before I do, I'm going to tell you that we are here to find runaway Chinese from the plantation and we aim to take them to prison."

"The Chinese here are finished with their labor contracts and are resting at my place before they go on to their new jobs. Now get off my land."

"Not before I round up everyone here and check them over. You've been making a reputation, Tana, for hiding contract breakers on your premises. Mr. Grant doesn't like that, and he aims to put a stop to your evil work. Now step aside while we go about doing our investigation."

For a moment John studied the horsemen. There were two white men, and four Hawaiians. One of the Hawaiians he believed he had met before. John returned his gaze to Larsen. "I told you that all these Chinese have finished their contracts. Get off my land."

"There are six of us to one of you, Mr. Tana. This is your last warning, step aside."

Twenty-one years ago, Grant men had come with whips ordering me from my land. Today, Grant men come again, delivering orders to be obeyed. Trying to control the rage rising in a torrent within him, John shouted, "This is private property. Grant has no power here. King Kalakaua told me of my rights once I owned land. You are violating the laws of the Hawaiian monarchy. You are trespassing. Get out."

"Listen to the little boy," Larsen sneered. "Your king is no more. Grant and the sugar people control the government now, so we are in our rights to do what we want." Larsen uncoiled his whip, reared back, and cracked it at John.

Yet the target of the leather snake did not remain stationery. Timing his movements to the tension in Larsen's hand, John leaped out of the path of the flying whip, seized a hoe dropped by one of the laborers, and squared himself for the next attack.

Larsen struck again with all the power in his arm and shoulders. John trapped the sinewy leather in the shaft of his hoe. Like a fisherman, John jerked on the whip-entwined shaft and yanked Larsen from his saddle into the dirt. Swenson's horse shinnied back into the other riders. Their startled horses stomped sideways to avoid the rearing animal.

Sprawled on the ground, Swenson screamed, "Get that damn kanaka." Only one rider responded to his command. The four Hawaiians reigned in their horses. Like a medieval knight the attacker charged, aiming to strike John down with his iron-pointed stick. The attack was clumsy, John easily danced away from the impaling strike. The rider reigned in his horse, turned, and was pummeled by a barrage of rocks and several Chinese striking him with bamboo rods. The animal reared and bucked nearly throwing its rider from the saddle. Finding an alley between houses, the horseman raced into it trying to escape the attacking Chinese.

"You son-of-a-bitching Hawaiians, I told you to get that man. If you won't, I will," screamed Larsen as he pulled a revolver from his holster.

A rifle shot whined overhead and Moana yelled, "Mister, drop that weapon."

Swenson searched for the voice and found Moana on the porch of a house, a rifle aimed at his heart. He let the pistol slip from his fingers onto the dirt. Then he raised himself from the ground and stared at the four Hawaiians. "Why didn't you obey my orders?"

"John Tana, good man. He let me, and my brothers live. Find jobs for us," answered one of the men. "We go home now."

John watched the strike breakers ride away and waved a silent thanks to the Hawaiian who had tried to assassinate Kalakaua many years ago.

CHAPTER 17

———

Two weeks later, John swiped a paintbrush along the trim of Joe and Nani's new home. He placed the brush in an old can, wiped his hands on a cloth, and then stepped back to survey the entire compound. The house built for Joe and Nani faced his own. Both were perched near the edge of a slope descending to a nearby beach and both bordered a path leading to the main county road. On each side of the path were two rows of buildings, cottages that housed the Alapai family and quarters for laborers finished with their plantation contracts. At the end of the cottages stood a large rectangular structure, the all-purpose building used by families for church services and special events.

From the county road, John heard the jingle of metal rubbing together. Out of the corner of his eye he saw a lone horseman heading down the path, dirt scuffed up by the horse's hooves swirling around the flanks of the animal. John studied the rider, wondering if the man was another representative of Grant, intent on causing him trouble.

"Aloha, I'm Deputy Sheriff Joe Kai, are you John Tana?" John nodded.

"I'd like to sit and talk with you about some trouble a little time ago."

"You from that guy Grant?" John demanded.

"No, Sheriff Lovell in Lihue is my boss, not Grant, but a fella by the name of Larsen who works for Grant made a complaint against you. He said you shot at him with a gun, roughed him and his partner up."

"Not true," John said and then explained the events that had occurred two weeks before. When John was finished he asked, "Are you going to serve a warrant?"

"What happened to the Chinese who were here at the time?" Kai asked, avoiding a direct answer to John's question.

"I took them to Hanalei, Anahola, and Kapaa where they are working in the rice fields. Look, Sheriff, those men finished their contracts with the plantation, they are not runaways as Larsen is claiming. You're not after them, are you?"

"Who is this fellow running up to us?"

"This is my son-in-law, Joe Still. But tell me Sheriff, why are you here?"

"Aloha, Mr. Still," Kai said, then returned his attention to John. "Answering your question, Mr. Tana, I told you Mr. Larsen made a complaint, but when he was asked if he wanted to swear out a warrant for your arrest, he mumbled something about his damn Hawaiian employees were no damn good and he left Lovell's office yelling that the sheriff would hear from Mr. Grant if he didn't do something about you. Right now, Mr. Tana, Grant's a powerful man so the Sheriff sent me out to do a little investigating."

"Is he powerful because of the news I've just heard coming out of Honolulu?" Still asked. "At the point of a bayonet, King Kalakaua signed a new constitution."

John stared for a moment. "A new—"

"Yes, I was just coming to tell you about it, a new constitution that strips him of all his power. The cabinet ministers are running the government."

John shook his head, sadness evident in his face. "I'm not surprised. This moment has been coming for a long time. We knew that once the sugar planters got their reciprocity treaty, they no longer needed Kalakaua."

"True," Deputy Kai said. "The reason our king finally lost his power is that he was trying to return the government back to the Hawaiian people."

Joe nodded his agreement. "Kalakaua didn't know how to play the game. That was the problem. What he needed to do was give the plantation people what they wanted: money for roads and bridges, railroads and shipping lines to transport sugar to the marketplace. Instead, he put money into a palace, a coronation, and plans to become the Napoleon of the Pacific."

John poured three mugs of passion fruit juice and settled onto a bench of a new redwood picnic table. He plunked the metal mugs onto the smooth wood. "A lot of that's just sugar men talking. David spent money on schools, culture, and the leper colony at Kalaupapa. If sugar people had paid their fair share of taxes, instead of making agricultural land tax free, our kingdom would have plenty of money."

A baby wailed, and all three men turned to see Mahealani coming out from one of the cottages, a little child in her arms. Kai took a swig of his nectar before returning to the conversation. "Speaking of Kalaupapa, this change of power is bad news for the lepers. The Board of Health has just announced that it's going to end the *kokua* system."

"No more kokua?" Mahealani cried, her fussing grandson leaning into her shoulder. "Why would they do such a mean thing to those sick people?"

"You didn't know?" Joe asked, the irony in his voice lost to no one. "Those people who run the Board of Health swear that leprosy is God's punishment for a wicked life. That's how they can justify not wasting money on healthy people who care for the sick."

"This is not the Hawaiian way; we take care of people who are ill." Mahealani moaned, the thought of dying alone created a somber aura over her. "And getting rid of the kokua?" she added with a shake of her head. "That means big trouble."

"I have to agree with you Mrs. Tana, getting rid of the helpers will return Kalaupapa to the evil place it used to be. All Father Damien's good work will be wasted," Sheriff Kai said, a note of sadness in his voice. "Well, Mr. Tana, I have to be on my way. Thanks for the hospitality."

"Wait up, Sheriff. I thought you had a complaint from Larsen to resolve."

"It's resolved Mr. Tana. I'm closing the file as of right now. Thanks again and I'll be on my way."

"Let me see you to your horse," John said, walking with Kai to where his animal was tethered. For several minutes the two men stood together in deep conversation before the sheriff mounted and rode away.

"Good man, before he came here he checked with the Hawaiians that were with Larsen. They confirmed my story. He's going to tell Lovell to close the file. He did mention that the other sugar planters on Kauai do not agree with Grant's methods. But the man has a lot of influence."

Mahealani sighed. "I was worried when I saw the sheriff. Without work for these many months and giving everything to the Chinese and Fijians that show up, if you were in jail, I don't know what we would do."

In the ensuing silence, John reached for his wife's hand. "There's something I need to tell you," he said. His voice was low. The last time he had spoken in this way was when he was dismissed from his position at the Kilauea plantation. "You know that we have been able to get by because of my security work in Hanalei, the dairy and pig pens in Anahola, and what we are able to sell from the farm."

Mahealani's eyes narrowed and John noted how her brow creased with concern. Unable to drag out his little charade any longer, a sly grin played over his face.

"You have something you're hiding from me!" she said, her voice tinged with both anxiety and hopefulness.

John suddenly broke into a wide smile. "Aren't you going to congratulate the new head of security at the Kealia sugar plantation?"

Mahealani released a robust laugh. "You good-for-nothing!" she announced then gave his shoulder a slap. "Why did you scare me half to death?" She leaned into John, breathed his *ha*, and kissed him warmly. "I'm so proud of you," she said, touching his face and then grandson Edward's. After a moment, however, her mood shifted to something more pensive. "Kealia? That's so far from here." When she saw his eyes shift away from her, she asked, "John, where will you live? I don't want to leave the child, not while he's still a baby."

John took Edward and bounced the boy in his arms, nuzzling his soft cheek. "I'll get a small place in Kapaa. You and JJ will live here. When it's the right time, we can talk about making a change." John passed the baby to Mahealani, who carried him into the house.

Joe had been watching, remaining silent as husband and wife made decisions about their future. "You were wise to let her stay. She loves her grandson so much, and its making her strong again being a grandmother."

John finished his juice and then made a sweeping gesture with his arm, the cup pointed toward the full extent of the compound. "I'm counting on you to take care of the Kilauea property while I'm away, keep helping the Chinese and the men from Fiji. Someday, all of this will belong to you and Nani. But I have to warn you, be prepared for unwanted visitors." He saw the confusion in his friend's eyes. "Sheriff Kai told me that a new heiau, a temple, is nearly finished on one of the islands. Tradition requires that when it's ready for its god, human sacrifices must be made to him."

At first, Joe smiled, but his expression turned serious when he realized that John was not making a joke. "I can't believe there are still people practicing that bloody craziness. Are you sure this rumor isn't just empty talk?"

John grasped Joe by both arms and looked straight into his eyes. "Don't—do not—ignore Sheriff Kai's warning. He is Hawaiian, and he knows what happened in the old days when a temple was built. The ancients buried slaves at each of the corners, and then they took prisoners and sacrificed them. I seriously doubt that warriors will come here to seize one of you for sacrifice, but it's possible."

Still took a step back, releasing John's hold upon him. "You're a Christian man, such pagan practices have been banned by the church for half a century. John, this talk is nonsense. Belief in the old religion is dead."

"When I ignored the old religion, I almost lost my wife. But this is not about my beliefs, whether they are Christian or pagan, we are talking about those still alive in these islands who believe in the ancient gods. Promise me that if you see any tattooed men, watch out, for they are the evil ones." Both men knew that the missionaries had outlawed the tattooing of the human body as a pagan practice. So, any man who has tattoos is likely to be someone who believes in the ancient gods and human sacrifice.

Averting his eyes from John's intense glare, Joe asked, "If there is trouble, how do I get hold of you?"

"There's telephone service at the Make plantation. If you have trouble, call me there. I'll be sleeping in the office while I do my security work."

Joe promised to keep a close watch on the family and the land. John could see that there was something else on his mind and urged him to speak.

"I didn't want to worry you. But have you noticed that the irrigation ditch isn't running as much water from the river as it used to?"

John thought about this for a moment and didn't like the first thought that came to mind. "I suspect the sugar people want our land. Kilauea plantation has just brought in some new steam plows and they can dig up as much ground in a day as four hundred oxen. This land would be a nice addition to their holdings."

"I heard about those plows. That equipment, plus the railroad, would increase their sugar cultivation. I'd bet they will want to get this parcel."

"Never! Just keep an eye on things while I'm gone." Two days later, John bid farewell to his family.

CHAPTER 18

——

At midnight a week later, Joe Still heard the alarm bell at the fishing hut on the beach clang sharply. Two more bursts followed then the ringing stopped. He jumped from his bed grabbing his trousers. A frightened Nani shuddered. "What is it Joe?" Catherine in the second bedroom whimpered, "Mommy, Mommy".

Still grabbed his wife's arm while still buckling his pants. "I don't know what's happening but take the kids and get over to the big house as fast as you can."

Nani hesitated, struggling to waken. "The ringing has stopped. Do you think it might have been the wind that set it off?"

"That was not the wind that rang that bell three times. Dress and go. I'm going outside to raise the alarm."

He seized the only weapon he had, his cavalry saber, and ran to a bell on his porch. In his excitement he pulled its chain with such force that the metal edge of the bell struck the overhang of the house.

Lights popped on in the Tana compound. Voices shrieked: "What's going on? What's happening?"

Moana came to the stairs of the cottage and called out, "Joe, what's up?"

Joe yelled above the strident ringing of his bell, "I don't know, but the alarm from the beach went off. John warned me of raiders looking for human sacrifices. Get your family and the others into the large building."

Moana disappeared into his home emerging within a minute with his wife Pua holding their new baby. They hurried toward the refuge.

"What's up?" Kunani yelled from a home near Stills.

"Don't know, maybe raiders. Get to the large house now."

"Peter, stop that! You're going to get a good licking," Kunani's wife, Heather, threatened her young son. Peter stood with his feet pushed into the dirt refusing to move. Kunani, his hands full with a club and spears, nudged his son with his knee. The boy wouldn't move, instead he settled to the earth screaming.

Heather settled the issue by seizing Peter around the waist and hauling him toward the refuge. The young boy's feet kicked out behind her like a frightened swimmer escaping a shark.

Despite the danger, Still laughed at the family squabble. He kept ringing the bell until he saw no one entering the large building. He released his sword from its scabbard and felt the power of the weapon. His hand tightened on the yellow cotton braid on the hilt crowned at the pommel by the head of a golden eagle. Its fierce look exhibited strength and courage.

Fierce sounds pierced the night - parents yelling, children screaming, animals making crying noises. A strong wind blew into the trees bordering the compound. Branches whipped against each other emitting loud crackling in the air.

"Who is out there?" Still demanded.

Wind hissed through the pines. A distant waterfall crashed into Kilauea River. The sounds of animals and humans faded to silence.

"Who are you?"

Darkness gave no answer.

"Damn, show yourself," he challenged, cleaving the air with his sword. Night rendered enemies invisible. Still agonized, *have I raised a false alarm?*

From the trail leading up from the beach he heard a new sound, the slapping of human feet on hard-packed dirt.

Still hurried to the all-purpose building, anxiety for his family speeding his movements. His eyes searched around to be sure that no one was outside, then Joe crossed the threshold into the refuge.

"They coming, brother Joe?" Moana asked.

"Yes, men are coming." In the semidarkness Still saw Moana with his brothers Kamuela and Kunani at the threshold, each man armed with a club and spear.

Deeper within the shelter Still could hear the fussing of children and words of comfort from their mothers.

"Moana, you, Kamuela, Kunani, stand to the side of the door. Be ready with your clubs. Nani, are you in here?"

"Yes, I am here. I am taking care of the children with Pua, Heather, Rose, and grandmother Alapai."

"Send Heather and Rose to me."

"Kamuela, Kunani, I need your spears."

Rose touched Joe's arm. He twitched with the shock. "Guess I'm a little jumpy."

"Eh, you're not alone, brother. We feel the same. Hard to deal with ghosts who come in the dark."

By Rose's side Heather asked, "Joe, what do we do?"

Sticking his sword into the floor Joe took spears from Kamuela and Kunani. "Take these weapons. Stand to my left side. Wedge your spears into the floor the best you can. Hold them in front of you at an angle. Let the enemy run into the points. Just remember that too much poking around can be more dangerous to your friends than to our enemies."

"Are the shutters locked and barred?" Still asked.

"Yes, they are," Moana answered.

"Be patient everybody. Be silent. Only one bad man at a time can come through the door. He will die from our weapons. The enemy may pound on the walls, but do not be afraid and run out. If you do they will catch you."

With the men stationed to his right at the threshold and the women to his left, Still faced the entry. He held his sword in both hands like a lance ready to skewer anyone charging through the door.

A year before, wooden walls and a roof had been added to provide more security to the large building. Closed shutters lined the walls of the building. Still believed they were safe from fire, but even if the enemy flamed the building he had a plan to foil them.

Outside the refuge hostile sounds came from the compound, smashing blows against wood, snarls of anger, bare feet slapping on wet dirt. The exterior noises drew cries of fright from some of the children.

A tattooed body appeared at the threshold of the all-purpose building. A spear thrust through the opening and probed the dark within.

A man leaped into the entry, his body framed by the threshold. Still thrust his saber into him. Clubs struck the enemy warrior, one weapon hitting a knee, the other glancing from his neck onto his shoulder. A grossly tattooed man fell outside, his feet blocking the threshold.

Jabbering voices screamed hostility. They urged the wounded man to get out of the way. He moaned, blood gushing from the saber wound to his side. He pulled himself slowly from the threshold.

Pounding, rapping, clubbing tested the strength of the walls. A shattering sound of breaking wood pierced into the refuge. A club smashed again and again against the damaged shutter.

Children whimpered. A girl cried, "Mommy, Daddy, the noise, I'm scared." The rain of blows shook the walls. Nani seized the frightened child before she could run out the door.

"Moana, go to the broken shutter. Report!" Still ordered.

"Frame is holding but starting to buckle."

"Heather, take a spear and help Moana. Pua, Nani, get weapons and come to me."

When the two women came to him Still said, "We need teams to guard the shutters. Kamuela and Nani, you are one team. Pua and Kunani, you're another.

I'm sure I can guard this door by myself. When a shutter starts breaking a team will go to defend."

Within moments there came severe pounding against the back wall. Wood began to break. "Kunani, Pua, go," Still ordered.

At Moana's post, the shutter splintered. A hand clapped onto the sill. Moana smashed it with a club.

At the side wall, there came more pounding and the breaking of wood. Stones thudded against the building. "Kamuela, Nani, go," Still ordered. He stood alone by the open threshold. *If the enemy makes a coordinated attack*, he thought, *they could finish us.*

A figure appeared at the door. Two spears probed inside. Still swung his sword, the fine Toledo steel clove through the protruding shafts leaving only stubs in the hands of the enemy.

At the back wall Still heard Pua yell, "Die, you bastard." Someone outside screamed.

There was whistling. The pounding stopped. Feet slapped on damp earth.

Soon there came an eerie silence.

"Regroup at the door," Still ordered. "It's time to reconnoiter." He jumped through the threshold and into the night.

A club hurtled by him striking the ground. Still whirled, slicing with his sword. The blade bit into flesh. The attacker howled and staggered into the darkness.

Two enemy warriors hurled spears. "You will die," they yelled.

Warned by the cries, Still ducked back through the threshold into the safety of the family refuge.

Calls and whistles disturbed the darkness. Voices jabbered outside. Then sounds of the stomping of many feet moving away.

Silence outside the refuge stretched from seconds into minutes. The only sounds breaking the stillness were that of fussing children inside. Finally, Still said, "I'll take a look."

"Let me," Moana answered.

Instead, Still jumped into the night flourishing his sword.

"This haole guy either crazy or one brave bugga. Come on Kunani, we better go outside and save the wild man." Moana laughed.

The three men stood in the darkness beyond the threshold searching the night. Except for the sounds of the wind the compound lay empty.

Despite the fear of ambush Still said, "Let's get torches and check around."

In the orange-yellow light the three men searched the compound. "Look like you got somebody," Kunani said as he raised his torch pointing his club to puddles of drying blood.

"Yeah, somebody is bleeding bad. Look, you can see the spots of blood heading to the trail that leads to the beach." Moana followed the dried drips of blood to the downward slope of the Tana compound.

"They're gone," Still said.

"Yeah, let's find out how the kids are," Kunani said. The three men returned to the large building.

"Where are Mahealani and JJ?" Still asked when he completed his third head count.

"Oh my," Nani suddenly remembered. "They went to the fishing hut to sleep. They were going to pick limu early in the morning when the tide is low."

Fear swept through Still. "They are the ones who sounded the alarm. I have failed John. I failed Mahealani and JJ."

"Moana, Kunani, go to the beach, find them," Still croaked, his emotions crushing him. "I'll go to the promontory and search the sea. The rest of you stay in the refuge. Wait here until we return."

CHAPTER 19

—

At the end of his first week at Kealia, John rolled into his cot exhausted after a round of arson checks at the sugar mill. He fell instantly asleep. The shrill ring of the telephone forced him awake and he wondered what fool would call at 5:30 in the morning. "What's up?" he demanded, yawning into the phone.

"John, Joe Still, we were raided last night by bandits. Mahealani and JJ are missing."

His heart raced against his chest and his hands shook so hard he nearly dropped the receiver. "What happened?"

"It'll take too long to explain. They were tattooed, just like you warned, and they're in a double canoe with a brown crab-claw sail. We think they're heading your way. Get on a hill and see if you can spot them. I'm bringing some of the boys to Kealia. Arm yourself, these men are vicious."

John slammed the phone onto its cradle, grabbed his telescope, and tore out of the office. Yelling for his assistant, he saddled his horse and mounted it. Manuel came charging to him, buttoning his pants and wiping sleep from his eyes.

"My wife and son have been kidnapped," John said his voice urgent. "I'm going to the Kealia point to see if I can spot them. Get weapons, rope, and load them onto a horse. Be ready to leave when I return."

He galloped to the lookout point and searched the water to the north. At first, he saw nothing. After an hour he spotted a double canoe a mile away. Waves buffeted the vessel and its sail was furled. With the telescope, he identified eight paddlers. Two of them appeared to be his wife and son. They had ropes tied around their neck. Two people were bound to the sail pole centered on the platform between hulls. One man lay on his back. The other had something wrapped around his arm and shoulder and appeared to hold a club.

John whipped his horse around, hurtling back to the plantation office. He clicked the phone several times before the operator woke up. "Get me Sheriff Lovell in Lihue, emergency!"

"This is Lovell, who are you?"

"John Tana. My wife and son have been kidnapped. There's a double canoe with six, maybe eight bandits, heading your way. Have you got ships in the harbor?"

"None in Kapaa, Nawiliwili, or Koloa," Lovell answered. "Damn! How are we going to get these guys?"

A brief silence ended when the Sheriff said, "The shortest route for the bandits is to come to Nawiliwili and then head across the channel."

"Can you call Honolulu?"

"There is no phone service to the capitol. Track these guys as they move down the coast. I'm guessing that, with this wind, they'll have to make landfall on Kauai before pushing across the channel tomorrow. I'll rustle up some men and two boats. Meet me at Kalapaki by nightfall."

John crawled onto the edge of a cliff searching for the enemy canoe. He spotted it still heading south, its sail unfurled, the ocean swells slowing its progress. "Lovell's right," he muttered. "They will have to come ashore for the night and resume their voyage in the morning. He watched the vessel round Kealia point then rushed to his office.

Joe had not arrived, and Manuel waited for instructions. "Get fresh horses for Still and his group and wait for them. I will watch the enemy. Tell everyone to meet me at the Wailua River."

For the rest of the morning John tracked the hostile canoe. Early in the afternoon, it crossed the wide mouth of Wailua Bay. As it did, the western sun blazed through heavy clouds hanging over the dead volcano of Waialeale. The bright light shone full upon the sacrificial temple at the river's mouth, its rays reaching out to the war canoe plunging through the waves, skimming across the bay.

John envisioned Mahealani tied to the temple's altar. Beside her stood the god Ku, his tooth-filled mouth gaping, thirsting for her blood. The priest next to the idol, draped in white robes, raised the sacrificial knife, plunging it—"

"No," John screamed.

Startled by the cry, the bargeman standing at the river demanded, "What's going on?"

"Nothing, just a bad dream."

Flood waters roared down the river and the boatman shook his head. "Plenty rain come down pretty soon, no can cross."

"Where's Joe?" John fretted, not sure if he should push on or wait. Just as the war canoe disappeared around the sacred temple at Wailua point, John heard the pounding of hooves. Over a low hill came Joe, Moana, Kunani, and Manuela, the four men galloping toward a frantic John Tana, their horses lathered with sweat. "Where have you been!"

Joe dismounted, running up to his friend, his cavalry scabbard jingling at his side. "We got here as fast as we could, sorry. It's nearly impossible in this rain."

John saw the scabbard. "You're going to fight with that?"

"It's one hell of a weapon," Moana interrupted. "I saw him put down several enemy with that sword."

"Okay, everybody on the barge," John ordered. He fought the fear welling inside him. He masked the tears in his eyes by seizing the traversing rope and yanking the barge into the river.

"Hey, wait until we are all in before charging off," Still yelled as he hauled himself into the barge.

"Sorry." John eased his grip on the traversing rope, letting Joe climb onto the barge as he shook river water from his boots.

The bargeman ordered the men and horses over to one side of the vessel while he helped John pull. The craft plowed into the river, dirty flood water filled with logs buffeted the side of the barge, the powerful flow of water threatening to upend and hurl it into the crashing waves raging at the mouth of the river.

"Joe, you and the rest of the boys grab those poles and help push us across this river." John yelled. "The boatman and I are barely able to keep this craft from spinning out into the sea."

"Push hard," the boatman yelled, panic in his voice as the barge turned toward the ocean. By their combined efforts, the men forced the vessel across the river, the barge finally crunching into its reed-filled south bank. They led their horses from the craft, mounted, and sped toward Kalapaki Beach.

CHAPTER 20

———

Two miles south of the river, John wormed his way through thick grass to the edge of Nukolii Beach, checking the progress of the enemy canoe. Rays of descending sun warmed his back as he peered through shoreline bushes at the sea. The hostile vessel was fifty yards from shore heading south.

Mahealani slumped in the canoe, her paddle trailing in the water. A tattooed warrior yanked on the rope around her throat yelling, "Paddle, you lazy bitch." The man prodded her on the shoulder with a spear.

John's heart urged him to leap into the water and swim to her rescue. Yet he knew he was too far away to help her. "Damn," he muttered, swallowing hard, suppressing his desire to bellow his anger. It would be stupid to reveal himself and compromise the rescue effort. Fighting his impulses, John returned to his companions and they continued their journey to Kalapaki.

In the growing darkness of evening Sheriff Lovell watched the enemy canoe sailing past Kalapaki Beach. "They are heading for Kipu Kai. They will spend the night there and then shoot off tomorrow for Kaena point on Oahu."

"I reckon you could be right," John answered, squatting beside him. "Right now, the wind would make it tough to travel across the Kauai channel at night."

"That's what I think. It's sixty miles of wild ocean and getting dark. Let's mount up and go after them."

The two men rode to the beach where the rest of the rescue team waited. They launched two outrigger canoes and headed into the sea, paddling their craft for the seldom-visited valley of Kipu Kai. Sheriff Lovell was in the lead canoe accompanied by his deputy, Kainoa, and John. In their wake came Still,

Moana, and Kunani. The sheriff was armed with a rifle, but John insisted that firearms not be used in the rescue attempt. "Gunfire in the darkness is too dangerous. We need to get close enough to identify the enemy, and then fight them hand-to-hand."

A howling wind smashed into the canoes pushing them toward massive rock walls at the south edge of Nawiliwili Bay. "You can see the headland to your right," the sheriff yelled. "Pull left. Pull left."

Water swirled into their vessels as the rescuers turned their crafts into the teeth of the wind and waves. "Bail, Moana. Kunani, steer left," Still yelled. His strident cries sent a shiver through John, as his canoe was also in danger of being swamped.

Did the enemy have the same trouble? But then he remembered they had a double canoe with more paddlers. Fear engulfed him as he recalled how worn Mahealani looked. *I know she would die if we do not rescue her. She would be sacrificed on an altar to a pagan god.* The muscles of his arms bulged as he drove his canoe up, over, and down waves that pounded in huge mountains of foam into the cliffs.

By inches the canoes escaped being ground into splinters as they slipped by the wave-smashed headland. John's team paddled into the less turbulent waters of a small bay. Many yards from the shore a bonfire blazed sending sparks shooting toward the stars. In the uncertain light, figures hovered around it.

The rescuers floated a few yards beyond the low surf breaking onto a fringing reef. "Those guys think no one's following them," John said.

"Do we rush the beach and charge them?" Still asked.

Lovell shook his head. "That would be a mistake. They'll know we're coming and might kill their prisoners. For now, we've got the element of surprise."

John nodded. "The last thing we want is to make a lot of noise and have them prepared to defeat us."

"John, swim to shore,'" Lovell said. "Check things out. Moana, Still, and I will follow. We'll meet at the high-water mark. He turned to Kainoa and Kunani. "Guard the canoes. When you hear me yelling *hele mai*, charge the beach."

John slipped into the sea and swam through the breakers. He reached the shore and moved upland to the grass at the edge of the sand. He studied the area around the bonfire and as much of the surroundings as he could see in the dim light of the stars. Then he returned to the water's edge and waited as his three companions crawled over the reef and worked their way to the beach.

John saw a streak blaze across the heavens, its light fading as the tiny rock from space burnt itself away. Scudding clouds blew past Kilohana crater, uncovering millions of stars, their distant light shining bright in the clear sky of a moonless night. John searched for Arcturus, the heavenly guide that had led early voyagers to Hawaii. If he could find it, the omen would be good for their rescue attempt. But then he thought that the men who had seized Mahealani and JJ were also searching the heavens for a sign that their deity was pleased with their sacrificial gifts. He shook his head realizing that searching for omens was denying God. He prayed for His help.

Lovell was with Moana, and Still joined John at the edge of the beach grass. "Maybe seven warriors. One is a lookout fifty-yards from us. Somewhere beyond the fire are the prisoners."

Lovell nodded. "How do you want to proceed? It's your family that's in trouble. We will follow your lead."

John thought for some moments. He glanced at the fire. A bird cawed, soaring overhead searching. He sorted through the possibilities and settled on a plan. "I'll circle around and approach the enemy from the rear. I'll try to find where the prisoners are held. Sheriff, you and Moana station yourself close to the lookout ahead of us. Joe, head down the beach maybe twenty yards. When I'm in position I will hoot like an owl. On that signal, rise up, scream like a thousand devils, and attack." With that, John scrambled over the brush at the high-water mark, dropped onto his belly, and wormed his way through the scrub.

—

CHAPTER 21

Despite a sense of urgency John moved slowly through the shrubs covering the valley floor. The beach fire suddenly flamed skyward. He stopped his crawl, watched the figures hovering around the burning wood. One man looked in his direction. Something in his eyes spread fear inside him.

Had he attracted the man's attention, but how? The wind blew into his face. The slight sounds of his crawling were carried away from the enemy. John remained still, his eyes locked onto the standing man. The delay worried him. Something terrible could be happening to his family.

Laughter drifted from the men at the fire. Someone handed the staring man a cup. He took it and squatted. The wind blew raucous noise into his ears. He became anxious as he thought he heard a voice pleading. But the warriors' voices and the crackle of burning wood were too loud. He could not be sure what he heard. He edged closer to the fire.

The smoke from smoldering driftwood blew over him. Mixed with it John caught the pungent smell of tobacco. He froze, searching the darkness. At the edge of the bonfire a man stood smoking. He quelled the wild beating of his heart. He stifled the scream of an owl that welled up in his throat. It was too soon to attack. He must locate his family first. But surely this man would see him?

The fire blazed high, but its flickering fingers did not reach out to him. He remained motionless, a crouching statue. The shroud of darkness that spread over Kipu Kai hid him, and the enemy warrior turned back to the bonfire. John thanked God for keeping the moon below the horizon. He slid deeper into the blackness working his way around the group huddled at the flames.

The ground sloped, and he scrambled up taking care not to dislodge loose rocks that could roll and alert his enemies. Except for the sounds of men carousing, the night remained silent. He rested his arm on a low boulder studying the ground below him. In the faint starlight he could make out shrubs and low rocks silhouetted in the bonfire. He could not find his family. He wondered what to do? Move to the attack, hooting like an owl? Wait until the fire died and the warriors were asleep? He knew that the only chance for JJ and Mahealani to live lay with him. If he bungled the rescue they would surely die.

His eyes fought into the gloom, straining to brush aside the ink of night. He spied, just beyond the fire, several bundles shaped like corpses prepared for burial. He heard an angry voice. At the fire he saw a warrior struggling with someone. There was the sound of flesh being hit.

JJ pleaded, "Stop. Please, stop." The beach fire flared away a curtain of shadow. A man had mounted his son like a dog in heat. John rose to attack. But where was Mahealani? Frantic, his eyes returned to the bundles. He heard the ripping of cloth. He saw the outline of a man, his body plunging down, uttering animal sounds as he pumped. Mahealani screamed, "No! Stop! It hurts!"

John ran hooting like an owl. A shrub caught his leg, he stumbled. Reaching down, he pushed off from a boulder and kept running toward the shrieks. He heard men at the fire laughing at her cries. In the firelight he saw a hand strike. He heard the rapist yell, "Shut up." The screams of Mahealani were replaced by sobs. He was closer now and saw the huge body of a man thrusting again and yet again into his wife.

Sickened by the ugliness of the attack, training, patience, planning blew away as John emitted a primal cry and ploughed into the sex-crazed man who rose from his missionary position exposing his torso. John's knife slid into the man's stomach and ripped up. Entrails bubbled out like a raw egg when its shell is cracked. The rapist howled. John seized his legs and yanked him from his wife. Screaming, he rolled onto his back, blood pumping from his cut belly.

The sound of breaking shrubs drew John from the wounded man, who blubbered as he tried to close the wound with his hands. Two warriors burst through the brush. One of them shouted, "Give 'em", raised a club, and smashed it downward to pulverize John like an insect.

He rolled away from the blow, pulled free a baton attached to his waist, and rose to a crouch. A spear nicked his side drawing blood. With a short stabbing thrust, John drove his hard, round stick into the gut of the spearman and watched him stagger toward the fire. Something sharp grazed his back, ripping his shirt, drawing blood. John twisted and swung his club into the shoulder and neck of his attacker. The man went down, incomprehensible words gurgling in his throat. Beyond the fire, Joe yelled in Hawaiian, English, and French. Lovell bellowed, "Surrender or die." A voice John did not recognize screamed, "Kill 'em" and grasped his feet. He kicked a bearded face. The man lunged in a clumsy attempt to tackle him. "It hurts," his wife sobbed. He heard the sheriff yelling, "Hele mai!" Moana screamed, "Where's my sister?" A guttural voice answered, "Eat shit."

Hands grasped his thighs. John swung down with his closed palm. He heard a grunt. His feet came free of clinging arms. He grasped hair and swung a knee into the jaw of his attacker. The man fell. John hurried to the groans of his wife. "It hurts," Mahealani moaned as John cut away the ropes that bound her arms. He whispered gentle words, as if soothing a frightened child. He found pieces of cloth and tried wrapping it around her nakedness, but she whimpered, "It hurts," and pushed his hands away from her thighs.

Battle sounds erupted from the beach. John saw figures silhouetted in the firelight, fighting, screaming, a howling bedlam of noise. He thought to aid his friends, but Mahealani sobbed, writhed on the ground in agony, her words incoherent. He realized that the kidnap and the terrible assault had pushed her to the edge of sanity. John folded her into him. He rubbed his palm over her hair and back saying, "You're safe. I'll protect you."

Mahealani's eyes widened. She stifled tears and pushed away from John. "Where were you?" Her fists beat against his chest. A sudden spasm of heaving erupted bile from her stomach and she vomited onto the sand. "Water," she begged. She vomited again and gasped, "Water."

Frantic, John searched the ground around him. The fighting had moved beyond the fire. Someone yelled, "To the canoe." Moana bellowed, "They're taking JJ. John, help." Mahealani heaved, her words garbled. "I'm helping, sister," John yelled and headed toward the flames. He passed the dying rapist, resisting an urge to kick him. Angry voices skipped through the darkness. Lovell shouted, "Give up the boy!" A deep voice answered, "Come get him."

John searched the ground near the burning wood. Beyond the flames he saw men edging toward the beach. He thought to join the fight, but Mahealani was alone. She was helpless. He must protect her from predators that could be lurking in the shadows. He found a gourd of water and rushed to her side. "Drink this," he urged, holding it to her trembling lips.

She coughed, the liquid stinging her throat. She begged for more. He offered her the gourd and she seized it, drinking her fill. Suddenly, as if awakening to terror, she cried, "Where is JJ?"

"I don't know," answered John, his voice breaking with worry for his son and wife.

"Find him. Find him."

CHAPTER 22

———

Weak light from a rising moon struggled to penetrate the heavy clouds that blanketed the Kauai channel. Giant waves rolled across the sea, pushing the outrigger canoe up then plunging it down in a dizzying series of rises and falls. John grasped the knob and long stem of his paddle and stroked it through the water to Moana's commands: "Pull on the right, one, two, and three. Pull on the left, one, two, and three." John, Sheriff Lovell, and Kunani timed their thrusts to Moana's cadence. The rhythmic beat sped the outrigger through the roiling water in pursuit of a double canoe with six warriors and JJ.

As he fought through the waves with the strength of a desperate man, John worried. *The rift caused by my Christianity, Mahealani's paganism, and the premature death of our son had just healed. Now this savage attack by men bent on human sacrifice has pushed her to the edge. Mahealani blamed me for her capture and rape. She blamed me for the loss of JJ. I know I must rescue our son, or I could lose her for all time.* "Pull harder!" he shouted.

"Harder?" Moana answered, his tone incredulous. But he increased the cadence plunging the canoe into the waves. The roiling waves smashed into the prow, splashed high, then fell back, dousing the paddlers in showers of salt water. The sudden surge of effort narrowed the gap between the pursued and the pursuer.

"This is the meanest, roughest water in the world," Lovell complained, paddling behind John. "Remember Kamehameha? He tried to conquer this channel a hundred years ago, but it conquered him. He lost half his army and almost joined the fishes. Maybe we should slow the pace and just try to make it to Kaena Point."

John shook his head. "If these are Waianae guys and they make it home, we won't stand a chance of saving my son. If they're not, we could lose them in the dark. We got to stick close. Catch them in this channel."

"I hear you. Save your son. I'm for that. But the only reason we are keeping up is that the wind is blowing against those bandits. They can't use their sail. If it changes, we'll never catch them."

A huge wave smashed the canoe. The curved outrigger that kept the vessel stable submerged. The canoe tilted at a dangerous angle and began to overturn. Paddling stopped as men leaned their bodies into the thrust of the wave. The outrigger surfaced. The canoe rode over the wave and slid into its trough. Another wave surged toward them.

"Lean on the left," Moana yelled.

"John, bail!" Lovell screamed as water ran the length of the canoe. Moana corrected the broadside drift of the craft and steered it into the rising swell. With great effort, the sheriff and Kunani paddled up and over the wave. John scooped water from the canoe, bailing as fast as he could.

"We lost headway when the last wave hit," John said, despair in his voice. The wind howled flinging his words back to him. He worried that they were beaten, the chase to save his son ended by the harshness of a powerful sea.

"Don't think so," Lovell yelled. "Those bandits might have a better canoe, but they're having trouble staying ahead of us. We're closer now than ever before." John stole a glance at the vessel ahead. He could see warriors stooped over, obviously exhausted. They're tired from too much paddling over the last several days, he thought. His despair turned to elation, and despite the dangers posed by the huge swells, he called, "Moana, faster."

"You're crazy. We almost turn over, and you want to go faster." Mahealani's brother laughed as he obliged and quickened the pace. The outrigger plunged up the waves, over, and down, again and yet again. The gap between canoes narrowed to twenty-five yards.

John thought that the warriors ahead were oblivious to their pursuit and he urged his team to paddle in silence. Slowly, the gap closed. The moonlight broke through the shrouding clouds, shedding a pale silver light on the chase. When they were less than sixty feet apart one of the warriors shouted, "Them guys are chasing us! Paddle more hard!" For a moment the enemy canoe surged ahead. "*Imua i na poki!* Go forward, young brothers," John shouted, uttering the battle cry of Kamehameha the Great.

The two vessels plunged over massive waves fighting to remain upright in the rough waters. There were tantalizing moments when, on the crest of a wave, John thought that he could reach below him and seize the mast pole of the enemy canoe.

Clouds scooted across the sky and the moon shone bright upon the water. The once boiling ocean calmed into long, slow swells, and stars winked upon the world. Less than twenty feet separated the two canoes.

John became energized, knowing that in a matter of minutes, they would reach the enemy. Then it would be a battle, man against man, savagery against cunning. He would fight for his son. Kill if he had to. A stone zipped by him and then another. He saw an unsteady warrior, standing with a foot on the platform between canoes, slinging stones. John smiled at his foolishness. The restless sea made it nearly impossible to hurl rocks with accuracy.

His laugh turned to a scowl as he sensed a shift in the wind. The slinger put away his weapon. The double canoe slowed, and John saw an unguarded JJ drag his paddle in the water. "Pull, pull," he yelled knowing that if the enemy sail was unfurled, the race to save his son was lost.

The slinger leaped onto the center platform and scurried to its sail pole. John's canoe surged forward, its prow just feet away from the enemy vessel. The slinger, a heavily tattooed man, pulled on the handlines rigged to the boom of the mast. The hala sail unrolled, spreading out as it rose up the pole. It billowed. Then the sail tightened as it captured the wind. The canoe surged forward.

John threw the three-pronged anchor of his craft onto the center platform of the double canoe. Iron hooks smashed into wood. The enemy craft slowed. John pulled on the anchor rope drawing the vessels together. He leaped onto the center platform. His hand reached to the three-pronged anchor he had used to grapple the double canoe and made certain that its barbs were deeply embedded into the fiber of the platform. He checked the anchor rope and assured himself that it stretched tight and secure between canoes.

The tattooed warrior by the mast pole stuck out his tongue, smirked, and said, "Goin' bust you up." He came at John. A man in the hull to his left poked his paddle at John's legs yelling, "Bastard."

He slid sideways to avoid the thrust, crouched, and swung a fist into the scrotum of the attacking tattooed enemy. The man's clenched hand pounded his back with little force behind the blow. The double canoe rolled up. John's opponent fell back onto the platform groaning, his head and upper body draped onto the left side hull. He saved himself from slipping into the water by grasping a crossbeam supporting the platform between canoes.

John pulled himself onto the right hull where JJ squatted. An enemy warrior turned and came at them swinging his paddle.

"Give me your stick," John said, wresting the broad-bladed oar from JJ's hands. A sudden exhilaration coursed through him. The chase was over. His son was alive and by his side. The enemy would never capture him again. He parried the wild swing of the warrior, the stems of the two paddles clashed together. Snarling, the man jabbed his weapon.

John slid his body to the side and countered the strike by smashing the broad leaf of the paddle at the head of his enemy. The roll of a wave tossed the canoe sideways. He missed the man's skull, but his paddle struck the warrior's shoulder. His opponent grimaced. He heard Kunani shouting and the sound of wood smashing into flesh. The wind blew strong against the hala sail, speeding both canoes bound together by the anchor rope toward Oahu.

Angered by the theft of his son, pushed to the edge of reason by the rape of his wife, John hacked his paddle into his opponent, splintering it against his body. Someone leaped onto the platform, and John thrust the jagged edges of his broken stick into the man. He yelled, "Sheriff, cut the rope." John grabbed JJ and rolled over the side of the canoe.

When they surfaced the enemy canoe had sped by them. His vessel rolled in the water a few feet away. John hollered, waved his hands. Moana guided the outrigger to where father and son bobbed in the chop of the channel.

CHAPTER 23

———

By dawn, John was back on the beach, his son safely by his side. They held Mahealani, soothing her pain, touching her bruises with care. But the internal injuries, the emotional scars, were painful. He knew it would be difficult for her to heal.

With loving tenderness, John brought his family back to Kilauea. He decided not to discuss the rape, choosing for his wife to speak of the unspeakable only when she was ready. The trauma of the attack lingered for months, during which Mahealani barely functioned.

Blessed by youth, JJ recovered rapidly, although he often awoke from terrible nightmares. It was always the same: the disfigured man who fondled him, toyed with him, and injected deep shame into his life.

Two months after his rescue, young JJ, now fifteen years of age, stood with his father and Moana at Pilaa beach. The three of them carried fishing spears, giving them the appearance of Hawaiian warriors.

"It's time a skinny guy like you challenged the ocean," Moana said. "And you don't have to be scared of Mano, JJ. When you're with me, nothing will happen."

John knew JJ still feared the great predator. He saw how JJ hung back from the water.

"Dad, are you coming with us?"

Moana gave JJ an affectionate slap on the shoulder. "Hey, no be scared of the shark, we'll be by your side!" With that, Moana and John waded into the water and swam out to sea.

John turned back and saw JJ hesitate. "Come on in!" he waved his spear. When his son finally plunged into the waves, bubbles and white foam frothed around him. JJ followed the surge outward and then, breaking through the swell, stroked hard through the clear blue water and joined the men.

"Eh, plenty game below," Moana exclaimed, treading water. "Look down." Under them swam a large school of fish. The boy looked up, eyes wide.

"Those are the biggest fish I've ever seen."

John had been afraid that JJ would turn and swim toward shore. He was delighted when the boy swam directly toward the finned animals. John followed his son. What he discovered was an underwater heaven filled with beautiful coral, great caves with many-colored fish spilling out and flitting around his son. After many dives, the three broke the surface and floated leisurely for a few minutes, before Moana swam further out. John kept an eye on his son, unaware of his brother-in-law's sudden frantic waving. "It's coming at you!" Moana shouted.

Something swam toward them. A grey fin knifed through the water. John swam toward his son.

"What's coming?" JJ screamed.

John plunged his head beneath the surface and saw that the current had pulled JJ toward a narrow channel, with brown reef walls rising on either side. He saw the long, cigar-shaped fish swimming toward the channel. JJ twenty yards away from it.

John kicked hard to reach him. Even if the boy made it to a reef, the water would still be over his head, making him an easy target for the shark. How many times had John told his son, "Fear is the enemy, you must conquer it. The coward gives up and dies."

John saw the shark dive at the boy's legs and then, turning, bare his teeth-filled jaws. As if watching a nightmare suddenly come alive, John saw JJ raise his spear and drive it into the shark's gills behind the crease of its jaws. John arrived at JJ's side just as the boy pushed his weapon deeper into flesh and slid his hands along the haft up to the gills to smother the shark.

Moana appeared at John's side and together they speared into the predator's gills. Together, the three wrestled the great fish toward shore. With huge effort, they dragged the shark onto the beach, where it flopped in desperation, the spears projecting from its body creating furrows in the sand.

"You are one brave young man," Moana announced, clapping JJ on the back. "A real warrior!" John added as he hugged his son.

"A warrior, yes, and now, my nephew is a killer of sharks." Moana laughed and pulled his spear from the predator's gills. "I will make you a trophy: a shark-skin belt and, from the teeth of the shark, a buckle."

The boy thrust his fist at the sea and called across the tossing waters, "I am not afraid of you, Mano!"

CHAPTER 24

———

Shortly after his victory over Mano, JJ showed his parents a rash that had appeared on his cheek and hand. John rubbed aloe on both and asked his son if he'd been with anyone who had open sores, a misshapen nose, missing fingers, or aching feet. He didn't want to frighten the boy, but a sense of dread ran through him.

"I haven't been near anyone like that," JJ said. A moment later, he added, "But do you remember the man who took me?" The boy released a shiver and leaned closer to his father. "He kept touching me and breathing over me."

John recalled the man, his disfigurements and grotesque appearance. When he was alone with Mahealani he told her, "I don't like what I'm seeing on JJ. He's got red rashes that itch." When his wife appeared perplexed, he added, "When I was on Molokai, the lepers told me that their troubles often started with rashes. What do you think?"

Mahealani stared dreamily at John, as if she had heard nothing. John knew she was traumatized by the sexual assault. Some days she was hardly with him, her mind drifting to places he could not see. "Those evil men dance in front of me. I can feel their harsh hands on my body." And then tears would well in her eyes and spill onto her cheeks. At times like these, John felt helpless. He would pat her listless hand and kiss her forehead, wondering if she would ever return from this world of hell where her mind dwelt.

John wasn't sure how to proceed with JJ, so he decided to wait. Several weeks later, he was thrilled to discover that the rash had completely disappeared.

Several months passed and Mahealani showed signs of improvement. She was taking walks with John and showing more interest in the people around her. He watched this and began to relax, finally able to tell himself that life would soon return to normal.

With the suddenness of a rushing storm, everything changed. JJ came to his father and showed him new rashes, these even more virulent than the previous outbreak. "I can hardly feel my toes and fingers," he complained, holding up his hands. "And my thumb is always so cold. I cut it the other day, Dad, and it didn't hurt."

John looked at the boy's hands, his own trembling as he studied JJ's palms. A large sore covered a quadrant of skin.

"It's been there for about a week. It doesn't get any better."

John pricked at the wound with the point of a stick. "Do you feel this?"

The boy shook his head, staring hard at his palm. He looked up slowly, his eyes searching his father's face. "Why don't I feel pain?" he asked, his voice rising in fear.

John found Mahealani in the kitchen, bent over the sink and washing dirt from fresh vegetables. When she heard him, she turned, her eyes blinking as she awoke to his presence. It took only a moment for concern to appear on her face. "What is it?"

John placed a hand on his wife's arm. "I've just seen new rashes on JJ." His voice was forced, emotion nearly closing his throat. "Our son has leprosy."

Mahealani gasped and her hand moved to her mouth, barely stifling a scream.

From the other room came an infant's cry. Nani rushed in, a baby in her arms. "What's going on?" she demanded.

Mahealani turned slowly to face her daughter. "Your father says JJ has leprosy," she whispered, tears filling her eyes.

The young woman stared at her mother for a moment and then shifted her gaze to her father. Had John not stepped forward, the baby might have fallen to the floor.

In the days that followed, the family agonized over their choices. John knew that time was not on JJ's side. As parts of the body were affected, the bacteria wreaked havoc on the nerve endings. Without those nervous impulses and receptors, injuries resulted. He also knew that the disease would spread. They could hide the sores on JJ's hands and torso, but what would they do when they appeared on his face? And after that, John's stomach turned over at the thought of his beautiful child becoming grotesque, a boy without fingers and toes. And the odor of decay!

While the Tana family considered their options, they also feared discovery. Informants were paid a bounty to turn in lepers. This left the afflicted only two choices: surrender to the Health Department and be buried alive in the colony at Kalaupapa or flee.

Nani was the first to insist that colonization was not an option. "JJ isn't going there!" she argued. "You said it yourself: the government doesn't take care of the people who are there. And now that kokua helpers aren't allowed, he'll be forced to rot and die alone, without anyone to love him or care for him!" The young woman burst into tears and rushed from the room.

"She's right," John said, holding his wife. "Our only choice is to help him run away."

Nani heard this from the other room and returned. "Yes, please, anything but that colony." And then, as if to seal the decision, she whispered, "We're talking about my little brother's life."

John did his best to reassure his family and started his own quiet investigation. Since the Bayonet Constitution, hardheaded businessmen controlled the Board of Health and instituted some harsh financial sanctions. One of those was to close the doors on those kindhearted souls who lived with the lepers. Funds to the colonies were being reduced and lepers were suffering the consequences.

John Tana knew too well that every family facing this decision suffered the same turmoil: What is the right thing to do? Thousands of Hawaiian families had suffered, and were still suffering, the terrible guilt of indecision. Do I choose what the government tells me? Or do I follow my heart and do what's best for someone I love?

Several days after the family's discussion, Mahealani called them together. "This is what we're going to do," she announced, no equivocation in her words. It was the old Mahealani, the woman who existed before the assault. Her voice was strong and sure. "We'll take JJ to Kalalau Valley, where many lepers are hiding. I will go with him," she added, raising a hand to silence John's protest. "He is my son, I am his mother, and he will not die alone."

Mahealani had spoken; the decision was made.

—

CHAPTER 25

Kalalau Valley, Na Pali, Kauai

On a warm, clear day early in 1889, when a soft breeze floated about the Tana compound and the world seemed ideal, John, Mahealani, and young JJ sailed for Kalalau Valley. As the boat moved farther from the shore, the boy looked back at his home. His eyes never left that spot until, finally, the boat rounded Kilauea point.

The family arrived at Kalalau beach, where they were welcomed by women bearing flower lei. They held Mahealani close, exchanging ha, giving her comfort, and JJ was treated with equal tenderness, taken by a throng of people to a long table where Judge Kauai anointed the boy a Chief of the Tribe. Celebration and feasting followed the appointment, and, for a moment, John was able to forget why they had come.

In the wide, pie-shaped valley above the ocean, John built a small house for his wife and son. It would be Mahealani who would convert this little structure into a home. They knew what awaited them—the horror of the illness and the separation from their loved ones—but the area was serenely beautiful, and they cared only about their son's remaining life.

John, Mahealani, and JJ spent hours hiking the area. They found streams that sliced into the rocks, creating pools for marine life to flourish. Moss fed by rain covered the rock walls of the valley and turned it into a great veil of green. Rock terraces rose from the beach, reminding these new inhabitants that there was a time when thousands of Hawaiians lived and prospered in this valley.

The night before John left, he sat on the bed, Mahealani stretched out beside him. His heart was filled with pain, the thought of living without his wife and son too difficult to fathom. He eased himself down and tucked his body against hers. Mahealani abruptly turned her back to him. "Damn it, this is my last night with you!" he complained.

She folded her knees to her chest.

John reached over, intending to force her against him, and then he stopped. A wave or guilt washed over him and swept away his anger. *It is my fault that our son is ill. My fault that my wife has moved from the warmth of life to the fear of men. That is why she is cold, because fear is still with her.* John stroked Mahealani's shoulder, as if his touch could release the terror from her soul. *He remembered former times, her happy smile, and the sweet, alluring scent of her body. His eyes filled with tears as he recalled the warmth of her ha mixing with his.*

The moment of departure arrived and those in the colony who were well enough to leave their homes came to the shore with flowers and aloha. John was deeply aware of the depth of his sadness, and that of his wife and son, yet he also understood that this was a choice of the heart, and it was the right choice.

Before he left, John promised Mahealani to pray to God for a return of health to her and their son. With listless eyes Mahealani looked at him and said, "Pray to the gods. Pray to the kahuna. They are the only ones that can save us now."

John left Kalalau realizing that he had lost his wife to the religion of the ancients.

CHAPTER 26

—

A very sad John Tana sat with his son-in-law on the veranda of his Koolau home. "It proved difficult to leave them, but I knew they would be well cared for. The hardest hit of all is Mahealani. Her mind is adrift. The rape and JJ's illness has pushed her over the edge of sanity."

"It is sad to hear that." Joe shook his head. "She had been making a great recovery from Edward's death and then the attack by the bandits. We should have killed them all when we had the chance."

"That might have been hard to do in that turbulent sea. We got JJ back, that's all I cared about at the time. Would we have killed the carrier of that terrible disease if we knew then what we know now?"

"I would say, yes. We are not saints. Aren't you glad you eliminated Mahealani's rapist for all time?"

"True, but I would be much happier if instead of satisfying revenge I had solutions to the illnesses of my family."

"I don't know what we can do for Mahealani, the mind is too complicated, but I just learned that the Chinese may have found a cure for leprosy."

"That's great news. What is it? What do we do?"

It's some kind of herbal medicine. You can't find it here. I think you'll have to go to Chinatown in Honolulu."

"Then I'll do it."

"What about your job in Kealia?"

"I lost it, gone too many days. Besides, management thought the arson risk is low in Kealia and decided to try making it without security."

"It's an unwise decision on their part. Do you need money?"

"I got enough to scrape by. You and the rest of the Alapai family can take care of the farm, my rice security work, and the other money coming in from the dairy and pig farm. Besides, I still have friends in Honolulu and I'm sure I could find jobs to do."

"When are you leaving?"

"As soon as I pack and say goodbye. What's the name of this Chinese medicine?"

"All I know is it's the Chinese cure for leprosy called *ta feng*. It's made from some type of flower. I'm not sure, I think it's called cannabis."

CHAPTER 27

———

John stepped off the steamer *Likelike* onto the pier. He searched the wharf for Aaloa but couldn't find him. He made inquiries of dock workers and finally got directions to a Fort Street Stevedores Office.

When John entered the room his muscular friend, although deep in conversation with another man, leaped from his chair, and embraced him. "Eh, brah, how you been? What you doing here?"

"Long story, but short version is I'm looking for a Chinese cure for leprosy."

"No talk too loud. Health department cracking down. They taking more people away to Kalaupapa since our friend lost his power."

"Things are bad for Hawaiians?"

"Bad for the king. Lots of locals mad with him. They no can vote if no have property. The guy gave up too much."

"You mean the Bayonet Constitution."

"Yeah, you remember we warn him, 'bring back the militia'? He no listen. Look what happen. Haoles have soldiers and scare him. Aue, Hawaiians no can vote, Asians too. Lots of grumbles."

"There's talk. Maybe get rid of Kalakaua and make his sister queen," a man next to Aaloa said.

"Eh, John, this Manuel. Portuguese guy working the docks with us."

The two men exchanged looks and nods. "Would Liliuokalani go against her own brother?" John asked.

"She is not happy with him," Manuel answered. "He spends too much, always needs more. Borrows from her and anybody else who will give him money. He

91

makes shady deals with a rich guy, Spreckles, tries to mortgage the kingdom to Britain. He spends everything on parties. Needs more money and sells an opium license twice."

"I heard about that. But he's still king with no plans to step down."

"That's why a revolution. There's this guy, Robert Wilcox, his mother is Maui *alii*. Kalakaua pays for his school in Italy. Big time military place, Turin Military Academy. He comes back last year. A good talker and gets lots of men to cause trouble. The haoles stop him. Kick him out to California. He's back, lives in Liliuokalani's Palama home, causing trouble again."

"Is he for Kalakaua, end the Bayonet Constitution and give him back the power?"

"What do you think if he is living in Liliuokalani's house?"

"Brother against sister, that only helps the haoles. How do I get to meet this guy?"

"Easy, he's holding meetings at the Palama house. He will talk to anyone who will listen."

"Aaloa, can I bunk with you while I'm in Honolulu?" "Sure thing, brah."

"Great, after I visit with Muk Fat in Chinatown to find cannabis, I'd like to meet this Wilcox. Manuel, you know him?"

"A little bit, I'll show you where to go then you're on your own. He likes to have Hawaiians come and listen to him, so you'll be welcome."

CHAPTER 28

—

Aaloa and John strode down King Street past its intersection with Beretania. "Manuel said we would see the Palama house on the right side of King. We couldn't miss it."

"I hope we doing a smart thing. Guy wants the haole control of the kingdom to end, but we still don't know if Kalakaua is with him or Liliuokalani."

"He's in Liliuokalani's house, isn't that proof enough?" John answered. "Can't say for sure. The Princess been living at her Washington Place house. Now she is on the Big Island. Maybe she doesn't know what's what?"

"That's why we're coming to the meeting. To find out what's going on. You said Kalakaua's reaching out to the old militia, trying to form a special group to protect him."

"Yeah, the king not sure of anything. Wilcox lives at Palama house. Newspaper has story that he should give up and let his sister be queen. Who can he trust?"

"I can see flaming torches over there. It must be the house. It's near the artesian well Manuel told us about. Lots of men outside."

"Okay, we go."

The two men strode from King Street onto well-kept premises of a two-story, L-shaped home with servants' quarters in back. A large gathering stood in a side yard. Several men stared at John and Aaloa, but no one raised an alarm. "I guess since we look Hawaiian we're okay," John said.

"Lots of guys here I don't know. Must be high class Hawaiians. Never mix with dock workers like me. I see some white guys. Not the typical haole-looking kind."

"Somebody's getting up to speak."

A six-foot-tall, slender man, with a narrow Roman-type nose, and tan skin urged silence. He stood dressed in a flaming red shirt and black pants. "I think most of you know me. For those who don't, I'm Robert William Wilcox, son of an American and Hawaiian royalty from Maui. I went to military school in Italy. There I studied to be a soldier, but most important: I learned about revolution from one of the great Italian leaders of all time, Garibaldi. All the people were under the control of the hated Austrians. Garibaldi and a few brave men started fighting. The corrupt Austrian government began to melt away and people of Italy regained their independence. Our nation is under the control of a wicked few men, no more than thirteen. It is time to end the Bayonet Constitution and restore power to the Hawaiians."

Wild cheering and applause broke out. John and Aaloa remained quiet and listened.

Wilcox continued to speak. "We have six Italians who have joined our cause. They know of the Risorgimento and the uniting of Italy. They are with us to end the control of the men filled with greed who oppress people. These few have taken away the power to vote of those who are without property and the Chinese. It is the Chinese who will provide us with the money to buy arms and ammunition. Let me tell you that there are other whites who will join our cause, Belgians, Germans. With their help you and I will restore the power of the monarchy to Hawaiians. From this day forward, we are 'The Liberal Patriotic Association'."

John whispered to Aaloa, "I've heard enough, let's leave."

The two men melted away from the crowd of people who had become agitated by the inflammatory words. As they hurried down King Street to Aaloa's home, John could hear shouts of: "Revolution! Hawaii for Hawaiians!"

CHAPTER 29

———

Bruce Jones placed a newspaper on Robert Grant's desk. "It appears that scoundrel Wilcox has returned to Hawaii. He's living in Liliuokalani's home."

"Are you thinking he is back to cause trouble?" Grant said. "We squelched the agitator in '88 and shipped him to San Francisco. The man should have been hung. But some of the business folk did not want to aggravate Hawaiians."

"From this account he's back and I believe is up to his earlobes in seditious talk."

"So, you think he'll start another revolt. Where is Kalakaua in all this?"

"The king isn't saying anything. He's playing a waiting game. The talk is that Wilcox wants to replace him with his sister."

"So, he wants to exchange Tweedledum for Tweedledee. If he succeeds there will be no change in this out-of-control monarchy."

"Except I believe Liliuokalani is braver than her brother. I would expect she would want a new constitution."

"Returning the power Kalakaua gave up in the 1887 Constitution to the monarch."

"Yes, we must be prepared for that eventuality. But until we can convince all our brethren that the monarchy has outlived its usefulness, we need to keep Kalakaua on the throne as a figurehead—"

"And squelch any revolution Wilcox is planning," Jones interrupted. "I agree. What is the state of our Honolulu Rifles?"

"We have been lax since there have been no threats for governmental change. Most of the volunteers have returned to their regular jobs. It's not reasonable to have men on a full-time alert for trouble."

"Best we get prepared for what may be coming. Maybe call up a hundred of the old hands to be ready to act. I'll get some of my boys to volunteer."

"So you can play major again." Jones laughed.

"I always thought I looked rather striking in an officer's uniform with medals and gold braid."

"Good, we are agreed on what to do. I'll start rounding up men and you do the same."

Jones left.

Grant ordered his clerk: "Get Larsen."

Sunshine and light breezes created a beautiful Hawaiian afternoon. Grant stood outside his office enjoying the ambience of the summer day. Light traffic rolled along the roadway with several passersby tipping their hats to him. He returned the salutes in the same way.

"Good weather," Larsen said, striding up to his employer. "Yes, it's marvelous. Come inside and we'll talk."

The big Swede followed Grant into his office. "You've been keeping up with your military training I trust."

Larsen shuffled his feet, shrugged his shoulders and said, "Too many other things to do."

"You mean chasing women and drinking up a storm." "Not as bad as all that."

"In the past what you did on your own time was none of my concern. But your habits must change for a while. There will be military action soon, and you must be ready. I want you to recruit a dozen men from my plantation. Everyone is to report to the downtown barracks for soldier training."

"What do I offer these men?"

"They should do it for love of country, but I understand that may not be enough. A silver dollar a week while drilling. If they must fight, it's a dollar a day."

"That will make them happy. I've been wanting to ask you about something."

"What is it?"

"I told you about this John Tana fellow hiding out chinks on his property. Lihue sheriff wouldn't do a thing about it. I got a score to settle with him. Need to get your okay to hire folks to squash him."

"I understand. I've been too busy with the troubles plaguing the kingdom. Right now, we have a revolution to deal with. Once we have matters under control, I will tell you how we will deal with Tana. We will squeeze him where it hurts, water for his land."

CHAPTER 30

———

With a wry smile, Kalakaua invited John into his Waikiki home. "What brings you to Honolulu?"

"I came searching for a cure for leprosy. There is a Chinese herbal potion that has been used for many years to stem the disease. It's from the flower of a five-leafed plant. The oil from it is called cannabis."

"I never heard of it. Don't tell me you have the *mai pake?*"

"No, I do not. Just say I am looking for a cure should the disease strike someone I care for."

"Any luck in getting it?"

"I have asked around Chinatown. One apothecary claims he has a shipment of the herb coming from the Orient. That is why I am still here and available to serve you. I have been at a meeting of 'The Liberal Patriotic Association'. Wilcox is planning a revolution."

Kalakaua shook his head. "It is only going to cause more trouble for the kingdom. What's he want? It isn't to put me back in power but give my monarchy to my sister if he is successful."

"I doubt that he will be. Aaloa asked me to speak to you. We understand you may have use for your friends from the old militia."

"Yes, I have reached out to them. It is hard to know who I can trust. The sugar people have corrupted the few soldiers we have. There are Hawaiian police who have indicated loyalty to my sister. If a revolt comes, I must be far away from the palace lest I be charged as a conspirator. Whatever the outcome of the fighting, I must be ready to flee by sea, seek refuge with one of the foreign war-ships in port, and find some advantage in the result."

John paused for some moments. "You have said some things I don't under-stand, but you are wiser about politics than I am. I'll work with Aaloa to put together a team of your old militia who will guard you when the time comes for action. But I will have to leave when I get the Chinese cure."

"That's all I can ask. You're a good friend. Tell me if you see trouble coming."

CHAPTER 31

—

A loud rapping at Aaloa's front door brought John instantly awake. He could hear his friend snoring and his wife beginning to stir. The knocking came again, and John called out, "Who is it?"

"Jimmy."

"Not locked, come in. What you excited about?"

A slender man with dark wavy hair entered the room. His face was pock-marked, and it was plain to see that he had survived the ravages of small pox that had decimated the Hawaiians. "Eh, brother John, you asked that militia guys keep an eye on the Palama house. Something big is happening. Dozens of men are gathering, some with rifles. They are all dressed in red blouses and dark trousers."

"The uniform of the Garibaldini revolutionaries. Wilcox admires what those Italians did to unify their country. The revolt in Hawaii has started. Aaloa, get up. We must get to the palace and protect the king. Jimmy, rouse the rest of the old militia loyal to Kalakaua. Meet us at Iolani."

Aaloa grumbled as he dressed, and the two friends armed themselves with rifles and ammunition. They marched onto King Street and headed for the pal-ace walk and the royal residence. A soldier stood at attention at the entrance. "My name is John Tana; the king has deputized me to be one of his special guards. I would like to speak to him, it is urgent."

"Wait here. I will wake my captain."

John chafed at how long it was taking to get past the soldiers and see the king. But he restrained himself to avoid creating an incident which might cause problems for him.

Sometime later, an officer, hastily buttoning his tunic, came to the entry. "John Tana, we've met. The king has a high regard for you. Why do you want to see him?"

"Revolutionaries will soon be marching onto the palace led by Robert Wilcox. They will want the king to sign a new constitution. We are to provide him security and take him to a place of safety."

"The king is not here. He instructed me before he left to secure the palace and let no one enter."

"He is at his Waikiki home?"

The officer paused, clearly mulling over what he should say.

"You have given me the answer. From this moment on close and secure the palace. Let no one in or tell them where the king might be."

At the bottom of the stairs he met Aaloa. "Kalakaua is not here. He is either at Queen Kapiolani's home at Queen and Punchbowl or at his boathouse. Wait for the rest of the militia and come to the boathouse."

At Houaka, Kapiolani's home, John roused the king. "Your majesty, rebels are on the march to the palace. I thought I'd find you there."

Kalakaua looked away as he dressed, his eyes evading John's gaze. "I didn't want to be at Iolani if, and when, Wilcox showed up."

"I understand he has a new constitution for you to sign restoring the power of the monarchy to you."

"Not to me!" Kalakaua pounded his fist into his palm. "To my sister! She can't wait until I'm dead to seize power."

"I'm sorry to hear that. I liked the Princess. Do we head to the boathouse?"

"Yes. But wait until I have instructed Kapiolani to go to the barracks and order the 2nd Hawaiian Infantry to remain neutral and not join with either side." John left the home and waited on the street. He wondered how this revolt would turn out. He suspected it would not end well. Wilcox must be relying on Kalakaua's cooperation to make his revolt succeed. But Kalakaua was running away and hiding. A puzzling set of circumstances.

Some of the militia had arrived at Punchbowl by the time Kalakaua left Houaka. The group proceeded to the harbor and the king's boathouse. Already, men were hurrying toward King Street, some buttoning jackets, others belting their pants, still others carrying rifles at their side.

John's group arrived at the boat house already occupied by a half-dozen of the king's retainers. With the addition of the militia Kalakaua would be well guarded, John thought. He approached the king and said, "There is an American warship in harbor—"

"America always has a warship here," Kalakaua interrupted. "They don't want any other nation to seize control of Hawaii."

"Are you going to ask for U.S. Marines to be landed to provide protection for your kingdom?"

"Let's wait upon events. See if the revolt succeeds. However it goes, I don't think I can lose. Do we have observers to advise us on the results of the rebellion?"

"Yes, I expect hourly reports. Here is Aaloa to give us information. What's up, 'brah?"

"A lot is happening, men in the palace grounds with four cannons, riflemen firing at them from the Opera building. The government house is occupied by revolutionaries." Aaloa looked directly at Kalakaua. "What's interesting is that Wilcox expected the king to be at the palace to sign the new constitution. There is talk of a double-cross."

Kalakaua looked away and then stalked off saying, "I need a drink."

Aaloa raised his eyebrows. "I know what you're thinking, the king made a deal with Wilcox."

"You got it. Why the change?"

"He found out Wilcox wanted Liliuokalani and not him to be the ruler of Hawaii."

"I see the double-cross, but his sister has said she doesn't want the throne."

"Who knows what is the truth? One thing for sure, this rebellion was hatched in Palama house, Liliuokalani's home."

"John," Kalakaua's voice boomed in the boathouse. "What's going on?"

"Don't know. I'll find out."

CHAPTER 32

———

John and Aaloa moved cautiously toward the sound of rifle fire. They wore dark blue jackets with a royal badge on their breast pocket signifying they were soldiers of the king. Both wore a light yellow, cloth helmet with a gold braided rope circling it, and the metal emblem of the monarchy fixed onto its front.

"Do you think what we are wearing will get us by as neutrals?"

John shrugged. "I don't know. We are not wearing red like the Wilcox guys, and what I could see from the men rushing to fight them at the palace, their clothes were different."

"Heard artillery fire for a while, now no more, only pop, pop of bullets."

"There's shooting from the tower of Kawaihao Church. It's close by, a good place to see what's going on."

The two friends hurried into the church yard and climbed the tower. They met two men there, one of them, Manuela, a Portuguese who Aaloa knew. "Eh, guys, we neutral in this fight. King send us, find out what's up?"

"Red shirt guys all over palace lawn," Manuela said. "They couldn't get inside. They got cannon from the Hawaiians in the barracks. Started shooting at the Opera House. We been firing back, drove the gunners away from their cannon."

"Who's winning?"

"Wilcox guys don't know what to do. They are surrounded, but not giving up from what I can tell. We keep shooting and they keep hiding."

"Thanks. Let's go back and report to the king." John said.

The two friends worked their way back to the church yard and began the trek to the harbor. Within moments after they left Kawaihao, a rifle bullet creased John's yellow helmet breaking the chin strap and toppling the head gear to the ground. "Down," John yelled.

Another shot smashed into the pavement near Aaloa. "Crawl behind that wall," John yelled.

Both men took refuge behind a rock fence. Bullets kept hitting it, sending slivers of stone flying. "What's up with whoever's shooting?" Aaloa asked.

"I don't know. Not wearing red, king's royal helmets on our heads. No challenge before shooting. It's very peculiar. One thing for sure, we are pinned down."

"We stay low. Follow this wall. I think it goes to Queen Street. Once we get across, make a dash for the harbor."

"Or find out who is shooting at us."

"I'm the last guy to run from a fight, but maybe—"

"Yeah, I understand, our first duty is to report to the king what we have found out. Let's go."

They got to the end of the wall. A gate led into the street. "We don't know who is waiting for us outside," John said. "I'll swing the barrier open. If no shots, I'll roll outside and provide cover fire while you dash across the street. When you are across go down and cover me until I get over to you."

"Okay, execute."

The gate swung open, John rolled out and lay down in a prone firing position. Nothing happened. "Aaloa head out, I'll cover you. Stay low."

The big Hawaiian, bending down, hustled across the street. John thought it odd there was no fire. Had the shooting been meant for him only? He would soon find out. "Aaloa, I'm going to shoot and then come across the street to you. Give me cover, fire diagonally across Queen Street. Here we go."

John took a snap shot, rose and began running in a zig-zag pattern across the road. Aaloa fired his Remington-Lee rifle continually as he crossed. Only one round of return fire occurred, the bullet striking the wall John had just left.

Lying in the grass next to Aaloa, John said, "We crawl away from Queen and head for the water. Use whatever cover is available. Let's go."

The two men wormed their way away to the waterfront without incident. Once they got to the sea, they stood and started hiking rapidly toward the king's boathouse. They could hear occasional shots from the direction of the palace three blocks away.

When they got to the king's refuge, John heard running feet, and a command, "Halt."

"Aaloa, get inside. Arouse the militia and be ready to protect the king. I'll confront whoever is trying to stop us."

The big Hawaiian slipped into the boat house. John assumed a firing position behind a post near the door. Five men rushed from Punchbowl Street stopping fifty feet away. The tallest of the group said, "You are a revolutionary and under arrest."

John recognized the man. "You are Larsen, Robert Grant's man. You have no power to arrest me. I'm a special officer of the king and since I'm not dressed in red you know I'm not one of Wilcox's men."

"Doesn't matter, you are out on the street. We part of the Honolulu Rifles and can arrest anyone we want. Surrender now!"

"I know the kind of person you are, Larsen. To curry favor with your boss, you'll take me and shoot me. You're just a coward and a bully beating up Chinese workers weaker than you are. Come take me if you can."

"You filthy kanaka, I'm going to beat you to a pulp and feed you to the sharks. You got no one to protect you like the last time we met."

"That's where you are wrong," Aaloa said as he and a dozen Hawaiian guardsmen stepped out of a side door of the boathouse. "Everybody stack your arms, so we can have a fair fight." He looked directly at Larsen's group of men. They complied with his demand. The Hawaiians did the same.

John set aside his rifle, Larsen surrendered his. The two men squared off against each other. John assumed the lua moku position, knees slightly bent, arms at his side, with fists clenched.

Already two inches taller than John, an erect Larsen with feet spread slightly apart and arms held clenched at stomach level appeared to tower over John. Aaloa shook his head, the Swede outweighed his friend by thirty pounds and stood much taller.

John moved to the left. Larsen turned and threw a roundhouse punch which missed its target. Larsen bore in, hurling a flurry of punches, obviously seeking to get close and grasp his opponent into his body with a bear hug.

John kept dancing away. Some of the blows hit him, but nothing powerful enough to cause severe damage. Larsen had a reach advantage. John had trouble getting close enough to gain leverage. He fought back with counter punches and succeeded in getting an occasional hit to the body. He didn't dare get too close or the Swede's massive arms would envelop him in a crushing embrace.

John knew he could not win the fight by constant evasions. He needed to find a way to bring the giant down to his level. He noticed that the constant swinging by the Swede made him breathe heavily. When his opponent paused at times to catch his breath, John would pummel his kidneys and even try to kick his knees. The big Swede would react with lumbering swings.

John thought back to the beach fight on Maui. It had been punctured with taunts to cause anger so that an opponent would rush into close combat. He began to badger Larsen with slurs and references to his manhood. He enraged the Swede when he said, "Your prick is so small it wouldn't get a woman excited."

Larsen screamed, "You will die, you bastard," and swung his arms like wind-mills. John retreated, letting the man continue with his berserk moves, noting how the Swede gasped for air as he advanced. The boathouse wall loomed behind John. Larsen's pals urged him onward. They appeared to sense that a crushing end to this fight was near.

John's body flattened against a wall. He saw Larsen spreading his arms to grasp him. John ducked under the encircling embrace, pushed off the wall with his feet and thrust his closed fingers deep into the exposed stomach of the big Swede. Larsen staggered back, dropping his head. John folded his fingers together and brought his clenched hands down on the back of his opponent's neck like an axe man decapitates his victim.

The Swede fell to the ground unconscious. John looked at Larsen's men. "You can take him home."

A discouraged group of men picked up their fallen leader and marched away. Kalakaua detached himself from the group of Hawaiians and walked up to an exhausted John Tana. "That proved to be quite a battle. Aaloa gave me a full report. I've requested that United States Marines from the *U.S.S. Adams* be landed to restore order in the kingdom. Wilcox's revolt is doomed."

The king's prophecy proved accurate. Wilcox and his surviving men retreated to a pavilion surrounded by an eight-foot coral wall. Without artillery the government forces resorted to the use of a baseball pitcher who hurled bundles of dynamite onto the metal roof of the pavilion. After three explosions and deaths among Wilcox's men, the revolutionaries surrendered.

———

CHAPTER 33

"By prompt action, we smashed the Wilcox revolt which saved Kalakaua's kingship. But he has failed to save us from financial disaster." Robert Grant pounded his fist on a green felt table, scattering poker chips and cards throughout the private room of the downtown club. "I say a pox on his kingship."

"Why are you so agitated, angry enough to ruin our poker game?" Donald Cartwright protested. "We were about to settle down to a friendly game of cards and you blew everything away. What's that monarch done this time?"

"It's not so much what he has done, but what he has failed to do. We have made millions on the reciprocity treaty, but I have gotten word that it is in jeopardy. United States Senator William McKinley is proposing a tariff act. Should it pass Congress our treaty will be negated. We will lose huge profits."

"What did the king do wrong?" Bruce Jones asked.

"You recall that he invited U.S. Marines from the *Adams* to restore order when the Wilcox rebellion was suppressed. Before that revolt he was making overtures to Britain, France, even Portugal, to take over his monarchy because of his unhappiness with the Bayonet Constitution. Those nations deferred to our Hawaiian League. They suggested that the king abide by what we had accomplished."

"Yes, I recall that," Jones answered. "We made him a puppet ruler. But what has that got to do with marines landing in Honolulu?"

"I see Robert's point," Cartwright interrupted. "Once the soldiers occupied the capitol, Kalakaua could claim his kingdom needed the protection of the United States and surrender his monarchy to America on terms favorable to him."

"I think that notion is a little far-fetched," Jones scoffed.

"It may be," Grant answered, "but I think he could have used that opportunity to a make a final deal for Pearl Harbor and bind America to the Reciprocity Treaty. He could have negotiated annexation."

"Would we have let him?"

"Many of our brethren would. It's too late now to speculate on what might have been."

"What do we do, have the king make overtures to America to get that country to make a favorable nation-to-nation agreement?"

"We can't count on the king's help. He has been buffeted by so many demands he has gone into a shell. He still tries to manipulate events, but without much success. We haven't decided what to do about the McKinley Tariff Act."

"We might still work a Pearl Harbor angle." "How so?"

"The last time the subject was dealt with, Kalakaua did make a deal to give America control of Pearl Harbor, with the stipulation that control would last only so long as the Reciprocity Treaty continued in effect."

"I see your point, we promise the United Sates a permanent naval base in Hawaii."

"That's our bargaining chip?"

"Kalakaua go along with this?"

"Maybe not, but if he doesn't, we isolate him. In the last revolt he feared a takeover by his sister. We play on that fear. We spread rumors that he plans to give Hawaii to Britain. That will anger both the annexationists and many Hawaiians. He was uncertain of the loyalty of his troops and turned to his old friends in the Hawaiian militia. We destroy each one of them. I have a special score to settle with an old nemesis, John Tana. He bushwhacked my servant Larsen and had a dozen of his thugs beat my man. I will shut off his water in Koolau and turn him into a pauper. He will be finished and then I will complete my revenge."

CHAPTER 34

———

A strong south wind gusted, whirling through the dried shrubs on a hillside at Kekaha, whipping up thin clouds of orange-red dust baked dry by six months of pitiless sun. John Tana squinted through the whirling dirt at a slender six-foot Hawaiian man dressed in simple clothes, shoeless, a broad-brimmed, dark hat shading his eyes. With him were a woman and a young boy.

"John Tana, this is Koolau, his wife, Piilani, and their son Kaleimanu," an elderly Hawaiian said.

Koolau, his eyes keen and searching, studied John for a moment then asked, "Why do you seek us?"

Scudding grey clouds misted the sea, bringing with the rain, cool air. John Tana shivered, uncertain if he was chilled by the rising wind or the determined look of the wiry man who stared at him. "I came to Kekaha looking for someone to take medicine to my family in Kalalau. The ocean is rough, and the continuing storm makes it hard to get into the valley through the cliff trail. Through friends, I learned that you and your family are leaving for the Valley. My wife and son live there. My boy has leprosy."

"You know much of what we intend. Yes, we go to Kalalau. A while ago a rash came upon my face, I showed it to my wife and she thought it was from the sun. It went away, only to return weeks later." His voice suddenly dropped, so that John was obliged to move closer to hear. "Our son's face and body developed the redness as well."

The man went on to reveal a story heard too often by John. How a government official arrived at their door and, wielding the power of the law, demanded that they see a doctor. This doctor diagnosed leprosy and ordered Koolau be sent to Kalawao.

"I asked if my beloved wife and son could come with me. But the answer was no."

John removed his hat and ran his palm across his hair. Koolau's story brought back all the agony of his family's decision. "My son was not turned in by an informer. I knew the symptoms, and I knew that we would never send JJ to the colony. Our family decided in secret that my son and his mother would travel to Kalalau and live there in freedom."

They stood together in silence, with no need to explain. The Law of Separation dictated that lepers be taken from their families and isolated. As unjust as this law was deemed, it was also inhumane. John nearly commented on the white man making heartless decisions about the lives of Hawaiians, but for what purpose? Koolau, a pure Hawaiian, knew of the injustices vented on the people by the dominant culture.

"When we married, we promised on the holy book to live together until death should part us. Now the government tells us that an oath made to Almighty God means nothing. That is why we're leaving for Kalalau."

John nodded and then glanced at Koolau's wife and son. They stood together, arms touching, a family unwilling to be separated. As it should be, he thought.

"You do realize that your defiance is now public, and they will send the law to get you?"

The man gathered his family to his side. "There is no fear in my heart, John Tana. My gun is our defender. I have loved it and cared for it and, in the days to come, it will care for us. When I die, we will be buried together."

Before John took his leave, Koolau agreed to transport the medicine and any messages to John's family. He knew that this Hawaiian man had a good heart.

But he worried. *The family had been identified with leprosy by a doctor and been ordered to Molokai. Would the law let him escape his obligation to go to the colony? What would happen if the sheriff pursued the family? Would those who had secretly gone into hiding in Kalalau be placed at risk of arrest and deported to the leper colony?*

John watched Koolau, his wife, and son begin the trek up the mountain to the remote valley. He had a grim foreboding that the decision that had been made would have fatal consequences.

CHAPTER 35

———

John rode into his farm in Koolau. Joe Still stood with his hands on hips waiting for him. "We have a big problem. Kilauea Plantation is shutting off our water."

"They can't do that! We have a right to take water from the river!"

"Not according to the manager. You remember a few years back, when water was trickling down the first ditch you dug? Since the river kept drying up, we dug a second ditch further upstream. This one connected to the first ditch and provided water to our fields. Now I'm told that we dug both ditches on their land."

John looked puzzled. "But how do they—"

"The plantation says we're landlocked. That we have no rights to water."

"What do they want?"

A wry smile appeared on Joe's face. "Are you serious? John, they want us out. And they're offering one-hundred-and-fifty dollars for the seven acres, take it or leave it."

"A hundred—"

"And they plan to start plowing in a few weeks."

John walked around the room, his head pounding from the pressure of being shoved up against yet another bureaucratic wall. "Typical plantation bullshit, surround the Hawaiian and squeeze him dry." Fists clenched, John appeared ready to fight. "I gave you and Nani those seven acres, so you must deal with this. But if you're asking me, I'd tell the plantation to go to hell, we're not interested in selling and we'll fight them. Hawaiians always had rights to take water from rivers and streams."

"I did tell the boss man to shove it up his anus. I got fired from my luna job for objecting. Strange thing, the manager apologized for shutting us down. He said his orders came from higher up the ownership chain. Somebody big has a desire to crush you."

"Yeah, I know the guy, Robert Grant. He stole my Maui land and now he is after what I have on Kauai. If ever I get the chance, I'll kill him."

"Murder is not the answer. We will fight him the legal way, in court. Nani and I have been working on finding a lawyer to sue. We've decided on an attorney in Lihue."

John and Still sat across a desk from attorney Charles Craig. "Mr. Still, you say the manager fired you because you wouldn't sell your land. And you were offered..." Craig shuffled through some papers and pulled out a document, "one-hundred-and-fifty dollars. What did you tell him?"

Joe Still gave a little shrug. "I admit, maybe I was a little excited when I talked to him, might even have said something like, 'You can stick your dang offer in your ear,' but that was the frustration talking. Of course," he added with a wry little smile, "it's possible that the manager might tell you something different." With that, Joe scratched his scalp and shifted in the straight-backed, unpadded chair.

"You mean, like stick it where the sun don't shine?" Craig said with a laugh. John listened, head swiveling from one man to the other. It was clear that they liked one another, which made him relax his tensed shoulders. Despite the levity, there was much at stake in this informal meeting.

"I reckon you might be right. I know the manager wasn't amused, he fired me. So, can you help us?"

Craig turned to John. "I think I've got this right. Around 1880, you bought seven acres in Kilauea from a Hawaiian. There was no water on the property, so the previous owner dug a two-hundred-yard ditch to the Kilauea River. When you got the land, you enlarged that ditch and improved it, which meant more water for your taro fields."

John nodded, impressed with the attorney's recall. "And it worked just fine for the next ten years. Two years ago, the river level fell and apparently the plantation diverted water from upstream to irrigate their fields. That's when your ditch started to run dry. You dug an extension up-stream, which improved the flow."

John pushed to the edge of his seat and gripped the end of the large oak desk. "Do we have a case?" Before Craig could respond, John added, "Remember, it's always been the Hawaiian way to share water. Have our traditions changed with private ownership?"

Craig formed a little pyramid with his hands and pressed his fingertips to his mouth. John wished the man would stop thinking, take a stand, and join the fight. When Craig spoke, his voice was less friendly, more professional. It made the hair on John's neck stand up.

"Mr. Tana, Mr. Still, we have several problems. The plantation owns the land around you, no one disputes that. However, by digging those ditches, you trespassed on their property. So yes, they have the right to shut you off from the river. The only way around this is to prove that you, as well as those who owned the land before you, had gained an easement over the plantation's property by adverse possession."

The law talk ran over John's head as he tried to grasp the concepts being tossed his way. Adverse possession, what did that mean? When he realized that the attorney was still speaking, he shook off the frustration and directed his attention to Craig.

"There are other problems. One is that you leased some of the acreage a year ago. Another is this issue of digging the second ditch within the last two years. And then," he went on, stopping only to take a deep breath, "we must deal with this issue of upstream water rights. It's what the law calls 'riparian rights', and it's only one of the many problems facing us."

"Problems aplenty," Joe groused. "But will you sue, and what will it cost?"

With an easy smile, Craig answered, "Yes, I'll file a lawsuit in which you will ask for an easement by adverse possession. There'll also be a claim for loss of riparian rights. And while we're at it, I'll add a claim for money damages, which will cover the loss of land use during the time the water was shut off." He reached into a drawer and pulled out a legal form. After writing on several of the lines, he pushed it across his desk to Joe Still. "A one-hundred-dollar retainer will get us started."

CHAPTER 36

———

A powerful wind blew sheets of water against the window pane of the second-story room of the Honolulu Downtown Club. James Kingsley fingered the lace curtain that partially covered the window. With a sigh, he turned back to the three men seated in the room. "Sugar profits for all the plantations are dismal since the McKinley Tariff Act passed. We need to do something, gentlemen, to turn the economic tide, or," he paused winking broadly, "we will all have to go to work."

"Ha, your soft hands have never known hard work. You should try laboring in the sugar cane fields, instead of always financing the plantations," Donald Cartwright scoffed.

"Let's not be too harsh on my son-in-law," Grant said.

"He's making a valid point. Our Queen, Kalakaua's sister, is as bad as her brother. Spends lavishly and doesn't tend to affairs of state by improving relations with America. Instead of fighting to blunt the effects of the Tariff Act on the sugar plantations, she refuses to make any concessions to the United States concerning Pearl Harbor—"

"I think it is time to get rid of the monarchy," Bruce Jones interrupted, wagging his hand around the room. "Let me tell you, gentlemen, that instead of tending to important matters, she is circulating a new constitution. Like her brother, she wants to return control of the government to the Hawaiian people, end all the benefits we reaped from the Bayonet Constitution of 1887. She wants to return Hawaii to the autocracy of 1864 and let Hawaiians without property and Asians vote."

Jones paused for some moments to let his words sink in. "Gentlemen, along with others, I have been in conversation with U.S. Minister Stevens. He is sympathetic to our cause." Jones waited, studying the three men. Speaking in hushed tones he said, "An American gunship is due in Honolulu in December of 1892, and when it arrives, I think Stevens would be willing to land U.S. troops in the capitol and rid us of this savage queen."

"I like the idea," Grant said, "but the old missionary types among our brethren still support the monarchy."

"I think not," Cartwright answered. "The Queen is spending beyond her means and is trying to get a bill through the legislature allowing her to sell opium licenses and institute a lottery."

"The majority of our legislature would never stand for that," Kingsley said. "You are probably right," Grant agreed, "but the woman is sneaky. Lots of Hawaiians support her views and they could get something passed by some subterfuge. It will be the Christmas season soon and the legislature will be on holiday. She could call a special session of those still in the capitol and get a bill passed to give her what she wants."

"If she did such a thing, coupled with trying to get a new constitution adopted, the business community will turn against her and depose her!" a furious Bruce Jones yelled.

"I would agree," Cartwright said, then asked, "Robert, how are you proceeding with your water manipulations and land grabbing?"

"I have acquired property along various rivers and streams in the monarchy and diverted the water to sugar fields that I control. As an example, I told you how we squeezed out Princeville Plantation by denying them water from the Kilauea and Kalihiwai rivers. As I told our brethren a time ago, I'm shutting down water to small farmers along the Kilauea River, and acquiring their land for peanuts. Kingsley, I sent you to Kilauea to carry out my plan. What did you find out?"

"Your concept is working. We claim all the land along the river, and we shut down any ditches leading from it. This has allowed us to acquire land for next to nothing. As you directed me, there is one farmer near the river, John Tana, who has a good-sized parcel, seven acres. He has been a pain in your side for quite some time, helping Chinese and other nationalities leave the plantation when their labor contracts are finished."

"You did order the manager to shut him down?"

"Yes, I did, but he's a stubborn man. He filed a lawsuit in adverse possession for an easement over your land."

"That scallywag troublemaker, you've hired a good lawyer to fight our case?"

"I got one of the very best in Honolulu. He thinks it's possible we may lose to a local jury but win on an appeal to Honolulu where we have more control over the court."

"Spare no expense, I want to crush that Hawaiian. Now, gentlemen, as to the queen, what do we propose to do? Jones, how about your Honolulu Rifles, can they help as in 1887?" Grant asked.

"We are not ready. We've been at peace for the last several years. After Liliuokalani became queen, we thought she would be a figurehead like Kalakaua. The Rifles more or less disbanded. It will take time to get them back in uniform and in fighting trim again."

"But the queen could call on no more than two hundred policemen and seventy-five royal guardsmen, hardly a force to be concerned about."

"That might just be enough to squash a disorganized revolt. Remember that there are many of our brethren who still favor the monarchy."

"Then to be certain of winning we will need the U.S. Marines from the *Boston*."

"Yes, if they just show up at the palace, the members of the Annexation Committee can occupy the government buildings and declare an end to the monarchy and the establishment of a Provisional Government. The queen will not dare fight a trained force of fully armed military personnel."

"How many members are on the committee?"

"Eighteen, none of them Hawaiian, fifteen of them are Americans born in Hawaii."

"Then to make this overthrow happen, we need Stevens and the marines on our side."

"Yes, and we have them on our side." Grant went to the sidebar and filled four glasses with scotch. He distributed the drinks, lifted his glass, and said, "Gentlemen, a toast to a successful revolution, annexation to America, and a return to profitability."

CHAPTER 37

––––

In late January, the trial to determine if John Tana and Joe Still had acquired an easement over Kilauea plantation land got underway. The two men and their attorney had prepared for months to win the case.

Seated at the table facing the judge were Charles Craig, John Tana, and Joseph Still. Next to them sat the attorney for the plantation and its current manager, Gordon Young. Adjacent to them was the jury of twelve, all white businessmen.

"Gentlemen of the jury," Craig said. "This is a simple case in which you must decide if Mr. Tana, Mr. Still, and the owners before them acquired a prescriptive easement to dig a ditch across the land of the Kilauea Sugar Plantation to carry water from the Kilauea River to seven acres of the plaintiffs' land. If you rule in our favor, you must then award damages to my clients for the plantation's wrongful acts that have prevented them from using that easement and receiving water from the river."

John tried to assess the jury members. He wondered whether they could be impartial when it came to the claim of a pureblood Hawaiian against a sugar plantation.

"What does it mean to secure an easement over the land of another by adverse possession?" Craig asked. "Simply this: the use of a water ditch must be open, obvious, and continuous for a specified time. My clients meet all these requirements. In fact, my clients and the previous owner of these seven acres have taken water from the Kilauea River by way of a ditch for more than thirty years. During that period water from the river has been continuously taken to provide for taro, vegetable fields, cattle, pigs, chickens, and people. You will also note that this use has been open and obvious to everyone in Kilauea."

John watched the faces of the jurors and was satisfied that they were listening attentively. Certainly, if they knew the facts and the law, they would vote in his favor!

"By the Kilauea Plantation shutting off the water from the Kilauea River for more than a year," Craig argued, "my clients have lost rent, fields of growing crops, and domestic animals. Today, by importing water and catching rainwater, the seven acres are barely serviceable for a family of four."

John noted that one of the jurors looked quickly at him and he was quite sure that the man's eyes were sympathetic. This process of explanations and trying to assess the sympathies of strangers was making John anxious. He was tempted to stand up and walk out of the courthouse.

"Mr. Tana and Mr. Still ask you for damages according to proof of five-thousand-five-hundred dollars for the wrongful acts of the defendant, Kilauea Sugar Plantation."

With that, the proceedings slowed to descriptions, maps, terrain, time lines, and a few comments from his adversaries that John felt bordered on lies.

Two weeks later, John returned from a visit to his wife and son. When he rode up to Still's new home in Kapaa, Joe rushed out and practically danced around him. "We won!" he announced with a laugh that was nearly a giggle. "The jury agreed that we had an easement and they awarded us more than three thousand dollars!"

Delighted, John slapped Still on the back. When they settled down, he thought to ask, "But what about our right to get water from the river?"

"You mean the riparian rights? The judge hasn't set that one for trial yet. He will make a decision as to how much is reasonable for you to take. I think his ruling will be favorable. The plantation has been storing much of the water in reservoirs and not using it. I'm sure he will require that they stop taking all of it and require they release water to downstream users like you.

"You also need to know that the plantation is furious. They've asked for a new trial. If they lose that one, they've already threatened to appeal to the Supreme Court."

John threw up his hands. "Delay, delay, delay! That's all these big-time guys are good for, damn it! Their legal maneuvers really work when it comes to starving out the little guy. We have sold animals, can't grow taro or vegetables, and we are spending money we don't have on a fight we could possibly lose."

"Look on the bright side. At least the jury gave us a victory and damages." Almost as an afterthought, he asked, "How was your trip?"

All signs of pleasure slipped from John Tana's face. "JJ is getting worse. He has sores all over his body and he's starting to lose some fingers. The Chinese medicine I got for him is not working. I don't know if Mahealani can cope with this." John's eyes misted over for some moments, and he gathered himself together. "She's happy there. That is, as happy as she can be under the circumstances. The people treat her and JJ with aloha, which is comforting, but there are times when she's in another world."

John was glad to be standing with his good friend, relieved to feel the release of so much of the tension he carried in his heart. "I have to admit that I'm glad the man who attacked her died on that beach. The harm he inflicted on my family will never go away. I'm supposed to be a good Christian, but I hate the bastard for what he did."

The two men walked toward Joe's house stopping just short of the sallow fields bordering it. "Sui Young is looking for you. He is making some noises about his people, his *hui*, possibly giving up on Kauai. That wouldn't be good for you."

John nearly made a crack about *when it rains it pours*. Instead, he said, "I got my Kealia job back again. But they aren't happy with me because I'm gone too much. They have a shipload of Japanese workers coming in, men with wives and children. I think the plantation will keep me on until these folks have settled. Then my job is over."

They went into Joe's house and sat at the kitchen table. "Is there anything new in Hawaiian politics since I left for Kalalau?" John asked.

"We didn't know this at that time but on Monday, January 16, U.S. Marines landed in Honolulu and bivouacked near the palace. The next day thirteen members of an annexation group occupied the government buildings, declared a Provisional Government, and required the queen to abdicate.

Faced with American military power, she yielded her authority '... to the superior force of the United States of America...until such time as the Government of the United States...shall...upon the facts...restore me in authority...as the constitutional sovereign of the Hawaiian Islands'."

"She caved in without a struggle."

"What could she do? Americans were well-armed. Hawaiians would have been killed by the hundreds."

"I still think she should have made a fight of it. The haoles are in power and Hawaiians are in big trouble. What's happened since the overthrow?"

"The Provisional Government rushed representatives to Washington D.C. The queen did also. The provisional folks are going to try to ram annexation through the Senate, before the new president, Grover Cleveland, is in office."

"Do you think annexation will occur?"

"I don't know. We need to wait and see."

"Nothing good for us will come from this. America needs to right this wrong. Only a few greedy people want annexation. Seventy-five percent of eligible Hawaiian voters are opposed to it."

John looked around the new home. It had three spacious bedrooms, a large living room, and a modern kitchen that boasted a kerosene stove. Low voices could be heard in another room and John knew that it was Nani and her women friends, quilting busily as their children played at their feet. "How do you like this place?" he asked. "What about your new job?"

"I love this home in Kapaa. Makee Sugar mill in Kealia is a great place to work, hop on a railroad trolley and in fifteen minutes I'm at the mill. But no matter how good it is, we need to win that appeal. Without water, the seven acres are lost."

"I hear you. I'm going to write to James Kingsley in Honolulu to see if he can help us. He owes me for the work I did for him a few years ago."

"Let's also say some prayers for the safety of our family in Kalalau," Joe said. "There is talk of leper roundups on the other islands and shipment of them to Molokai."

CHAPTER 38

———

Robert Grant studied Ezekiel Jones, Marshal of the Provisional Government of Hawaii. The middle-aged man was stout in build, with a full head of hair, mutton-chop sideburns, and a closely-cropped beard. A breeze warmed by the morning sun blew the sounds of a bustling metropolis through an open second-story window. He heard the clang of a street bus, carriage wheels grinding on pavement, horses prancing on the roadway, and the strange clacking sound of a revolutionary new machine.

Grant thought the automobile a nuisance: noisy, puffy, and with a shrill tooting horn. But he felt satisfied, for these were the sounds of prosperity. It boded well for his continued profits. The overthrow of the monarchy by the Committee of Thirteen was good for business. The deposed queen was under house arrest. His militia policed Honolulu. All was well except—"

"Major, you're asking me to hold off on any more leper hunts," Jones said. "You say the powers-that-be are worried about this guy Blount and his investigation."

Grant's voice assumed a conciliatory tone. "Marshal, we all appreciate your great work on Hawaii island, rounding up the lepers there and shipping them to Molokai. Those people disobeyed what is the right and lawful thing to do, which is to turn themselves in for relocation to the colony."

"But you're saying that enforcement of the law must be stopped, because of this fellow from Washington?" Jones said his voice incredulous. "What are you worried about?"

"Marshal, there are treaties of friendship between America and the Hawaiian monarchy. President Cleveland is saying America broke these treaties by landing

U.S. Marines in Honolulu to take over the Hawaiian government. He is saying that the overthrow of Liliuokalani was engineered by a handful of business men and not because she was booted out by a popular revolution. Blount's on a fact-finding mission. We don't want a lot of publicity by unhappy Hawaiians over leper roundups."

"I see your concern," the marshal said. "If the government wants annexation to America, we have to keep these islands looking peaceful."

"You have it. Avoid incidents that could be trouble."

The marshal studied his desk for some moments. "I can hold off on my end, but I got a hot-head sheriff from Kauai due any minute. He wants to do a roundup in a valley called Kalalau."

There was a sharp rap on the office door.

"That could be him." The rapping came again, loud and insistent. "Come in," the marshal said, irritation in his voice.

The door swung open and a tall, lean, good-looking man strode in and said, "I'm Louis Stolz, Deputy High Sheriff of Waimea." Then he caught sight of Grant, who had been partially hidden by the entranceway, and asked, "Did I interrupt something?"

"No," the marshal answered, a genial smile on his face. "Let me introduce Major Robert Grant of the All Hawaii Militia."

"Everybody calls me Lui," the sheriff said, extending his hand, then added, "A militia major. Do we need an army to protect us?"

Grant took the proffered hand, irritated by the man's insolence. But instead of rebuking him he chose to be reasonable and said, "Hawaii is in a perilous position. So far, America has rejected annexation. Foreign countries are poised to take advantage of our weakness, Japan in particular. Liliuokalani has not actively fostered sedition, but there are those who hate the new government. Even now a petition opposing connection to the United States is circulating among Hawaiians. Military power is necessary to save our revolution."

"Harsh enforcement of the law is your best guarantee against dissension," Stolz answered. His handshake made Grant wince, and he withdrew his fingers from the sheriff's grasp, flexing them to ease the pain. "That's why I'm here to talk with the marshal about disobedient lepers in Kalalau."

"What about the lepers in Kalalau?" the marshal interjected.

Lui inclined his head toward Jones seated at his desk. "Maybe one hundred are holed up in that valley. They have a grand little community there. It's time to arrest them. Ship them to Molokai. You did a great job on Hawaii Island. You became famous for rounding up hundreds of those lepers. That island is now clean of the unclean." The sheriff laughed and looked at the sugar planter seeking appreciation for his crude joke.

Grant compressed his lips in a slight scowl of disapproval. This man was too self-assured. He would be difficult to control. The marshal interrupted his thoughts. "Yes, we rounded up hundreds of those scofflaw Hawaiians and sent them to Molokai. Hawaii no longer has lepers hiding there." Jones smacked his desk.

"Yes, you did a great job on the island. The Provisional Government promoted you to Marshal of Hawaii. It is because of your success that I need your help. There is a serious problem on Kauai, maybe an armed revolt in the making," Lui said, his eyes fixed on Jones.

Grant was surprised by the sheriff's claim. Lepers were usually docile. Was this man seeking a reputation? Maybe even a government promotion to a higher office? He said, a note of incredulity in his voice, "Are you saying that there is a revolution brewing on Kauai?"

"It hasn't come to that, yet. But we have had trouble in Waimea with armed lepers. If you don't destroy a growing bee hive, the insects could someday sting you to death. I want the marshal's authorization and help to proceed with a Kauai cleanup and the capture of a trouble-maker Hawaiian called Koolau. A former cowboy from Waimea, and a crack shot."

"You sound like you want to prove that you are better than this man," Jones said. "But right now, the government doesn't want trouble. No fighting with rebels that might hit the international news."

"That's right," Grant said, his voice stern. "We are being investigated by Washington. A fellow by the name of Blount is snooping around. The provisional government wants to keep everything quiet. We want to keep the investigator thinking that the revolution by the Committee of Thirteen is popular with the Hawaiians."

"Which we all know it is not," the marshal interrupted. "But what Washington doesn't find out helps the cause of annexation to the U.S."

"Who's this Blount?" Lui asked, relaxing into his chair, a puzzled expression on his face.

"When our 'beloved' Queen was deposed by the committee," Grant answered, "she yielded her authority under protest 'to the superior forces of the United States'. She said she wanted to avoid 'any collision of armed forces and perhaps the loss of life'. Liliuokalani was wise to do so. The one-hundred-sixty-two marines and their Gatling guns landed from the *U.S. Boston* would have mowed down the pitiful Hawaiian Royal Guard. But, when members of the Committee of Thirteen rushed to Washington D.C. to secure annexation, President Grover Cleveland would have none of it. He told Congress that the United States had taken over a defenseless country in violation of peace treaties. Blount has been sent by Congress to investigate."

Lui asked, "So what's the provisional government worried about? Isn't Blount one of us? Isn't kicking out the Queen what everybody wanted?"

Jones stared at Lui in disbelief. "Where have you been? The overthrow of Liliuokalani occurred because she wanted to adopt a new Constitution returning the power of the government to the Hawaiian people. When the news of her intentions got around, a handful of business people and the marines booted her out. It was never a revolt by the Hawaiians." The marshal glanced at Grant before continuing, "Rumor has it that Blount is a straight shooter. The major thinks that his report will not be favorable to the cause of annexation."

"I understand the problem," Stolz said. "But now is the time for action. I am told the lepers are engaging in target practice in Kalalau Valley. Soon it will be surf-bound, then the only way in is by foot trail. A few trained riflemen could hold off an army trying to get into the valley. Action is needed now."

"Patience, sheriff," Grant said. "Let Mr. Blount leave Hawaii, then the marshal and I will come with our men to help you rid Kauai of Koolau and all the lepers in Kalalau." He watched Stolz leave the office without a word of agreement on his part. The man was clearly dissatisfied. Grant thought that Stolz would do something foolish, maybe arrest Koolau by himself.

CHAPTER 39

—

Grant reviewed the papers on his desk, an appointment from the Provisional Government of Hawaii to Major in the Hawaiian Militia. He wasn't certain about the extent of his powers. He could suppress any form of insurrection, that he understood. But could he execute a man without a trial? Could he authorize an underling to do so?

In the past he had not concerned himself with such technicalities. But his experience at the docks in 1887 and the British Minister made him cautious about conducting a lynching as an official of the realm. As he thought about it, there was a difference. The man to be hanged, Gibson, was white and the Premier of the monarchy. The Hawaiian is dark and a member of an inferior race. They must yield to the better people, the Anglo-Saxon.

He thought about the Japanese. Already some contract laborers had completed their agreements and gone into business on Oahu. They competed with merchants of the ruling class. This must stop. Beatings and even hangings were justified to end their attempts to challenge the superior race.

Grant's reverie ended when his clerk entered the office. "Mr. Sven Larsen is here," he announced.

"Let him in." As he watched the big Swede enter Grant made up his mind as to what to do. "You're back in fighting shape I trust?"

"Never better!"

Grant shrugged. He could smell the reek of alcohol. When he first hired Sven he believed the man was not a coward, but since the Wilcox revolt he had changed. He still bullied the weaker workers, but when given more confrontational assignments he fortified his courage with alcohol. Even with this support, he had been known to back down. Despite this, Grant had no one else who might carry out an assignment for a lynching.

"I have a special job for you. You're to go to Kauai, find John Tana, and hang him."

Larsen's eyes widened, he stepped back, and began to shake. "Man is dangerous. I can't do it."

Grant pursed his lips then hissed the words, "You're afraid of him. Why? You're bigger and I would wager stronger than that brown man. You have good Teutonic blood in your veins, maybe a Viking heritage. You are superior to any Hawaiian."

Larsen began to sweat. He took a kerchief and mopped his brow. He stood silent for many moments. "I hang Japanese, Chinese for you. Okay. They small, no big problem. This guy is tough, my neck still sore. I can't do it alone. Why you want lynch him? Shoot him from a distance."

"When you see a man hanging from a tree, it's a sign to others that you don't mess around with someone else's property. I want to teach a lesson to anyone who resists the power of the Kilauea Plantation."

"Okay, I see why you want to use the rope. I want a dozen men to back me up. I say, just shoot him."

Grant shook his head. "A dozen men! The kanaka is that dangerous?"

"Look boss, we in his home territory. Last time I try, Hawaiians I hire left me. Complain to sheriff, he did nothing. No way I can handle this guy without a lot of help." Larsen rubbed the back of his neck. "I'm lucky I can walk. I get pain into my leg."

"Is that why you're hitting the sauce?" Grant said, a look of disgust on his face.

Larsen smirked. "It kills the pain."

"All right, I can't find a dozen men to do a lynching on Kauai. How many do you need to back you up to do a shooting?"

Larsen fingered his jaw for some moments. "At least four besides me."
"Four!"

"Take care of opposition."

"You find three and no more to help you. The Portuguese have been very supportive of the Provisional Government. They are a good source. When you recruit, say you're on a mission to eradicate revolutionaries. I'll give you an order saying that. Once U.S. Minister Blount leaves Hawaii, be prepared to execute."

"You'll give me the money, rifles, and ammunition?"

"Yes."

CHAPTER 40

—

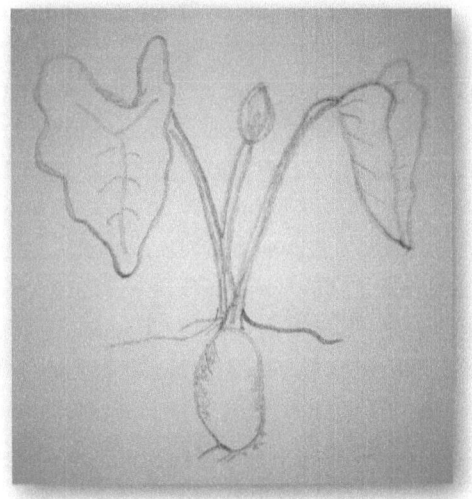

With his feet in the mud, John thrust a taro corm into the wet soil. Next to him, Joe Still complained, "This is hard work for a tall guy like me."

"But look at it this way: once the field is full grown we'll have enough taro to last us for a year."

"Yeah, but only you loves that purple paste."

"Nani loves it and the grandchildren thrive on it. With what I get from the sea, our food problems will be over."

"For me, I'll eat the sweet potatoes. At least they grow faster than this root and have a taste I like. But John, I got to caution you. We beat them on the new trial motion, the judge ruled for us on riparian rights, but there is still the appeal to the Hawaii Supreme Court. If we lose that we are back to where we were a couple of years ago."

"You got to hope for the best. At least Nani and the kids love it here. We are going to hang in the best we can. At least you can get time off from your Kealia job to come see us."

"It's not too bad when we work in Anahola, a long ride, but I can make it in an hour. Otherwise, I'll stay at the house in Kapaa. I guess your security days are done?"

"With the plantations, yes, but Sui Young is still in business in Hanalei. Rice sales are good. It's the number two export from Hawaii. Chinese in California love rice. What's the political news?"

"I'm hearing that Mr. Blount is reporting to the president that U.S. Marines assisted in an illegal takeover of Hawaii. That Minister Stevens exceeded his authority in ordering the military landing and recognizing the Provisional Government."

"Does that mean Liliuokalani will be Queen again?"

"I don't know about that. The government's recreated a militia. They are buying guns and ammunition. Even if President Cleveland says America did wrong in the overthrow, the plantation boys are going to hang onto the power they got."

"You're saying Hawaiians must fight to get Liliuokalani back."

"I think that's right. America isn't going to send armed forces in again to overthrow the Provisional Government."

"I don't like what I'm hearing. The plantations will run these islands until they can get annexation. That means they are the boss and we have no rights. Goodbye to our winning an appeal."

"Don't give up hope. We still have some rights. I need to head back to Anahola and be ready for work in the morning. I'll say goodbye to Nani and the kids. Take good care of them until I'm back."

"You can count on me."

Some prescience forced John awake. Darkness hid whatever sinister thing might be outside the home. Is it the conversation with Still that made him uneasy, or could his aumakua be warning him of trouble coming to visit him? He knew the revival of a haole militia is a dangerous sign, and Grant is involved with it.

John stepped out of bed, kneeled by his window, and listened. There were only the usual night sounds, nothing for him to be disturbed about. Still, he sensed something. He strained his eyes to pierce through the dark. There, he saw it, heard it, the movement of men in the dark.

Shoving on his pants, he hurried to Nani's room. "Get the children, hurry out the back door, go to the beach house and wait for me."

"Dad, what's wrong?"

"No time to explain. There are men approaching the house. Leave now."

John went to a locked closet, opened it, and pulled out a Remington rifle. He grabbed several five-round magazines and hurried back to his room. He smelled the odor of kerosene and realized the nocturnal visitors planned to set his house on fire and kill anyone who fled outside.

He listened and waited. His eyes became accustomed to the darkness. The light from the stars revealed hovering bodies outside. A child shrieked in the back of the house. John fired two bullets into the dark forms outside and rushed to the back door.

Nani wrestled with a man. John smashed the butt of rifle into his head and clipped his jaw with his fist. The assailant went down. "Take the children and go." John heard footsteps. He fired. Whoever approached fled. He went to the ground. A fusillade of bullets struck his house. He squirmed away from the gunfire searching for a vantage point where he might see the enemy and protect his family as they made their escape.

A torch flared, its sputtering flames revealing two men. John fired at the light. The burning brand fell as a man howled. Red flashes pierced the dark. John felt a sting on his shoulder, burning on the top of his head. He rolled away from the blaze of gunfire.

The fallen firebrand ignited something on the ground. Flames erupted, spreading rapidly. In the sudden brightness, John saw three men. He levered the bolt of his rifle but realized that he had fired the rounds in the magazine. Ejecting it, he thrust in a new one. Before he could chamber a round, he heard a voice yell, "Retreat!"

John watched as the figures melted away. He fired in the air. "That will keep them running," he muttered.

Bullets whined in the dark. John kept low, his eyes on the flames burning stacked wood. It gave off enough light that he could see enemies approaching. If he didn't shoot, darkness would hide him.

Far away, near the government road, he heard a yell, "Where's Gilberto?" Aiming for the voice, he fired two rounds into the dark.

There came an anguished cry, "Go!"

Horses' hooves pounding hard dirt rent the stillness of the early morning. John listened as the galloping faded into the distance. He remembered the man he had struck and returned to the rear of his house. A body lay prone in the dirt. He checked to see if the inert man lived. Satisfied, he got rope and bound his wrists and ankles.

John hurried down the beach trail to the seaside cabin. He worried that Nani and the children might have been injured. He called out as he neared the small building, "Nani, it's Dad. Is everyone okay?"

"Yes," came a firm reply.

John entered, swept his family into his arms and wept with happiness.

CHAPTER 41

—

Grant received word to report to Marshal Jones' office immediately. When he arrived, he found the lawman and a stranger in his office. "This is Deputy Lana. He just arrived from Kauai. He has a terrible story to tell. Stoltz couldn't wait for us. He imagined that people spoke of him behind his back. He thought they had doubts about his courage, that they questioned his fitness to be sheriff. Two weeks ago, he announced to Lana, 'It's Koolau's fault. The damn leper is making a fool of me. Lui is the law. By God, I will show him who has the power'."

Grant shook his head, realizing with mounting horror where this story would lead. "Despite our caution not to act you and Stoltz marched into Kalalau."

"I didn't know that. Luis never told me, but it is true that we crossed the mountains into Kalalau."

"What happened when you got there?"

"Stoltz demanded that all lepers meet at the beach in the morning. He made it a point to look for Koolau, but his wife Piilani said, 'he is picking taro'. 'Tell him to be at the beach at sunrise'."

"Is that when trouble started?" Grant asked.

"No, the lepers came. Lui ordered everyone to prepare for departure to Molokai in a week. He looked directly at Koolau. 'Will all who have the leprosy obey my lawful order to be transported to Molokai?' Koolau whose cheek showed the redness of leprosy replied, 'Will my wife be allowed to go with me'?'

Lui answered, 'Piilani cannot go. That is the law'."

"What did the Hawaiian say or do?" Grant asked, his heart beating faster as he listened to the unfolding tragedy.

"Am I to be denied the helping hand of my wife, and the cord of my love for her is to be cut? This is a wrongful law that separates a man from his wife. While I am alive I will not obey this law."

"Dramatic stuff," Jones said. "Did Lui take him into custody?"

"No. He said, 'I will be back in a week with a boat. I order all of you with leprosy to be at the beach.' He pointed a finger at Koolau. 'I expect you to be here when I return.' Koolau walked away without another word."

"Those two men have too much pride," Grant said. "Old proverb: 'Pride goeth before a fall.' Something bad would happen to one of them."

"What happened a week later?" Jones asked.

"We returned with a boat. A dozen lepers waited for us. Lui asked, 'Where is Koolau?' One person answered: 'He will not go to Kalawao.' Lui swore. 'Damn that pig-headed Hawaiian. He is too stubborn, too filled with pride. I will show him. I will show all of you who has the power in Kalalau. When I capture him you will see him cry. If he fights me he will die.'"

"Tarnation," Grant said. "Two stubborn men, you can see this collision was inevitable. I understand that Koolau is a crack shot and has a rifle that he treasures."

"Yes, he calls it 'death from afar in a wink'. The battle between the two didn't need to happen. The lepers told Lui that Koolau would remain in his home in the hills tending to his taro fields. Only if the sheriff came to take him would there be a fight. I tried to discourage Lui from going the mile uphill to Koolau's home, but he said, 'When it is dark we will take him'."

"Night time! That is foolish. It is easy to ambush someone in the dark," Grant said. "Where were the lepers? Were they helping the Hawaiian?"

"Yes, we were told that a group of them had taken refuge with Koolau. They did not want to go to Molokai. I'm sure they spied on us. I could tell as we trudged up the hill through the brush in the night that watchers ran ahead of us to warn of our coming."

"You didn't follow the trail to Koolau's house?"

"No, Lui decided not to use the beach path. He wanted to surprise him by working our way through the low shrubs until we got to the house. From a protected spot Lui decided to challenge him. It seemed like a good plan. We thought if Koolau was going to ambush us he would lay in wait along the trail.

"As we pushed our way through the brush I thought the shrubs shivered as if in fright. I did not like what I saw. Near the house, a full moon came out from the clouds. It cast weird shadows on the boulders near Koolau's home. It revealed where we were, and I'm sure the leper spies had warned Koolau of the route we were taking. The sheriff got ahead of me, moving forward while bending low. He reached the edge of the rocks. He rose slightly and called, 'Koolau—'. A shot echoed through the valley. I heard Lui say, 'Hui, it hurts.' Then he collapsed. I saw no one. I was frightened. I ran."

Grant looked at Jones, disgust plain on his face. "This is a king-sized mess, a sheriff murdered and lepers in revolt. We will have to act now before this insurrection spreads."

"Can you get military to help me?" Jones asked. "A hundred lepers in revolt, an armed rifleman, and maybe more with guns. I need support."

"You will get it. I'll visit the government offices today and get the authority to rent a ship to transport militia and pick up lepers for Kalawao. You send marshals to seal off the trails into Kalalau. Stay out of the news. We don't want interference, more revolts, or leaks to Washington. I'll be ready to act within the week."

CHAPTER 42

———

On the beach at Kalalau, Major Grant issued orders. "First Platoon, fifteen of you head up the hill to Koolau's home, Deputy Lana will show you the way. Seize him and any lepers and bring them to the beach. If they resist, shoot to kill. Second Platoon, round up any other lepers that are in the valley. Use whatever force that is necessary. Load the lepers onto the *Waialeale* and ship them to Honolulu."

Dressed in cast-off faded blue outfits worn by American Civil War Union soldiers, thirty-five militia of the Provisional Government proceeded to their assigned tasks. Grant watched with satisfaction as his mix of Portuguese and Caucasian troops responded to his orders. He turned to his underling standing by his side, "Good men, they will get the job done right, unlike your attempt to kill John Tana."

Larsen gave a surly look at his master. "We had a good plan. Somebody betrayed us."

"You've been saying that ever since you returned from the botched venture. All I got out of it is one wounded man and another missing."

"Gilberto showed up, the kanaka let him go. We lost nobody."

"That is fortunate for me. It would have been difficult to explain the loss of a man in an aborted raid to kill an insurgent. Look, there is fire. Our men are at the homes of the rebel lepers."

After many minutes, rifle fire filled the valley with smoke and noise. "We are fighting these renegade Hawaiians. Larsen, head up the path, bring me a report."

Sporadic rifle fire continued throughout the day. It was not until nightfall that Larsen returned. Grant sat in a captain's chair beside his tent. "What's your news?"

"Our men got to Koolau's home and the shacks of other lepers. All were empty. We set fire to the houses. The soldiers captured a leper who pointed into the hills where he claimed Koolau was hiding. Our men began shooting and slowly advanced up the mountain. A single bullet fired back. A soldier was hit and died. Everybody started fleeing downhill. With the help of a sergeant I got them to stop running. But no one wanted to climb back up to where Koolau must have been hiding. The soldiers decided to fire into the hill from safe positions."

"We don't know if the man is dead?"

"He never fired back. He must be—"

"I need a body. Capture any more lepers?"

"The one we caught and two who surrendered. I think there are more hiding in the hills."

"Disappointing reports. Tomorrow we will take twenty men and finish that Hawaiian if he is still alive."

In the late morning of the next day, Grant assembled his militia at the ruins of Koolau's home. "You men advance in skirmish order to where we are told the leper is hiding. Once near his hangout, a party of four will advance into his lair. The rest of the detachment is to provide cover fire for the attackers. Since Private Jones is a Civil War veteran he shall be the point man for the assault. Now execute."

Grant watched with satisfaction as his blue-clad militia toiled up the mountain. "This time we will get him. He can't escape the net."

Larsen nodded his agreement.

It wasn't long before rifle fire began, the sound of bullets whining off rocks echoed through the valley. One shot sounded louder than all the others for it was accompanied by a horrific scream. All shooting ceased. To Grant's dismay, he saw blue coats running downhill.

"Damn those men, routed by a single Hawaiian! Larsen find out what happened."

Many minutes later, the Swede returned. "The Hawaiian shot the lead man, Jones. He fell, knocking down the rest of the assault team, one was badly injured. Another soldier running away shot himself."

"A first-class disaster, three dead, one man injured, and nothing to show for these losses. Have the men form a firing line and shoot into the hills. Pepper the hiding place with rifle shots. That might do the trick. Tomorrow the *Iwalani* will be here. We will shoot up Kalalau with our artillery, load up lepers, and leave."

Leper Colony Site
– Kalawao, Kalaupapa, Molokai Island

CHAPTER 43

———

On July 4th, 1893, an agitated Joe Still rode into the Tana compound. The minute he saw John, he blurted out, "Lui Stolz, the sheriff, is dead, shot to death in Kalalau."

"My God, what happened?"

"Lui was told to wait until the marshal could help him deal with the lepers in Kalalau. But he went ahead and acted against them anyway. In the valley he warned the lepers that he'd come back in a week with a boat big enough to take them all away. He directed his order specifically to Koolau. That's when Koolau demanded to know if his wife, and all the other helpers, would be allowed to go as well. Lui told him 'no' and Koolau said, "l not obey this law'!"

John shuddered and intuitively knew what happened next. Koolau was a crack shot and owned a rifle, what he had once called 'death from afar in a wink'. "Please don't tell me that it was Koolau—"

"A week later Lui came back, determined to take the lepers and especially Koolau to Kalawao. Lui snuck up on Koolau's house at night, but your friend was waiting for him. I'm sorry John, but he killed Lui. The provisional government is going crazy, calling it an armed insurrection by the lepers. The last I heard, an army has gone to Kalalau to kill Koolau and any lepers who resist."

John looked frantic, his eyes wide with fear for the safety of his family. As if reading his mind, Joe said, "The trails into the valley are blocked off. Everybody in the valley, whether sick or well, is to be arrested and hauled out. That's about a hundred-thirty people who will be rounded up and deported."

John leapt from his chair. "We must go there now, find a way to get Mahealani and JJ out!"

"But how? All the land entrances are blocked. The sea routes are being watched. It'd be suicide to try."

"I will get there."

Kee Lagoon view of Na Pali Coast

Heavy clouds covered the sky. Late summer winds blew with an intensity that created large waves that rolled swiftly over the reefs and onto the broad, sand beach of Kee lagoon. The rock ridge called Makena towered sixteen-hundred feet above the sacred hula school where the goddess Pele once danced with Chief Loahi. For miles beyond, and barely visible in the darkness, massive humps of rock towered thousands of feet above the sea.

The faint light of a guard's cigarette glowed at the base of the trail leading to Kalalau Valley. John could see that Joe's information was correct: all passages into the leper community had been closed off. In the trees near the shoreline, John shared his plan, and Joe whispered, "You're crazy! No one can swim around that point and reach the Kalalau trail."

Studying the flickering light of the guard's cigarette, John asked, "What choice do I have? I can't just walk up to the man and ask permission to go in, and there's no way to get into Kalalau by boat without being spotted by the soldiers. So where does that leave me?"

Joe grabbed his friend's arm. "That's two miles of treacherous water, with waves that smash into the rocks. The currents will pull you right into the sharks. There's got to be a better way."

John had been harboring something that he never intended to share. But now, with his friend nearly frantic, he felt he had no choice. "I've kept this from you because I was sure you wouldn't believe me." He paused, sorted through his words to choose the ones that would be best received. "On two different nights, an *uhane*, a spirit, has come to me in my dreams. Both times, the *uhane* has called me to Kalalau."

Joe's expression changed not a bit, giving John the encouragement to go on. "I've been living in hell for four years. No," he said, raising a hand when Joe started to speak. "No matter how you feel, I know that I failed my family, especially when my son and wife needed me most. I wasn't there to protect them from being brutalized and I'm not with them now. Believe me, Joe, if I do not listen when the spirits call me to Kalalau, I will never be able to live in peace. I failed them once; I will not fail them again." He saw how Joe peered into the darkness, as if hoping to conceal his own emotions. John wanted to explain more.

How my Christian beliefs could live in harmony with my Hawaiian spirituality. A god worshipped in the white man's church could be loved and revered. At the same time, Hawaiians would listen to their native spirits, the uhane who came in the night.

"You have no idea how much I want to turn back that clock," Joe finally admitted. "But I know it's impossible. Perhaps this is our chance." He placed a hand on John's shoulder. "You must go, I will not stop you. But first, please know that, in my heart, I failed them, too." He informed John that he would watch for his return. "If you aren't back in three days, I'm coming after you."

John slipped into the lagoon and swam with the current towards the ridge. The tide's pull carried him to the open sea and Niihau Island. He fought its grasp and moved closer to the waves that shattered against the sheer rock walls of the ridge. More than once seawater clouded his vision, and a steady rain added to his misery.

Occasionally, he dove underwater, swimming below the sea for as far as his lungs would carry. Within an hour, he first heard and then saw waves crashing on the beach. Knowing too well that a sea entry into any small valley is dangerous, he warned himself to be patient. How many times had he explained to JJ that a wave builds quickly as the ocean gathers itself, moving into shallow water. Soon it becomes a mountain of compressed water that uncoils with great force onto the sand. Spending its energy in its rush up the beach, the water flows back into the ocean to repeat its curl, coil, and fall, over, and over again.

The sandy bottom brushed against John's chest as he swam under the cresting wave, the water twisting above him. As the wave unleashed its power onto the shore, John extended his body and rode it onto the beach.

The moment he got his footing, he pushed through the mushy sand and moved upland. He sensed danger. Only one phenomenon of nature would cause a sudden rise of fresh water and send small rocks buffeting his legs. He stopped and listened. He heard higher in the valley the rumble of crashing rocks, the sound intensifying as it blasted toward him. Terror gripped him as the flash flood headed for the sea through the tight funnel of Hanakapiai Valley. Water swirled around him as he struggled to reach higher ground.

In seconds, the overflowing water from the nearby swamp rose to his hips and would soon be over his head, thrusting him into the open sea. A vine brushed his hand and he grasped it just as the water's force tore his feet away from the rocks. John pulled hard on the plant stem, his arm and back muscles screaming with his effort, but the water's force was too great, and the plant was ripped from his hands. He thought of death, of his need to make up for all that he had not given his wife and son.

CHAPTER 44

———

Desperate, his feet sought a foothold on the rocks of the streambed, the churning flood waters drawing him to the sea. John searched overhead, his outstretched hand sliding by large tube-shaped roots of a hala tree anchored firmly into the rocks. Stomping his feet onto the loose stones of the stream bed, John found a hard surface and pushed himself upward through the raging waters. He seized a thorn-encrusted tree root. The creeper bent from his weight and the current. John ignored the pain from the little needles of the root puncturing his hand and muscled himself upward.

Root after root, hand over hand, he inched up, the water threatening his death, rising as high as he climbed. Soon it covered the branch on which he finally stood. With a sinking heart, John realized that leaf-covered branches prevented him from climbing higher. He clung to the thorny leaves, praying to hold on long enough for the flash flood to reach its peak and then subside.

Later, he would not be able to say if it was seconds, minutes, or hours before the raging waters dropped, and John swung from the hala tree—the magnificent growth that had saved his life—onto the trail. The first sheltered spot he found became his bed and, exhausted, he slept, dreaming of the Menehune Queen, Hanakapiai, who died in the valley when her little people were fleeing Kauai and the oppression by the big people.

Sunlight streamed onto John's face, awakening him from this dream. He glanced at the sky, it was cloudless. The dawn had brought a beautiful day, a day to save his family.

The stream below him meandered to the sea, such a stark contrast to the violence that tore at its banks only hours before. He reached into his waist pouch and was astonished to find a stick of dried fish still there. As he ate, he found his way into the small valley and then climbed to the crest. He would have remained, feeling blessed by the spectacular view, but his wife and son needed him. Thousands of white flecks danced upon the water. He turned away just as a great green turtle appeared. In the sky above, a tropicbird cried, its sharp voice echoing along the sheer cliffs of Na Pali.

John squared his shoulders and set off following the bird as it soared above the sea, gliding high over the rounded tops of the cliffs, and then along the great walls of clinging green moss, ferns, and flowers. It plummeted thousands of feet downward to the water, skimmed the waves, and then disappeared. John trudged along the trail bordering the ocean, using every native sense to get to his wife and son in time to save them.

From southwest of where he hiked came an eruption of gunfire. John felt his heart pounding, as if trying to escape from his chest. *What was happening in Kalalau? What was happening to Mahealani and JJ?*

The trail became a narrow, slippery foot path, bordered on one side by a thinly vegetated rock wall, and a treacherous vertical drop on the other. Suddenly, far up ahead, artillery shells whined and exploded, followed by the crashing of boulders onto the valley's floor. Despite the imminent danger of slipping and free-falling into the ocean, John flew over the path, his anxiety increasing as rifle fire, artillery shelling, and heavy smoke rose from Kalalau.

Wind whipped around him, the relentless sound of crashing waves struck his ears. Mixed with nature's noise came the terrible mechanical sounds of war that beat upon him. John was pounded by the clashing sounds, and he wished he could turn off the cacophony that increased his fear.

He rounded an outcropping and saw a steamer riding the swells of the sea. A whiff of smoke floating lazily from its funnel was soon lost in a dense cloud of grey fumes streaming out of Kalalau Valley. The whining of shells and the ceaseless tattoo of rifle bullets faded away just as John climbed up to a bluff.

Kalalau Valley

Spread below him was the valley, its red hills glowing in the light of day. Along the beach, huge fires consumed the homes of the lepers of Kalalau. He looked inland and saw that other fires were burning as well. Mixed with the smell of smoking wood was that of exploded gunpowder.

John saw movement on the water and realized that the steamer was leaving, its decks awash with people. He shielded his eyes against the glare of the water, but he could not make out the figures of Mahealani or JJ. Frantic, he began to run, finally crossing a stream and making his way along the beach.

To the north, the government steamer chugged towards Hanalei; to the south and west lay a scene of devastation. Fire licked at blackened skeletons of homes, once a shelter for sick people who had lived in freedom in the valley.

When he moved closer, he saw the extent of the devastation: burnt wood everywhere, the acrid smells a signal that a battle had concluded. Great scars scorched the cliff walls. Trees and shrubs had been mowed away by soldiers and violence. Despite the carnage of war, thin rainbows arched over the torn landscape creating a bizarre beauty.

John ran along the beach, looking for the home he had built for his wife and son. When he found it, there was nothing but charred wood and embers. He shouted for them; there was no response. He searched the burnt, black wood, for clumps of bodies. There were none. Frantic questions rose in his mind: *Are they dead? Are they bleeding but alive? Are they hiding, or have they been taken on that ship?*

He raced around shouting,

"Mahealani! JJ!"

———

CHAPTER 45

As he rounded the skeleton of a house, a voice called to him. "John Tana, are the haoles gone?"

He looked and saw Paoa, a shoeless leper. "Yes, they are. But where is my family?"

The man stumbled from the bush and into John's arms. "Water," he begged. John found a canteen and helped the man drink. When Paoa was finished, he stepped away and demanded, "Where are my wife and son?"

Paoa pointed to the far end of the valley. "Over there, they fell into the water over there." He went on to tell John how they had been together for three days, while the soldiers fought Koolau. "Today, their big gun fired all over the valley, great chunks of hill collapsed, and shells exploded. Boom! Boom! Boom!"

The man was nearly mad from fear, yet John was desperate for news of his family.

"Metal whizzed all over like angry bees flying from their nest," Paoa went on. John held up a hand to stop this recounting, but the leper needed to speak. "Your wife was going crazy. She jumped out from our hiding place and ran to the beach. JJ, he limped after her. And then an artillery shell blasted near the water." Paoa pressed both hands over his ears. "The noise was terrible! We were so afraid! Rocks flew everywhere, and I don't know if they were hit. But over there," he cried, pointing to the sea. "They fell in over there."

John raced to the low ridge where waves lapped onto the shore. The dying sun blazed on the red dirt hills of the valley turning them deep orange, but John ignored its amber beauty. Reaching the end of the valley, he dove into the ocean, swimming with a frenzy that scattered schools of fish scuttling in darts of dark green away from his churning arms.

Up and down the coastline he went, searching for bodies until the dark of night spread its blackness over the sea. A cave yawned in front of him, the remnants of an old lava tube. Water surged in and out, partially covering its entrance. Within its recesses he saw a floating bundle of rags. Diving under the water, he swam for many yards and then surfaced within the tube. Floating beside him was the body of his son.

John held JJ to him, stroking the boy's face as they bobbed in the darkness. Blinded by tears, John struggled from the cave, using one arm and powerful kicks to force his way through the current. He pulled his son to shore and lay the boy on the sand.

Paoa was waiting for him. Together, they dug a grave near the south ridge of the valley. John removed the belt that circled his son's waist, the buckle made by Moana still emblazoned with the tooth of the shark killed by the boy.

John wept, remembering his son riding the waves, swimming through the water, playing jokes on his sister, standing bravely at the water's edge, announcing "I am not afraid of you, Mano!"

It was too dark to search for his wife. He knew it best to wait until morning. With Paoa's help, they buried JJ, placing rocks upon his body and wailing their grief to the dark night.

The emotions were profound, yet John was burning to know what had happened in once-peaceful Kalalau. He built a fire and beckoned Paoa to join him. "Tell me of my wife and son!" he snapped, as if this poor leper had brought harm to his family. "Tell me what happened here!"

Paoa cringed, inching back and away from this grief-stricken man. He opened his mouth a few times, as if to speak, and then said nothing.

CHAPTER 46

———

John looked at Paoa's grotesquely disfigured face and realized that it mirrored his inner fears. "Please, Paoa," he said, his voice softer. "Tell me what happened. I promise, no harm will come to you."

Paoa seemed to gather his courage and nodded. "We in the valley were doing well. The women knew your wife's story: her stillborn son, the kidnap, the cruelty of the warriors, everything. They came to her house daily to help her and your son, treating them with love and kindness, with aloha. I think her mind was clearing of its clouds. But then, three days ago, the government soldiers landed at Kalalau." Paoa paused, his eyes wandered over the valley, as if looking for the homes of his friends. Looking for those he once knew.

"How many people were here when the soldiers came? How many lepers? And what did the soldiers do?"

Paoa's eyes seemed to be in a dream, as if he somehow envisioned the happiness of mothers and fathers holding their children in their arms.

"Tell me," John pleaded.

Paoa turned his head and looked at John, as if for the first time. "We all knew that when Koolau killed Sheriff Lui, trouble would come. Maybe forty soldiers arrived to get him. They captured a hundred-and-forty-eight of us. And these soldiers," he added, his face expressing disgust, "they walk around like big bosses, they search for guns. 'Koolau is the only one in the valley with a gun', we tell them, but they don't believe us. And then Mahealani, JJ, three others and I run into the hills, looking for Koolau. We want to hide with him, not surrender. "When we warned Koolau of the soldiers and asked for his help, he told us that we must separate from him, that the soldiers wanted him, and we should not put ourselves in danger. He tells us that these *kolea* birds have come to fatten upon our land and eat our people. That they should feast upon his body, not ours. And then he tells us that we can surrender and live out our days alone in Kalawao, while he hides in these hills and fights them until he dies.

"Koolau's wife, Piilani, was determined to stay with her husband and keep her promise to God to live together *until death do us part*. They took their child and fled, leaving the others behind. This is when Mahealani, JJ, and I moved farther away, while three other lepers went to the beach to surrender.

"The next day, soldiers climbed near Koolau's refuge hollering and screaming, firing their rifles and making a terrible noise. Around noon, a single shot rang out, its echo bouncing across all the walls of the valley. Soldiers flew down from the hills, yelling as if a monster chased them, and then they stood on the beach and fired into the hills where Koolau hid."

After a long moment, and a gentle urging from John, the leper resumed his story. "The next day the enemy fired thousands of times at the place where Koolau hid. After much shooting, they moved uphill again. Some soldiers sought higher ground above the place where he was sheltered. They hoped to find him from above and kill him.

"When the soldiers reached the crest of the ridge, a single shot rang out, loud and pure." Paoa stopped, as if reliving images riveted into his mind. "A soldier rose from the ridge, one hand clutching his heart. And then his rifle clanked over the crest and bounced down the walls of the cliff. He staggered forward until he came to the edge and then he fell, striking other soldiers who bounced with him down the mountain."

The leper told John that the rest of the soldiers ran down the hill, firing wildly and blasting to pieces the mountainside where they thought Koolau was hiding. "In the early morning, the soldiers buried three men. After this, they brought out a cannon and fired at the hills. Until then, Mahealani, JJ, and I had been safe."

John gripped Paoa by his shoulders. "Did they fire where you were hiding?" Looking into John's eyes, Paoa whispered something. John had to lean closer, straining to hear. "The shells marched closer to our hiding place, yes. Rocks, metal, everything came down; shrubs and trees were crushed. It was as if rain from hell creeped toward us." Paoa stopped, his voice becoming lower. "You know the rest." The next morning, with early light clearing away the darkness, John swam around the southwest ridge of the valley searching the coastline. The weather was good, the sea calm, and at any other time he would have considered it a glorious dawn. He swam on, stroke after stroke, until he reached the shore of another valley, this one more verdant than the last. From the water he could see the sand and, behind it, a waterfall. At the base of the cascade lay a mass of white cloth. His heart began to pound, and his stomach churned, until food and then bile erupted from his lips, but he continued to swim, stroking powerfully as he raced toward the beach.

Mahealani was battered with angry cuts on her face and body, the wounds no longer bloody, having been cleansed and purified by the salt water. John kneeled before her, threw his head back and wailed. He wailed mightily, in the tradition of Hawaiians in mourning; and he wailed for having failed her. He wailed for rejecting traditional beliefs and accepting Christian teachings; and he wailed for their life and their future now lost.

John drew Mahealani into him and held her close. He touched her nose, searching for her warm ha, but there was no more breath to mix with his. *He remembered how she smelled and the warmth of her skin, her laughter and how the moonlight played in her eyes. And he remembered her gentle cooing as she excited him, and they gave each other pleasure.*

He rose, Mahealani in his arms, and walked aimlessly along the beach. Tears washed freely from his eyes and his breath came in short, rasping sounds. He fought to control the shaking of his body. He was bewildered by his loss.

Finally, John placed his wife by a little cave in the wall of the valley. Stripping the rags from her body, he prepared her for a Hawaiian burial. With the blessings of the gods supporting him, he cut open his Mahealani and removed her organs, which he then cleaned with loving care. Over the next three days, John salted and dried her body and watched how this shell of his beloved shriveled in the sun. He wailed as he did his work, crying out *"I love you, why did you leave me? Why did you go away like this? I miss you! I will never forget you! Forgive me!"*

In the afternoon of the third day, John took the remains of Mahealani and wrapped it into a ball. He placed his wife inside the cave and piled rocks atop and around her grave. And then he took the locket that had hung around her neck and placed it into a pouch at his waist.

Exhausted, racked with coughing, John collapsed onto Mahealani's grave. As his mind slipped away, he recalled Leinani, and how she recited words of a long dead English poet:

"...to sleep-perchance to dream
...in that sleep of death what dreams may come..."

———

CHAPTER 47

John vaguely heard a man say, "I'm afraid there's little I can do. Your father has pneumonia. His pulse is weak. His fever is high. Pour as much liquid as you can into him and bathe him with cool water to reduce his temperature. The next twenty-four hours are critical."

He saw Nani and Joe standing beside him. He watched, as during the day they took turns tending to him, alternating cool compresses with urgings to drink whatever fluids they could coax between his parched lips.

The doctor came several times, but it was evident that his efforts were for naught. "Dad," said Nani, "I'm calling in the kahuna," determination in her voice, as she glared at her husband, stilling any protest he might have made.

John nodded, his expression conveying that, at this point, they had nothing to lose.

Kahuna Kainoa arrived and went to work. He extracted the juice from mashed herbs and applied it to John's body. Next, he created a tent around the feverish man, in which he placed a steaming pot of herb-filled water. John struggled for breath, triggering coughing spells.

"Dad," Nani wailed. "Please don't leave me, I can't lose you, too," and then she fell sobbing into the arms of her husband, striking feebly at his chest. "If only you had found him sooner!"

Joe held Nani and spoke into her hair. "Sweetheart, we sailed for Kalalau as fast as we could. Besides," he added, separating himself from Nani and smiling at her, "he's the strongest man I know. If anyone can make it, he will." They remained at John's bedside, working together to save him.

Two days passed, the nights were arduous. John's fever burned, his coughs harsh, rasping, like a death rattle. When Joe suggested that a priest be called to administer last rites, Nani screamed, "How can you say that! You promised he would live!" And then she wept, helplessness etched across her face.

Another dark night turned into morning. John woke. His head ached. He saw Nani asleep next to his bed, the sunlight streaking through a window touching her haggard face. "Water," he croaked.

Startled awake, Nani looked at her father and heard no rasping sounds coming from his chest. She pressed a hand against his brow and smiled. "The fever has broken!" she announced, and then ran to fetch water.

It took several days before John could sit up and take nourishment, and the fear and grief that had gripped Nani and Joe released its hold upon them. "You're looking pretty chipper for a guy we gave up for dead," Joe said, smiling at his old friend.

John managed a grin. "Thanks to you and Nani, I cheated the devil."

"I never thought I'd say this, John, but it's because of that kahuna fellow that you're still here. Whatever that evil-smelling stuff was that he poured over you, it did the trick."

John smiled again, although this time it transformed his face into the old John. "Take my word for it, you don't want to know."

The men sat together in that kind of comfortable silence that comes from many years of friendship and trust, from sharing joy and grief. After a lengthy pause, Joe shifted on his chair and then coughed, as if he had something more important to discuss.

"Out with it," John said. He had known this man too long not to recognize the signs. Something was on his mind and it was not going to be pleasant.

"John, I didn't want to mention this until I thought you could handle the news, but..." Joe's voice trailed off.

"Joe, it's okay, tell me." When he said nothing, John sighed. "Come on, out with it. What's up?"

Joe glanced toward the window, through the bedroom door, everywhere but into John's eyes. "You remember how Sui Young's hui got that lease on the Anahola land? Well, the lease just ended, and the plantation took over the property. Our friend is moving to Oahu, giving up on growing rice on Kauai. And," he added, holding up a hand to curb John's response, "without a lease, Cabral and Ito aren't permitted by the sugar plantation to run a farm, so they've left for Honolulu."

John leaned back into his pillows and folded his arms across his chest. "So, all I've got left is the lawsuit."

"Speaking of that, a letter came for you from that fellow Kingsley. I held onto it until you were better. Here it is," Still said, handing him an envelope.

John's hand trembled as he reached out and took it. He paused for a moment, afraid to open it.

"Come on, get on with it. Maybe he has good news for us."

Breathing deeply, John slit open the wax-sealed envelope and unfolded the letter:

August 3, 1893
Dear Mr. Tana,

Responding to yours of June 18ᵗʰ, 1893, I regret to inform you that I may not be of any assistance to you. My father-in-law, Robert Grant, has a substantial interest in Kilauea Sugar Plantation.

My advice is that you accept his generous offer to purchase your land and end your meritless claim against the plantation.

James Kingsley

"Damn him." John crushed the letter and tossed it across the room. A burning anger welled inside him. Tension returned. *If I lose my suit against the Kilauea Plantation, I will have nothing left.*

"This money guy, Kingsley, won't help us?"

"No! And he's telling me Leinani's father, Grant, is behind all our troubles. That man has hounded me since I lived in Kahului. If ever I get the chance, I'll get even with him."

"Fellow like that is too powerful to take on unless—"

"Yeah, that's exactly what I'm thinking, finish Mr. Grant for good," John said, making a cutting motion with his finger across his neck. "If we lose the lawsuit, I am back to where I was a long time ago, a poor Hawaiian."

Joe shook his head. "You've got it all wrong. We have the land and the house in Kapaa, and don't forget about my field supervisor job at the plantation in Kealia. There's plenty for all of us. And I don't want to hear any talk about doing in Mr. Grant, killing someone solves nothing."

John's hand trembled as it reached out and grasped Joe's hand. "I couldn't ask for a better son-in-law and friend, but you have Nani and the children. You don't need me added to your burden." He coughed, nodding his thanks. "I'll stay here, in Kilauea. As soon as I'm well, I can make my living from the sea."

CHAPTER 48

—

John stood still, melded into the black rock at the edge of the reef, his hand thrust back behind his head, holding a harpoon. His six-year-old grandson, Edward, watched, motionless, near him. In a tidal pool a large blue uhu (parrot fish) bit on seaweed growing on the rocks. Its tail flicked idly defeating the surge of the waves and keeping it close to its food.

The uhu turned sideways as a foaming wave washed over it. John flung his harpoon into the big fish. He scooped up his weapon from the water.

Edward clapped his hands reaching out to the wildly flapping fish. Its wide tail slapped the side of his face. For a moment the surprised child appeared to cry, but John reached to his grandson and brought him to his side, whispering to him. Instead of tears cascading down his face, the young boy laughed.

His grandson's toughness pleased John. "Good boy, that didn't hurt. But what did we learn in our lesson on fishing today?"

"How to catch a blue fish while standing on a rock?"

"We could call the lesson that, Edward, but we learned if we want to catch a fish be patient, still, and wait for our chance."

"Still, that's my last name, so you're saying: 'Still is to be patient and wait for his chance'."

John laughed at his grandson's twisting of his words. "You are one smart little man. What I meant is: don't move, be patient, watch for an incoming wave. When its foam hits the rocks, it will hide your movements from the eyes of the fish. Aim your spear at the upper part of the animal, water always affects your aim. Then throw it." John reached down and took Edward's hand.

"Where are we going, Grandpa?" Edward asked as he skipped from the reef and onto the sand.

John scooped his grandson up to his shoulder. Hugged him against his body giving his cheek a mushy kiss. "We have our dinner, Edward, what do you say we find your sister Catherine and head up to the mountains to see what we can find?"

"Yeah, yeah." Edward clapped his hands and began to sing, "To the mountains we will go. To the mountains we will go, high ho the derry ho, to the mountains we will go."

At the Tana compound, John found Catherine. He took his grandchildren by their hands and marched upland following the Kilauea River. Nani accompanied them for a short time. As tears welled in her eyes she said, "You are happy, Dad."

John stopped his riverside walk and held his grandchildren close. "They have eased the pain of what I have lost. Their happiness brings joy to my heart."

Nani smiled, wiping away the trickles of water that moved slowly down her cheeks. "Have a good time everyone. Children, mind your grandfather." Her smile broadened as they answered, "We will."

Trudging on the river's bank John pointed to the water. "There is a lot to eat in there."

"What's to eat Grandpa? All I see is running water," Catherine said as Edward picked up a rock and threw it into the river.

"Watch." John pointed towards the ripples as they moved away from the point where the stone had crashed into the water.

"Watch what? Look at what?" Edward and Catherine chorused.

"See the goby fish scattering under the shallow rocks at the edge of the bank? Watch the shrimp scooting away from the ripples."

"I don't see anything," Edward said defiantly. "There is nothing in the water."

John reached into the water with his scoop net. He poked it under a broad flat stone lying at the water's edge. When he pulled the net from under the rock there were two fish in it and several flopping shrimps that snapped about, bouncing against the mesh.

"Can I hold one?" Edward asked, then reached into the net and grabbed a squirming fish. He held it in his fist like a banana. The goby slipped through his hand, plopped on the bank, and flipped itself into the river.

John laughed, chiding his grandson, "You should have waited until I said 'yes' before you grabbed the fish, but that's okay, we didn't want to eat it. Let me show you a fresh water opihi." John's hands went under the rocks near the bank, feeling their underside.

"Grandpa won't something bite you or grab your hand?" Catherine squealed. John pulled his hand from the water. In his palm were two soft round limpets. "There isn't anything that will bite you in this river, Catherine. Look, this is fresh water opihi. It's a little different from the ocean opihi, easier to catch, and sweeter in taste. You should never starve when you're near a stream."

As they enjoyed the cool breezes blowing from the mountains, John pointed to green vines covered with purple fruit. "This is lilikoi, passion fruit. Watch as I break it open. There is sweet nectar inside. You can suck it out of its shell or add the nectar to water or other juice to make a great drink."

They kept hiking into the hills. In a ravine of the mountain John pointed to a forest of tall stalks of round, yellow wood. "This is bamboo. It has many uses. One of the main reasons for harvesting bamboo is to build a frame for your shack. Once you have built a frame you take grass and bundle it over your house to protect it from wind and rain. The young bamboo shoots may be eaten. Wild pigs love them. If you want to catch a pig you can build a trap and stock it with bamboo shoots."

"Did you ever catch a wild pig, Grandpa? Did you ever see one and fight it?" Edward asked as he reached over to a slip of bamboo trying to tear it from the soil. It held fast to the earth, refusing to budge from its roots.

John took out his knife and cut the slip from the ground and handed it to his grandson. He looked at Edward for many moments before saying, "Once, a long time ago, I think I killed a huge black boar. I was never sure I did since it got away from me. We saw a lot of its blood but never found its body."

John reached down, lifting Edward into him, hugging his grandson. Edward clung to his grandfather, hopping in his arms, filling his fists with John's hair, rubbing his nose on John's cheek. The happiness of his grandson wrenched John's heart. He blinked several times to clear his eyes of the tears that blinded him as memories of a lost child, a happier time, flooded over him.

"Grandpa, are you all right?" a worried Catherine tugged at John's arm. "Yeah, I'm okay. I was just remembering," John muttered as he released Edward from his grasp. He took each child by the hand and headed home.

On the way the small family picked juicy, red, mountain apple. As they chewed the fruit John pointed to other useful items, the mulberry bush for the making of tapa, the koa tree for its rich brown wood and seeds.

"These koa seeds are boiled to soften them. Then they are strung together to make brown lei. You can make lei from a lot of things. When we get back to the ocean I will show you shells from which you can make beautiful lei."

At the Tana compound, John took thorny, light brown leaves from the lauhala tree. "What you do with these leaves is dry them in the sun, strip away the thorns from the sides, then cut the tip. Take the leaves and fold them over each other to make mats, baskets, and all kinds of things."

"Can you make a hat or other stuff?" Edward asked, then let out a yowl as he nicked his finger with a hala thorn.

John took Edward's hand and wiped away the droplets of blood from his grandson's finger and examined the break in the skin. "It's okay, just a little ouchy. Come on, you two, let's go to the coconut tree and I will show you how to make a hat and a little bird."

From a fallen limb John stripped away bunches of green leaves. He sat on the ground cross-legged. Catherine and Edward snuggled up to his knees watching intently as Grandpa weaved a hat. "Next to the taro, the coconut tree is the most important plant that our ancestors brought with them on their voyage to Hawaii. From the coconut tree you can make a hat and many other good things. Let me show you."

John pounded a dried coconut against a rock. After tearing away the husk he pointed to the fibers. "You see this? Pull it apart and you can weave the fibers into rope. Open the seed and there is food and drink. From what is inside you can make oil for rubbing or fire. Use the shell for water or to put food in it. The trunk of the tree can be used to build houses, make statues, or walls." John finished his lesson by plopping a broad-brimmed hat onto Catherine's head.

"How pretty you look." John smiled.

"Grandpa, Grandpa, how about me?" Little Eddie begged as he snatched at the new hat. Catherine leaped up and ran behind a coconut tree. Eddie pursued her.

"Nah, nah, you can't catch me," Catherine teased as she eluded his grasp and ran to a second coconut tree. John laughed as his grandchildren played 'catch me'. Forgotten were past sorrows as they ran about the compound, the coconut hat jiggling on Catherine's head, its green leaf brim barely escaping Edward's grasp.

CHAPTER 49

—

Many years after John was gone his grandchildren told their children about tutu man's traditional methods of fishing and his story telling. Catherine would sit in the family parlor, her children at her feet, spinning fantastical tales of her grandfather with such awe and wonder that John Tana became legendary.

In the dimness of candlelight, her children's eyes wide as saucers, Catherine spoke with an air of mystery in her voice. "We would sit on the shore in our coconut hats, your Uncle Edward and me. Your great-grandfather would set his net across the channel. Edward would tease tutu man yelling, 'Hey, Grandpa, you can't catch fish in the daytime. They will see the net and run away.'

"Tutu man would just wink at us. 'Wait, wait,' he would say.

"Then he chanted in Hawaiian. He used words that I did not understand.

"Nothing would happen. Edward and I would snicker and lose interest in crazy old Grandpa's antics. He had been sick for a time, and your uncle and I thought that the illness had taken away some of his mind, especially when he began wearing his malo, loincloth, all the time.

"After a short time, he would chant again in Hawaiian. Nothing would happen. Your uncle and I would dig up clumps of sand and hurl it at each other. It was a glorious fight, but, oh, did the sand sting when you were hit.

"As we flung our missiles Grandpa called out, 'Look to the sea'.

"Wiping sand from my eyes, I searched the deep blue of the ocean. At the mouth of the channel, a great fin appeared and then a second. The fins began to zigzag back and forth between the reef walls, their movements driving ahead whatever lay before them. As the fins reached shallower water the fish swam into the net. They gilled themselves in the webbing, trapped by its cords.

"Tutu man waded out to the grey sharks. They swam around his legs like happy dogs while he spoke to them in Hawaiian. Then they swam away.

"Yet the most awesome of times was at night," Catherine whispered to her children. "Tutu man had a large fishing hut at Koolau beach. After the evening meal of fish and poi, your great-grandfather would lay a fire in the center of the hut. All of us, Uncle Edward and Joseph, Grandma Nani, we would sit around the fire and he would tell us stories and legends of the past.

Pele

"Many years ago, Moana, a Chief of Kilauea, challenged all comers to a sled race. Moana was an expert at holua (sled racing). He had never been beaten.
"The course was set for the backside of Kahili crater. It had the right incline and length to give the racers a slide of a mile ending at Kilauea village. At the appointed time, Moana and the three other contestants came to the starting point. Just before the race began an old woman appeared from the side of the dead volcano. She asked Moana for his sled to race against the other men.
"Moana refused. 'A champion needs to ride his own sled to win a race'.
"The old woman asked Moana's brother Kiawe if she could use his sled. Kiawe had been properly taught to be respectful to elders and kind to strangers so he agreed and surrendered his sled to the elderly woman.

"Down Kahili the four raced. It was clear at the outset that Moana's sled was the fastest, yet the old woman's sled was almost as good. The two other contestants rapidly dropped out as the man and woman outdistanced them.

"For a time, Moana was in the lead. Then the old woman would catch up and pass him. This jockeying continued back and forth until the two sleds crossed the finish line.

"The judges could not pick a winner the finish was so close.

"'I challenge you to a second race,' the old woman demanded. Moana laughed and agreed. 'You were lucky the last time. This time I will win.'

"Back to the top of Kahili Crater the two contestants climbed. When they reached the starting point for the race the old woman said, 'I think that we should change sleds. Let me use yours and you may have mine.'

'Ah, you are nothing but a dirty old hag, you cannot beat me. I will not let you have my sled.'

"With these words, Moana leaped on his sled and began to race down Kahili. Enraged by his cruel words, angered by his unfair advantage, the old woman changed. Her stringy hair turned to long, flaming strands of red. Her face became young and beautiful with cheeks that were rosy like fire. The white cloth wrapped around her body became strips of black writhing about her like slender snakes. A wooden pole appeared in her hand.

"Pele stamped her feet and thrust her staff onto the ground. Land melted into boiling red liquid fire. The angered goddess slid after the rude chief. A wave of molten lava followed her.

"As Pele sped faster and faster downhill, her flowing red hair smoked. Her black garment burst into flames whirling around her like fire sticks. At her feet a great wave of molten lava flowed, building to gigantic heights.

"At the finish line the horrified villagers saw fiery Pele charge towards their homes dragging a stream of molten rocks. An elder yelled out, 'It is Moana who has angered the goddess. Pele is after him. He is a bad chief. Chase him from the village.'

"The people raced up Kahili carrying logs, stones, wood, thatched grass, and all manner of obstacles. They created a low wall in Moana's path which curved away from the village towards a deep ravine.

"When Moana saw the obstacles, he steered his sled along the curve of the artificial wall, Pele behind him. The people gaped with horror at the charging goddess. Her eyes glared as she and her hot lava churned toward them. As one person, the villagers turned and fled, trampling old people and children in their hurried flight.

"As the flaming wall reached the first barrier Kiawe stood alone in front of the hot flood of rocks. Pele swerved her molten wave away from him, away from the village, and pursued Moana. Sweeping along the barrier, Pele followed the rude man, leaving a deadly trail as wood and grass of the artificial wall burst into flames.

"Moana realized that he was racing to his doom and tried to steer toward the barrier only to be driven away by the hot flames. As Moana glanced behind him Pele's heat scorched his toes. Like a surfer the Chief of Kilauea dug his fingers into the earth speeding his sled away. He gained some distance from Pele, but the gap closed as the goddess and her hot rocks inched towards him.

"With a mighty pull of his fingers and arms Moana drove his sled forward launching it into the air, and the sled soared over the edge of the ravine. Moana flew for a short time then plunged to the rocks below. Pele followed him and devoured Moana and his sled, changing them into molten rock.

"Kiawe became the King of Kilauea and ruled wisely and well. During his life he was always kind to strangers, especially old women."

CHAPTER 50

———

John spent months in rehabilitation, exercising to rebuild his strength, and his recovery was steady. He finally felt strong enough to practice lua with Moana, and together they sharpened their martial arts skills. Over time, he regained full health and strength and was able to resume a normal and active life. During the school holidays, Nani and Joe's children stayed with him and he taught them the Hawaiian ways of land and sea. In the evening, he treated them to legendary stories of heroic men and women, Hawaiians who created the fascinating and colorful tapestry of a nation's history and lore.

The plantation lost its bid for a new trial and appealed to the Hawaii Supreme Court. John's attorney explained that if the plantation lost the appeal, John would win his claim for riparian rights and would be entitled to water from the Kilauea River. On the other hand, if the plantation was successful in its appeal, John's land would be worthless.

Despite the legal proceedings, the plantation plowed the land up to his ditch and along one side of John's seven acres. Plantation work crews dug a canal diverting water from upstream of the Kilauea River into the newly plowed land. Where John's ditch had trickled some water into his land, the aggressive new moves of the plantation ended all flow from the river. On several occasions John confronted plantation supervisors who invaded his property, challenging property lines and his rights to the land. Finally, both sides reached an uneasy truce. Yet John knew that if he lost the appeal the plantation would move aggressively to hem him in and drive him out.

In the winter of 1894, John received word from Joe Still that he should make a journey to Kapaa. Arriving in mid-morning, the two men greeted one another.

John sensed that he had been beckoned for something important. As Joe chatted on, John's impatience rose.

"You've been a second father to me," Joe said. "My aloha is great, and my home will always be yours."

John tried not to scowl, nor did he want to offend Joe by brushing aside these loving comments. He knew this man and understood that something important, perhaps something unpleasant, needed to be said. "I'm guessing there's more than aloha and being welcomed into your home that you want to discuss. So out with it: what's going on?"

Joe walked around the room, rearranged a few books. "Your grandchildren always talk about you, and there's awe in their voices when they speak of the knowledge and strength of their *tutu* man. They love you very much, as do Nani and I, and—"

"Cut it, Joe," John interrupted. "What is it you're trying to say?"

Joe stopped fidgeting, walked over to where John was standing, and faced his friend. He sighed once and then stated, "We lost our case."

John felt a dagger thrusting into his heart. His knees buckled and only Joe Still's grip on his arm saved him from falling to the floor. Collapsing into a chair, John felt grief turning to anger. He struggled against hateful thoughts and an instinct he rarely experienced: a desire for revenge. "What happened?" John whispered, fury rising in him like a young fire fanned by strong winds.

"It's a little hard to explain," Joe began, as if he, too, was trying to make sense of this disastrous news. "Our lawyer talked about dominant tenement and servient tenement, but I found it all confusing. However, the bottom line is clear: the court threw out the jury's decision about damages, and it rejected their finding that we had acquired an easement over plantation lands."

"On what grounds?" John demanded, his hands clenched into fists.

"They said we had no right to alter the size of the ditch or its course, and that these acts broke the adverse use of the waterways we had dug to the river."

John appeared incredulous, eyes wide and head shaking from side to side. "Are you saying that we lost on some garbage technicality? But that's not fair!"

The moment John made that declaration, the men fell silent. The expressions on their faces said it all: The Supreme Court of the Republic of Hawaii was stacked against the Hawaiian, the commoner. With the court made up of plantation bigwigs, self-important men who wore judicial black robes and played the role of wise judges—while not giving a damn about the real Hawaiian people—men like John Tana would never be given a fair chance.

John rocked in his chair, his fingers thrust through his hair. "So, I'm back to where I was when Grant kicked me off my land on Maui." He was too angry to recognize the irony in this, that decades later his own frustrating history was repeating itself, just like the history of his people.

"That's not true, you have Nani, your grandchildren, and this house." He placed a hand on John's shoulder and winced when it was pushed away.

Silence descended on them, a quiet that was neither pleasant nor hopeful. John struggled to gain control of his emotions, but it was impossible. *Waves of grief fomented by a lifetime of losses flooded over him. So many losses, all due to king sugar and the damned new Republic of Hawaii, who strong-armed the legal system and took from John Tana all that he had left.*

His Aunt Malia's words ricocheted around his head. *"Hawaiian man has no land, no money, he has nothing."*

Emotion finally won out and John began to tremble. Joe rushed from the room to find a blanket, but John called him back. "You don't have to worry about me," he said, his voice bitter, edgy. "I won't succumb to this and die. No, I intend to seek revenge."

The expression on Joe's face could best be described as shock. "Revenge against...the Republic of Hawaii?"

The muscles in John's jaw were pulsing from pent-up rage. Unable to contain it any longer, he bellowed, "Yes, Joe, that is exactly what I mean!" Calming himself with several deep breaths, he finally added, "Remember when I saved King Kalakaua from assassination?" When Joe nodded, he continued. "And you remember how I let those men go, and then got them jobs at Makee Sugar? Well, we've remained friends and they owe me."

"Owe you...how?" asked Joe.

John weighed how much he wanted to reveal to Joe and then nodded. "Manuel came to me last week. A group of royalists are planning a rebellion. They've raised lots of money and one of them left for San Francisco to buy weapons. He's expected back by the end of the year."

Joe stared at his friend for a long beat and then said, "You can't intend to join in a conspiracy to overthrow the new government?" There was surprise, concern, and disbelief in his voice.

John shook his head. "Now that I've lost this case, what can I lose by rebelling? Anyway," he quickly added, "I've already decided. I'm going to Honolulu with Manuel and Kaleo and fight those bastards." Again, his hands balled up into fists. "They took my land, my wife, my son, and left me nothing!"

Joe seized John by the shoulders, the younger man's towering height dwarfing the older. "You have a lot to lose, damn it! Your reputation, your good name, even what's left of your family. My God, man, do you really think that rebelling is the answer to your troubles? Work with the system! Become political and find a peaceful way!"

John put both hands onto Joe's chest and gently shoved him away. "You can't teach an old dog new tricks, isn't that what they say?" His voice rose to nearly a shout when he added, "I don't understand their laws and I never will! But I know how to fight, and I know how to use the land and the sea to feed and care for my family, and no one will deny me that right!"

Joe Still fixed his eyes upon John Tana, both men burning with emotion. "Rebellion only results in one thing, and that's death. Have you forgotten that I fought in the war between France and Prussia? Do you have any idea what it's like to watch men—no, boys—fall on a battlefield because Napoleon believed that Bismarck had insulted him? Insulted! Europe was torn to shreds over an insult, damn it! And for what? France lost the war, Napoleon abdicated, and the French elected a new government, which was fought by French rebels in Paris! Called themselves the Paris Commune, a bunch of liberals with fancy new ideas."

John glared at Joe and began pacing the room. "I don't see what France and the Paris Commune have to do with my trouble."

Joe threw his arms in the air, his face red. "It was all about equality for everyone, and social welfare programs, and for what? The French prisoners of war were sent home by the Germans to fight for the new French Government against the Commune. My friend Pierre La Follete told me all about it. The French government went crazy and ordered the soldiers to kill without mercy, maybe fifty thousand Commune supporters died." Breathing heavily, he took a step closer to John and said, "How's that different from your friends' plan, huh?"

John spoke slowly, restrained fury in his voice. "This is Hawaii, not France, and equality is not the issue. It's Hawaiians having a right to their own government. And yes, I'm talking about our right to share the *aina*, the land, and not have foreigners take it away." It passed through John's mind that "foreigner" might also refer to Joe, but he said nothing.

Joe was not to be deterred. "It's like the Indian Wars, and all those Indians rampaging, beating up on settlers who were taking their land. And then—"

"And why shouldn't they rampage!" John erupted, cutting Joe off. His anger felt strangling and he heard his voice rising. But it was too late to stop, too late to ignore the century of hatred, discrimination, and greed. "It was their land! Why shouldn't they fight the thieves who were stealing it!"

"Let me finish, please," Joe begged.

John fell into a sullen and brooding silence. If his son-in-law needed to give him a history lesson, he'd take that time to regain his composure. *But do I really need to be told about the Indians and how the government corralled them into dusty, isolated reservations? Who didn't know about Custer, his defeat, and the revenge the army took on those Indians?* After listening with a patience that surprised even John, he finally blurted out, "We're not Indians!"

"Look at your friend, Koolau. You see any difference there? A leper colony, a man who refuses to obey the law—" The sentence was left hanging, as if John would get the connection.

"Koolau had a valid reason to disobey the law." When he saw the disbelief on Joe's face, his ire grew. "Are you saying I was wrong in sending my wife and son to Kalalau? Don't forget that this colony was considered lawless, too!"

Joe rolled his eyes. "Sheriff Lui was sent to Kalalau to enforce the law."

"A law created by a bunch of Christians who hated Hawaiians! It was our monarchy that encouraged the kokua system, remember? And it was the Christians who ended it! You of all people should know that if the compassionate system were still intact, none of this would've happened. Koolau would've have gone peacefully to Kalawao, instead of having to flee to the safety of Kalalau.

You're not making sense! Should Koolau have gone with the sheriff instead of shooting him?"

"Yes, that's exactly what I'm saying."

John flinched under the intensity of Joe Still's glare. All that guilt he had suppressed over the abandonment of his wife and son rushed back, bringing with it ugly memories. He turned his face away from his friend's harsh look.

"So, tell me, John. What should the provisional government do? What should any government do when there's an uprising? Where a lawman is killed? The answer is: You fight force with force and stamp out the rebellion."

The room became eerily quiet as two old and trusted friends considered the possible end to their friendship. Into this silence, Joe Still spoke. "I don't have any excuses for soldiers burning houses, shooting up the valley, maybe killing my wife's mother and brother. But let me tell you this: Whenever you let loose the dogs of war, there is only death and misery, everyone loses."

"Are you saying that you know what will happen if we rebel against injustice?"

"I fought in war! I lost friends to war! I lost my homeland to war! And what do I have? Scars of battle and no family, except the one you've given me. And believe me, John, I do not intend to lose them!"

"David Kalakaua was my friend," John said, his voice lower, more controlled. "After he was made our king, the sugar people stripped him and the Hawaiian people of power. When his sister, Queen Liliuokalani, tried to return power to her people, America and a few rich men got rid of her as well. Whether you like it or not, Liliuokalani is my queen; she is also my friend. In my mind, and the mind of my brothers, her overthrow is unjust." He walked to the window and gazed out, his body now relaxed with the certainty of what he must do. "A few rich men will not determine the future of Hawaii. I will no longer remain passive; it is time to act."

CHAPTER 51

—

"By the right flank, march," Robert Grant bellowed at a company of volunteers parading in cast-off Civil War uniforms. "No! Right flank, turn on your left foot, not your right foot."

"Major Grant, your sharpshooter company doesn't know right from left." Donald Cartwright laughed.

Fuming, Grant brought his militia soldiers to a halt and dismissed them for the day. The tired men rushed to their temporary barracks to store their rifles and left for their homes. With a disgruntled snort he said, "Captain Cartwright, I don't think your Citizens Guard is any better."

"Maybe not, but they're good enough to squash plantation strikers and put them in prison."

"I heard about that, two hundred Japanese who were complaining about abuse from their supervisors marched forty miles from Kahuku Plantation to Honolulu to protest to the government. Dumb fools, they should have known that they had signed a contract to work and couldn't strike," Grant said, then smirked. "I wouldn't be so proud of your achievement; they had no weapons and were too exhausted from the long march to fight."

Cartwright pursed his lips before answering, "Look here, I think my boys are better than those National Guard types who took on that Hawaiian in Kalalau and lost. You'll see, when the revolutionaries make their move my boys will do them in." Cartwright paused before continuing, "When do you think the rebels will swing into action?"

"My information is that this fellow William Seward left for California in October to buy weapons for royalists who want to return Liliuokalani to the throne. The man I talked to in the government of the Republic of Hawaii thinks Seward will be back around Christmas time. It's his thinking that the shooting will start after U.S. warships leave Pearl Harbor the first of January."

"So, the rebels must be thinking that they lost the monarchy in January of 1893 because U.S. sailors overwhelmed the pitiful Palace Guard of Liliuokalani, and without the help of the U.S. military in January of 1895, the Republic can't stop their revolution from being a success."

"You have it right, Captain Cartwright, but where there were only thirteen businessmen who took over the monarchy two years ago, we have fifteen hundred men under arms today. Besides, the rebels will be in for a big surprise, most people support the Republic. Our government is financially prudent, unlike the spendthrift monarchy, and we put money where it counts, into public works."

CHAPTER 52

———

Before the New Year, three men sailed for Oahu in John's double canoe. Manuel and Kaleo put their strength into the paddles and the trip was made without incident. When they landed at Diamond Head, they split up, with John walking into Honolulu intent on gaining information, and the others seeking contact with the rebel leaders of the Hawaiian revolution.

John followed Waikiki Road, pausing at the gate to Aunt Malia's house. The place was well-maintained, its white picket fence newly painted and the yard a lovely scene of grace and tropical flowers. John opened the gate and approached the front door. He knocked and was immediately greeted by Malia.

"Come in, you no good!" she declared, her face beaming with pleasure as she led John inside. "How come you no see Auntie long time?" she complained, pulling him to the kitchen table. "You sit right here, I get poi, *lomi* salmon, *kalua* pig, dry fish. Eat plenty, you too skinny."

John laughed at his aunt's fussing. How he missed this. To the Hawaiian woman, her family was always too skinny and being fat indicated happiness. Anyone who was lean was either sick or miserable. "Your house looks great," he told her, looking around. "It's so much bigger. But tell me, Auntie, what are all those gadgets on the wall?"

Malia's wrinkled brown face broke into laughter. "Mr. Kingsley sure good to me. He rebuilt the house, so I have three bedrooms, inside toilet, big parlor, nice kitchen. On the wall, I got electric lights, and over there," she added, pointing proudly, "a telephone. I call all over Honolulu!" She slipped another plate of food in front of her nephew. "Now, tell me about you, your family."

John had meant this visit to be light and merry, but Aunt Malia was the last of the elders and he thought of her as his mother. She still wore her dresses long, covering her body from neckline to toes. Today, it was a white dress decorated with a simple brown, leaf print. He noted how her hands appeared withered, yet they warmed him whenever she touched him. And when his aunt smiled, her face projected love, a beauty that emanated from within. John noted how this gentle appearance was heightened by the white hair peppered with strands of black.

Overcome by Aunt Malia's expression of acceptance, John could not restrain the flood of emotions. He unburdened it all: the deaths; the raid; the loss of land. Perhaps most painful is his sense of guilt for having failed his family.

Aunt Malia listened to the retelling of John Tana's sorrows. As he spoke, her hands reached out slowly, until they finally enveloped his. When he fell silent, she took a very deep breath and exhaled loudly. When she stood, she stumbled into John and he caught her. "I no walk as good as I used to," she said with a laugh. And then she kissed his forehead and ran her fingers across his face, smoothing the worry, relaxing his eyes and temples with her fingers. "My poor boy," she said, her voice almost singing. "You had much trouble, come stay with Auntie, I take care of you. Make you feel better, give you happiness."

Malia's tenderness soothed John, but it did little to lift his heart. "Nothing you can do for me will replace what is gone, Auntie. I'm afraid that the burden of my loss will remain with me forever."

"What's a matter you?" Malia retorted, giving him a feeble slap on his arm. "You think you the only one who suffered losses? Me, I bury my husband and three children. All I have is David, and he's in prison. You think Makanani family got plenty? They lose taro lease, now scattered all over the place, living on air."

"But Auntie—"

No 'but Auntie' me! If I quit when somebody die, or when I get hard time, where you think I be today? Six feet under, that's where!" Her brow furrowed, and she leaned closer to John. "You stop feeling sorry for yourself, stop it right now! Everybody has troubles. Go any house you want, you find plenty trouble. Now wash mud out of your head and get on with life!" She put both hands on her hips and glared at him, as if daring him to defy her.

The woman's words stung John. She was as tough and as strong as his grandfather and this reminded him why he had come to visit. He was desperate to learn from her wisdom, from her knowledge, and her lifetime of experience. If anyone could place him on the road to healing, it was Malia.

Hoping to quiet her scolding, he shifted to another subject. "You haven't mentioned Leinani. How is she?"

"Eh, Leinani doing real good. Kingsley worship her, she has two grownup kids. Even though she rich, she do lots of volunteer work, especially at the hospital. Never worry," she added with a laugh, jabbing him with a bony finger. "Your cousin no need help from you."

The comment stung, but John was unwilling to let that show. He forced himself to join in the laughter, while reminding himself that it was Malia's wisdom that had led him to make the right choice for Leinani. "Auntie," he finally said. "You do know that she's not my cousin. Grant is her father and her mother is not related to our family."

Malia lapsed into silence and then smiled, reaching out to stroke John's hair. John waited for her to respond, but she said nothing. After several moments, he told her it was time to leave.

Malia walked him outside, the two standing amid a pageantry of green foliage and startling flowers. "You always welcome," she said, kissing John's face. "You come back anytime. God be with you."

CHAPTER 53

———

John walked the streets of Honolulu and marveled at the changes. In the five years of his absence, the roadways had been paved and were bordered with sidewalks. There were horse-drawn wagons everywhere, along with carts, carriages, horses, and more people than John could have imagined. Trolley cars rumbled along iron tracks set into the roadway, the clanging of bells sending out warnings and clearing their path. Electric and telephone lines crisscrossed the roadways, providing modern services to those businesses whose buildings lined street after street. Honolulu was no longer the dusty, rustic town he once knew. Today, it was a bustling metropolis.

John enjoyed the crowds, even the elbowing, shoving, and intimidation used to clear paths through the throngs. Beneath the surface of this normal activity, however, he sensed a sinister undercurrent, a kind of foreboding. In addition to the bustle and the modernization, there were also armed men patrolling the streets.

He passed the government building that guarded the harbor and came across soldiers engaged in small arms drill. Artillery stood in neat rows, ready to defend, perhaps ready to attack, and it worried him. What if news of the rebellion had been brought to the attention of the government? If so, what was the chance that John and his cohorts could be stopped before they had time to execute this overthrow?

John needed to speak to Aaloa and headed to the waterfront. He recognized a stevedore from his militia days, and called out to him, asking if he'd seen Aaloa.

The man peered at John, as if uncertain of his identity.

"You must remember me," he said, recalling the man's name. "Kimo, I'm John Tana. Do you remember that we stopped the lynching of Chin Sing? We fought Shaw together."

Distrust and suspicion slipped from the man's face and he smiled. "Ayah, I remember you! You John Tana, one tough guy. You looking for Aaloa? You not know he's dead?"

The pronouncement nearly felled John. He clutched his stomach and tasted bile in his mouth. "What happened?" John asked.

"Heart attack."

In a flash, memories flew through John's mind: The battle in the street with the bone crusher; arm wrestling in a saloon; staring down sailors who were bent on lynching Chin Sing; the fight with the counterfeiters. *One more person was gone; one more person who has left me with nothing but memories.*

"Who's running the stevedores' union?" he asked. "And where are the others who served with us in the militia?"

Kimo looked around as if making certain he could speak safely. "The old militia is no more, and the government broke up the union. That means we can't strike. Listen," he added apologetically. "All the guys you knew are dead or they've left the waterfront."

Had John been alone, he might have sat down and wept. As it was, he walked away from the harbor and headed to the restaurant. Maybe Ah Sam could answer his questions. Were the Chinese being persecuted under the rule of this new government? And would they support a rebellion? He felt uneasy as he walked through this place he hardly recognized, a city not crumbling under the rule of a new government, but prosperous and booming.

John arrived at the restaurant and found his godson, Choi, standing at the door. Now a fat, jovial-looking man, he bubbled with delight when John appeared.

"Uncle, it's been a long time since you've been here," he said, hugging him. "Come inside. Did you know that my sister runs the place now? What can I get you to eat?"

John and Choi entered the restaurant, with Choi shooting question after question at his visitor.

"So much to tell you and to hear." John laughed. The two men sat at a table near the window. "What's happened since I left?"

Choi smiled and nodded. "Plenty, plenty, the family is well. Mama takes care of the grandchildren in the main house and Papa spends time in his den with Muk Fat, enjoying retirement. I have an import/export business just up the street. We do very well," he admitted, satisfaction on his face, "especially since we snuck in some family from China to help out." At that, Choi laughed.

Suddenly, the front door flew open and Choi's sister, Leinani, walked in. When she saw John, she let out a scream and rushed to embrace him. "We've missed you so much. You're a bad uncle, not coming to see us for so many years." "Forgive me for neglecting your family," John answered his voice half-tease, half-apology. "There has been so much I've needed to do." He looked at the young woman's face. "And you? Are you happy? Is business good?"

The young woman sat in the chair across from John and smiled, her hand grasping his forearm. "Everything's terrific, we do very well. Lots of good customers come to the restaurant, especially downtown business people. But what brings you to Honolulu, a holiday, business, visiting old friends?"

John knew better than to speak the truth to Leinani. To mention rebellion would be to put her at risk. "I have a question," he countered, hoping to change the subject. "Do the Chinese people support this new republic, or do they want their queen back?"

Choi studied John for a long beat before responding. "Uncle, business has never been better, so we like the new republic."

Leinani released her hold on John's arm. Any happiness that had illuminated her face moments before suddenly disappeared. She took her time before speaking, as if contemplating how she would respond. After a silence, she said, "I'm sorry that the queen lost her throne, but I think it's better now. The queen's brother spent too much money on unnecessary things, and so did she. Did you know that the monarchy was bankrupt? Change was needed to make business better." Having spoken, she shifted in her chair and then folded her hands in her lap. "Uncle, I hope you're not here to bring the monarchy back."

The bluntness of her statement surprised John. He did not want to lie to her, yet he knew that an honest answer might compromise the rebellion. "I'm here to find out whether the Chinese support the monarchy or the republic," he said, comfortable with this half-truth.

"Stay and eat with us," Choi invited, saving John from making any incriminating remarks.

Over a meal, John told them about the death of his wife and son, the loss of his land.

"Come live with us," Choi insisted. "We'll take care of you and you'll have nothing more to worry about."

John looked at Leinani, who was nodding eagerly, and he felt warmed by their love. "You're a smart business man. But your Hawaiian side is showing. Don't be like so many Hawaiians—give, give, give without expectation of reward. Trust me, too much giving does not pay off in the end."

The young man stopped eating and looked at his godfather, a deep hurt in his eyes. "How can you say that? You, who have given so much to our family? You saved us in Lahaina. You saved us when the bad seamen would have killed all of us. You paid to rebuild our restaurant. You've been a good friend to the Chinese people. It's not my Hawaiian side that's showing, but my love for you and what you've done."

John, Choi, and Leinani sat together in silence, all of them teary-eyed. John had so much bad news. He had so little to hold onto in his fight for freedom. "Uncle, please come live with us. We will take care of you." Leinani begged. Her hand reached to him, touched his arm. He felt the softness of her fingers on his skin. The warmth of her palm as it covered his hand. He knew there was love for him with this family that transcended ties of blood.

He needed to leave. "I must go," John said. "Thank you for the food and your kindness. Your family will always be in my heart."

As he left, with Choi and Leinani standing at the door and waving their farewell, he heard her call out, "Come back soon, Uncle John. Our home is always yours."

"E komo mai," John answered her, the tone of his voice bitter. "I wish I could say those words, 'my home is yours.' But I have no home and no country."

Leinani Sam gasped, tears welled in her eyes, overflowed down her cheeks. "No, Uncle, don't say that. You have a home here with us." She studied John for a moment then said, "To go with hate in your heart is to die. Stay and learn to love again."

John shook his head, touched by their kindness. They meant well. But he did not want to burden them with his troubles, nor end his days in a dark room smoking opium like Muk Fat and Ah Sam. He waved. The love of the Chinese family reached out to him, tugged at his heart. *I feel that I am leaving the warmth of the sun and descending into a hell of turmoil and danger.* He hesitated for a moment wondering if it was too late to turn away from rebellion. Then he made up his mind, waved once more and said, "Thank you for your aloha."

Then set himself on a path toward Waikiki and an uncertain future.

CHAPTER 54

———

Grant sipped his absinthe as he passed out cigars to his two companions, Bruce Jones and Donald Cartwright. "That was a marvelous claret you served at dinner," Jones said.

"I provide only the very best for my friends and their wives. Here, I'll fire up your cigars." Grant lit a match and applied it to the stogies of the two men. He borrowed one of the newly lit cigars and applied it to his own. Soon the opulent den of red furniture, carpet, and burnished brown, koa wood walls filled with aromatic smoke.

"You have a magnificent portrait of yourself in your major's uniform hanging over the mantelpiece," Cartwright observed.

"Yes, I had it painted after I returned from Kalalau following our capture of more than a hundred rebellious lepers. I think I told you gentlemen the story."

"Not that I recall," Jones said. "I understood that a company of militia was sent to that valley to seize a Hawaiian who killed a sheriff. Was he among those that you took into custody?"

Grant paused for a long moment. He stroked his hair and cleared his throat. "If you must know the truth, we did not. My men tried in every way to capture him, but he eluded us. We ended our attempts by firing numerous artillery shells into the hills and setting fire to every building. The rebel certainly died from the rain of death we poured into the valley."

"And the provisional government promoted you to a full major instead of a brevet one." Cartwright added.

"Yes, I have the power to call up militia, to suppress insurgents, and be paid for my services."

"Do you need the money?" Jones asked.

"Don't we all need cash? Ever since that dastardly McKinley Tariff Act my profits from sugar sales have been almost nil. I scrape by, being prudent, and squeezing all the labor I can from my workers. Even my son-in-law Kingsley is hurting. There are no startup sugar mills for him to finance. We need annexation to the United States to reopen a tax-free market place."

"That may be a mixed blessing," Jones commented. "Since the American Civil War, that country's constitution prohibits slave labor. Our contract laborers would be set free from their agreements."

"We will find a way to keep them suppressed!" Grant retorted with a hearty laugh.

A rapping at the den door interrupted the conversation. Grant, his cigar on the left edge of his mouth, blew a lungful of smoke into the room. He strode to answer the knocking and opened the door. He faced a nervous manservant. "I regret bothering you sir, but one of your soldiers is at the main door. He claims he has urgent news for you."

Grant nodded, and within moments Sven Larsen appeared in the hallway. In an excited voice he blurted out, "Major, the rebels are bringing in arms. A riot is in the making near Honolulu Harbor at Kakaako."

Irritated by the interruption, Grant received his henchman's news coldly. "Larsen, why are you bursting into my home at this late hour? There have been rumors of royalist troublemaking for weeks, but nothing has come of them."

"Perhaps we should hear out your sergeant," Bruce Jones said. "My information is that a schooner is due from San Francisco with arms. Possibly it is offshore as we speak."

"It is," Larsen answered. "I am at the barracks with some of the boys. This Hawaiian guy came and told us that a ship is off Waikiki, near the Sans Souci, with guns and explosives."

"The Sans Souci! Isn't it a small hotel where Robert Louis Stevenson used to live?" Grant asked.

"Yes. And the place where the Princess Kaiulani would visit Stevenson," Jones answered with a smile on his face.

"Kaiulani," Grant repeated. "She's the one that some of the Committee wanted to put on the throne to replace Liliuokalani. And that Stevenson, he is not a friend. He was a crony of that scalawag Kalakaua and a supporter of the monarchy. Yes, Sans Souci is a logical hive for royalists and seditionists to meet."

"Larsen, what else did you learn from this informer?" Jones asked.

"He says to me that most of the guns will be stored in a small warehouse at the base of Diamond Head, near Kahala. Some of the guns will be taken to Liliuokalani's home and buried there. There is a safe house in Waikiki where the leaders will meet tonight and plan their attacks."

"Then we have no time to lose," Grant said. "We will end our meeting now. Jones, gather up as many of your Honolulu Rifles as you can. Suppress the rioters at Kakaako. I think it's a diversion to keep our eyes off Waikiki. Cartwright, see Jones' wife home. Larsen, return to the barracks. Muster as many of our All Hawaii Militia as may be available. I will meet you there at ten o'clock. Be ready to march on Waikiki."

"Yes, sir. Rifles only?"

"Bring along the Krupp field howitzer that was used at Kalalau."

CHAPTER 55

Waves rocked the longboat, spread around it, and then washed onto shore. Several men oared onto the sand beach at the foot of the Sans Souci Hotel. Mangrove trees thrust their long roots into the brackish water. Coupled with the darkness of the night, the revolutionaries were well hidden.

Whispering, glancing furtively, the six rebels unloaded the armament purchased in San Francisco. Lifting the weapons, they trudged through the sand and over a low embankment. When they reached the narrow roadway, they stopped. Robert Wilson pointed to the boxes and oilskin-covered Springfield rifles. "You four, John, Manuel, Peter, Pekelu, take the bombs and a few rifles to Washington Place. You'll meet some of our men there and they'll tell you what to do."

"What do we do after we deliver this stuff?" Pekelu asked.

"I'm taking the rest of these weapons to Diamond Head," Wilson said. "Meet me in two hours in Waikiki, at the safe house. And watch out for militia patrols. I'm pretty sure the word is out that something's happening, because the police pulled off a raid a couple of nights ago and took some Hawaiians into custody."

John hoisted a box of bombs onto his shoulder. "I've seen lots of militia wandering around these last few days. All of them knew about the newspaper articles regarding a rebellion and weapons being smuggled into the islands. Maybe we should call this off."

Wilson's eyes flared, his body stiffened. "You're not a coward, are you, Tana? Because there's no place for cowards here!"

"I'm just speaking the obvious. Someone's ratted on us and the government knows what we intend to do."

Wilson checked the contents of a box about to be carried off. "I reckon you could be right about us having a snitch or two, but with the weapons here and planning underway, it's too late to pull back. So, deliver that stuff and hope for the best." The four men carried their load toward the home of Queen Liliuokalani, darkness concealing them from casual view. They moved warily, shifting their heavy burdens from shoulder to shoulder, stopping often to listen, peer into the night, searching for hidden enemies. After what seemed to John an eternity of marching, they arrived at the queen's home. Two Hawaiians, Kaulana and Eleu, met them in the garden and told them to bury the weapons. "And keep the noise down," Kaulana said. "The queen can't know we're hiding this stuff in her flower beds."

John and Kaulana worked together to bury a large carton. "What are the bombs for?" John whispered.

"The plan is to blow up the Church across the street. It will be a diversion. We want the militia to come here. If they try to capture the queen, we can defend her. Wilson and the others will swoop down and take control of the government buildings, then we'll persuade Liliuokalani to issue a proclamation for all loyal subjects to join the revolt. We'll know more once we get back to the safe house."

"Are you saying," John asked, feeling a wave of revulsion, "that you haven't asked the queen if she'll go along with this revolution?"

Kaulana stopped shoveling, his eyes glinting in the dark. "Look, Tana, we didn't want to compromise her. What if the rebellion didn't come off, or we tried, and it failed? If she was part of the conspiracy, she'd hang."

Incredulity crept across John's face. "But isn't this the same plan that failed in the rebellion of '89?"

The man raised his shovel and stabbed it into the earth. "What do you mean by that?"

John was not to be intimidated, not after having come this far. "What I mean is that, in 1889, a hundred revolutionaries went to the palace. They wanted to get rid of the Bayonet Constitution and substitute a new constitution, one that would give Kalakaua back his power. But Kalakaua didn't want anything to do with the rebellion, and he hid out. I helped him. Many rebels were captured, and many people were injured, some killed. Did you not know that?" He stared at the man, as if challenging him to argue.

"It'll be different this time," Kaulana grumbled. "Just finish filling that hole and don't make any more trouble. This time," he added, his voice almost taunting, "the rebellion will succeed."

After the weapons were buried, Kaulana ordered the men to scatter and meet up at the safe house. "Don't forget the curfew," he reminded them. "If you're stopped and arrested, don't rat on your friends."

John fled the garden and, holding close to walls and shrubs, moved covertly toward the safe house. At Waikiki Road, he cast his eyes about and found that, except for an occasional light filtering from houses that bordered the roadway, all was clear. With each cautious step his regret for having joined this rebellion increased. Unless the entire republic and all its soldiers were asleep, there was not a flicker of hope for success.

A booming voice broke into his thoughts. "Who goes there?"

John stood his ground, his Civil War kepi shadowing his features, the bridge over the Apua Stream only a few feet away. "A friend," he whispered.

"Come forward and show yourself," the bridge guard said.

With slow steps, John approached the sentinel, noting the light from a distant lamp glinting from the steel of the man's bayonet. He saw that his easy stroll had caused the guard to lower his rifle as he peered in the darkness studying John.

Within a few feet of the soldier, the man said, "Halt right there!"

John ignored him, continuing to move forward. Alarmed, the guard swept up his weapon just as John made his move. Leaping to the side of the rising bayonet John leveled a sharp punch into the man's stomach.

"Mother," the guard gasped dropping to the ground, his rifle still clasped in his hands. He struggled to breathe, trying to force air back into his lungs.

"Hey, Abe," a voice yelled. John saw figures materializing out of the darkness. He did not have time to wrest the gun from the winded soldier. He bent low and raced for the stream.

"Alarm, alarm," voices punctured the night. A rifle fired, a bullet whining over John's head. He reached the edge of the stream and slid into it, shivering as the coolness of the water covered his body.

Men pounded up to the bank yelling curses, firing wildly. As he swam underwater, John could hear the bark of rifles that sent bullets plunging into the water. He broke the surface and checked the far bank for enemies. He heard boots stomping across the bridge, a voice yelling, "Stop shooting. Cover both banks, we will get that rebel."

John knew the Apua Stream and swam for a large clump of reeds growing along its far side. Taking a deep breath, he dove, crab-crawling his way into the reeds. His progress was slowed by the thick spiky growth, but he knew that they would also slow the pursuit. To his left a voice cursed, there was a splash, a man slid off the bank into the stream as his rifle discharged, the sound of the explosion muffled by the water.

Other men cursed nearby, and John could hear thrusting sounds. He guessed that they were probing the reeds with bayonets, afraid to fire for fear of hitting one of their own. He moved into the upright stalks, his feet sticking in the gooey mud. With effort he pulled deeper into the dense growth, his feet searching for hard ground.

Ankle deep in mud, he heard a swishing sound and saw a bayonet smashing across the reeds. The tough green stalks resisted the blade, bending then swinging back as the slender dagger scythed into them.

John's feet touched hard stone, and he knew he was near the earth bank. The stalks were less dense, yet still full enough to hide his enemy. He huddled low in the water as a long bayonet thrust above his head. For a moment he thought he had been discovered, but soon realized that the owner of the weapon was holding the butt of his rifle and thrusting it into the reeds.

Like a seamstress sticking pins into a green cushion, the bayonet kept poking. John realized that the man stood at the water's edge, blocking his exit onto the bank. He watched, timing the thrusts, the soldier uttering low grunts as he probed. The bayonet slid into the plants, the barrel of the rifle sliding by John's head. He saw a man's hands clasping the butt of the gun.

Grasping the iron tube of the rifle, he yanked. The soldier gave a low yelp, stumbling into the growth, and onto John's body. John whipped his elbow into the man's face. He heard the crunch of broken bones. Blood spurted over his eyes. The man howled, John grasped him by his shirt collar forcing the soldier into the reeds. He thrashed in the stalks, blubbering unintelligible words. A voice yelled, "Miguel, you okay?" John shoved the man into the brush and clambered up onto the bank. In the dim starlight he saw the outlines of men bearing down on him. His heart sank as he realized he might not escape capture.

CHAPTER 56

———

"Major Grant, we caught a couple of rebels and they been telling us where their safe house is and where their armament is stored near Diamond Head. One of our pickets got waylaid by the Apua Stream, and the men are searching for the rebel who did it."

"Good report, sergeant. You can lead the squad to this safe house. Corporal Gaines, go to the rear and tell the artillerymen to hurry up and bring the howitzer forward. Troopers, move out, follow Sergeant Larsen."

Grant strolled after his platoon as they hurried across the Apua Bridge, their boots thumping in rhythmic cadence. He smiled, his 'Sharpshooters' had learned the art of soldiering. He thought that they were now good enough to put down this rebellion without any help from the other militia. Tonight, his unit coupled with his leadership, would prove its worth to the new Republic of Hawaii.

Gunfire interrupted his reverie. Angry voices screamed in the darkness. Grant heard the howl of a man and rushed across the bridge, eager to capture the scoundrel that he believed his men had shot.

The injured soldier thrashed among the reeds. Militia in cast-off Civil War kepis and uniforms rushed toward the sound, firing their rifles into the brush. John heard the man in the water howl. Bullets struck the ground, smashed the reeds, plunked into the water. He smiled as he slithered along the bank; his enemies were hurting themselves in their chaotic search to find him.

He moved along, using his elbows to dig into the loose soil. The man in the water screamed for his friends to stop shooting, a soldier passed a few yards from John rushing to the reeds. Two others hovered at the edge of the brush, yelling.

Someone called, "Don't shoot. Stop firing." Soldiers gathered by the rushes leaving the roadway into Waikiki and the way to the safe house unguarded. John rose to a crouch and padded away from the stream. He glanced behind him and saw more figures materializing in the dark. "What's going on?" a commanding voice asked.

"Major, one of the boys got hurt. We're fetching him from the water right now."

"Detail some men to get torches. Find that rebel before he does more damage. First Squad, follow me, let's get to the rebellion's safe house before they escape."

The major's voice was familiar, but John could not conjure a face to match it. He gave up searching his memory and focused his senses on escape. He bent low, scuttling alongside the Waikiki Road. He thanked the many days that he had lived and worked in Waikiki as he easily found his way in the dark.

"Who goes there?" a voice challenged. John froze, holding his breath, squatting to the ground. He saw figures approaching. "It's only us boys, Abraham," a man's voice said. "You sure are some jumpy picket, seeing ghosts everywhere."

"Yeah, well, you'd be scared too with all the gunfire, and screaming that be going on."

Footsteps came within a few feet of where John lay. "What's up, Garcia?" someone asked.

"We're going to barbeque them rebels, Abraham. We know their plans, and the Major says to catch 'em red handed before we kill 'em."

"You got it wrong. Catch 'em with the goods, that's what we got to do, then turn the dumb bastards over for court martial. There'll be a lot of hangin's in Honolulu soon. I sure will enjoy seein' that fat brown queen swingin' on a rope." A third voice yelled, "Hey, guys, wait up for us, you're gettin' too far ahead."

A dozen men passed John, all of them rushing toward Waikiki beach. He waited until the tramping faded and then followed the retreating footsteps. *I must get to the safe house before they do, he thought. Warn everybody. But how do I do it without getting caught?*

Diamond Head loomed above him, starkly outlined in the faded light of the stars. Ahead of him came the sound of marching feet, then a low command, "Halt." John went to the ground, crawling along the shoulder of the road. Anxiety made him move faster, but a cautionary voice buzzed in his head. "Always keep your opponent in sight," his grandfather had warned. John slowed his pace, crouching in the shadows, staring into the darkness. Only a few yards ahead, he spotted figures moving near the safe house and scurried into a ditch beside the road.

He heard a muffled command, "Everyone in skirmish order." His heart raced. He pressed his body into the dirt. He heard shuffling steps of men spreading out. Gunshots flashed, a scream, lights in the safe house went out. Everything around John was sinister, oppressive.

Burrowing deeper into the ditch, John hoped that it concealed him from his enemies. He heard the shallow breathing of soldiers moving closer. He sensed that a man was just a step away from his hiding place, one more move and –

More gunfire erupted. John heard a rifle shot above him. A metal bolt ratcheted, and a shell casing fell by his face.

"Stop firing!"

Bullets whipped through the trees. John's head throbbed. In the dim light he caught a glimpse of a face he had seen before. It was Robert Grant. For a brief moment a desperate urge to leap up and strike the man down overwhelmed him. Yet, he realized he would fail if he attacked into the thick of the enemy soldiers. Right now, his responsibility was to help his friends in the safe house. His vendetta against Grant could wait for another time.

The soldier near the ditch moved away. John raised his head and peered over its edge. He saw dim forms several yards ahead of him. He dug his elbows into the dirt and pulled his body over the opposite side of the trench. He rose to a crouch and scurried crab-like into the cover of a stand of coconut trees. His feet crunched on fallen branches and he tripped, sprawling to the ground.

A staccato of rifle fire sprayed the trees. The bullets shattered splinters of wood all around him. John judged the men were firing blindly, motivated by fear, bolstering their courage by shooting their weapons. *They were just like the soldiers who attempted to kill Koolau. He smiled remembering that day two years ago when the Republic's men destroyed Kalalau valley frightened to death by one Hawaiian man. Then he scowled. Koolau's victory would be the only win that Hawaiians would ever have against the sugar people. This rebellion was finished before it even began.*

John dashed to another coconut tree, the sounds of his movement raising a fusillade of fire, some bullets plowing into the stout trunk serving as his shield. He shrieked, feigning being hit, then scurried to the next tree.

A soldier yelled, "We got that rebel."

John moved from tree to tree, searching the night for the safe house, guided to it by the sporadic firing of the soldiers. Over the noise of battle, he heard a chilling command, "Corporal, order up the artillery. We'll blast these rebels to hell."

He shuddered as he heard the order.

Artillery, what chance do men with rifles have against cannon? Should I find a way to escape this trap? I pledged to others I would revolt. But knowing that the revolution is doomed wouldn't it be wise to abandon my compatriots and save myself?

CHAPTER 57

—

Major Grant crouched near the rebel's safe house irritated by the disorganization of his men. "Sharpshooters," he scoffed. "They fall apart, Larsen, the moment a rebel challenges them. We started with a full company, thirty men, but once that scallywag attacked they scattered, running amok, shooting everywhere and anything. It's a wonder we weren't hit. How many men left of my command?"

"I been able to round up ten, counting you and me."

"And the artillery?"

"I send soldier back to bring up the gun, but nothing so far, Sir."

Grant peered into the darkness as his eyes adjusted to the scant starlight and a crescent moon hidden by clouds. He could make out the outlines of a house ahead. It stood silent and unlighted in the night. A sporadic pop, pop of rifle fire punctured the dark behind him, but there was no action in front of him.

"This is the safe house we were informed about?" Grant asked.

"Yes, sir," Larsen answered. "Turncoat rebel say it's at end of this road and there it is."

"It's very quiet inside. No lights. Maybe whoever occupied it is gone."

"Only way to find out is to get into it, attack, break door down."

Grant considered his options. They needed to get into the building to find out. But what lay ahead might be a trap. He could spread his men out in a firing line and blaze away at the house and the shrubs around it. Charge forward with all hands and break in, *a coup de main*. But maybe what would be best would be to send a small patrol to test if there might be resistance ahead.

"Larsen, send two men ahead. They are to approach the house with care and when near it, order surrender. If no response they are to break in. The rest of us will form a fire line to provide cover fire if needed."

"Yes, sir!" Larsen picked two men and they scurried toward the house. "Let there be no resistance," Grant muttered. "I don't want losses."

Near the silent building one of the men in the patrol yelled, "We are the soldiers of the Republic of Hawaii. Anyone inside is to—"

A fusillade of bullets erupted from the house. Grant heard a shriek. "Give them cover fire," he ordered. A half dozen of his riflemen blasted away at the wooden building. Within a minute the shooting from the house stopped.

"Hold fire, Larsen, take two men and work your way around the left side of the house. You two men come with me around the right side. The rest of you stop shooting. The password is 'sugar', that means friend. Anyone who is silent, uses the wrong word, or shoots at you is an enemy. Kill him. Private Stewart, Corporal Jonas, fix bayonets, cover my left side as we sweep around the house."

Crouching, Grant and his detail stumbled toward the safe house. Someone moaned in front. Feeble starlight barely outlined the waving palms of the coconut forest and the roof line of the rebel refuge.

"I'll end this rebellion tonight. Then the Republic will owe me!" Grant muttered as he advanced. "Maybe give me command of the army. What power I will have."

Grant's gloating was interrupted by the whispers of one of his soldiers.

"Charlie is there someone behind the house?"

"Don't know," Jonas said.

"Move slow. Keep alert. You two swing out further to the right where those shrubs are. You'll have a full view of the rear of the house from there. Keep your rifles ready." Grant watched his soldiers creeping toward the brush.

CHAPTER 58

———

Sheltered by a coconut tree, John could see the silhouette of the safe house. Except for distant gunfire, the area near him and the building lay silent. Had everyone left for Diamond Head? He had to get into the house to find out.

To John's left he heard a voice. He could not decipher the words, but it had an authoritative sound and he suspected it to be the enemy. He went low and began to crawl forward, careful to keep the noise he made to a minimum.

Suddenly rifle fire erupted from the house followed by a fusillade of shots into the building. Some bullets whizzed by him, smashing into the wood of the coconut forest. He saw shrubs ahead and crawled into their shelter.

As suddenly as it had started, the shooting ended. John heard shallow breathing of men approaching. Men edged toward his hiding place. He searched the ground groping for a weapon. His fingers curled around large stones. "Better than nothing," he thought as he rose to a squat, his body shielded by the low growth, and waited as his enemies approached.

The back door of the safe house flew open. A head appeared. In an instant, two riflemen rose leveling their rifles. John hurled a rock at a fence bordering the house. Swiveling to the sound, the soldiers fired.

John flung himself into the nearest man. He swung his rock-filled fist into the throat. Stunned, the militia man sliced his bayonet downward. John hammered his fist into the soldier's jaw. The man fell, his weapon thudded to the earth. John dove to the ground. A bullet whizzed by in the darkness. He did an acrobatic flip and stabbed his feet into the groin of the second soldier. With a sharp cry, the man released his rifle and fell.

Bullets thudded into the house, whined over John's head. He heard Grant yell, "Stewart, Jonas, what's going on?"

John lay prone between the bodies of the two soldiers. One man twitched, the other groaned. He saw Grant as his face and body were lit by faint light coming through the rear door of the safe house. His pistol hand shook. He jerked the trigger. The weapon clicked. In one smooth motion, John rose from the ground, leaping into the major. The sugar baron turned to run.

John tackled the fleeing man. As he fell, Grant whipped his pistol into John's shoulder, but he felt no pain from the blow, his anger boiling into savagery. He grabbed Grant's pistol hand as the man tried to work the trigger. The gun clicked again. John applied a twisting lua move. He heard a cracking bone, and the pistol dropped. Grant flailed with his left hand, and John smashed an open palm across his face.

Grant howled, his arms falling to his sides. John pushed him down, straddled him. He studied the face of the man who had dogged and destroyed all his dreams for a happy life. His fingers fastened about the throat of the writhing plantation owner. He would end the life of his nemesis tonight.

His fingers tightened. Grant pleaded, "Don't kill me."

"I'm going to kill you," John spat, his anger mounting as the dead faces of his wife and son swam in front of him. *The thirst for revenge increased as he thought of the land that had been lost to this man.*

Grant's hazel eyes bulged. John shivered. *Leinani was looking at him, her pupils boring into his, begging him. Words rushed through his head. "Nothing good happens from war. There is only death and misery. You hate, you die."*

Behind him, the bolt of a rifle ratcheted. John swung from the inert body of Robert Grant. He saw one of the soldiers fumbling with his gun. John leaped, driving his shoulder into the chest of the rifleman. They fell in a heap. John smashed an elbow into the soldier's jaw and drove his closed fingers into his stomach. The militia man moaned, then ceased fighting, releasing his grip on his rifle.

Grant struggled to his feet. He stumbled along the side of the safe house. "Rebels," he screamed.

John grasped the soldier's rifle. "Password!" a frightened voice yelled.

"Rebels! Help!" Grant screamed, hysteria in his voice. John fired twice into the darkness.

Answering rifle fire boomed in the night.

There was a cry of pain. A moan of, "Oh, oh." Then more shots. John heard a voice yell, "Retreat to Diamond Head!"

He shouldered the rifle. There were more shots. A scream came from the safe house. John crouched and followed several figures scuttling for the weapons cache at the base of Mount Leahi.

Someone yelled, "Unlimber the cannon. Prepare to fire."

CHAPTER 59

———

Artillery shells crashed against Diamond Head, stones and hot metal erupting from the explosion rained onto the mangroves and shrubs. John met up with other rebels who were huddled near the shed that stored their weapons. Terrified, they buried their heads in their arms as another round whistled though the air. Many of the men searched the sky, hoping to track each missile and determine where it would land, but it was impossible.

A shell struck the arms cache and the earth chugged upward, followed by the powerful blasts of bombs and ammunition. The violence threw hot metal, slivers of stone, and body parts everywhere. Something metallic struck John, knocking him to the ground and driving the breath from his body. A rock glanced off his head, and his face was covered in blood. He shook away his dizziness and wiped his face with his sleeve. Then he looked down and realized blood was pumping out of a wound in his chest.

A fear-filled voice yelled instructions and a ragged group of rebels ran along the base of Diamond Head, dodging artillery fire at every turn. John staggered after them, stumbling often on the rocks while willing his legs to move. When he finally realized that he could not make it to the safety of the hills, he turned toward Aunt Malia's home.

With every movement, searing pain burned through his chest and down his legs. He hobbled to the stream and paused, feeling for the wound. What he found was sharp metal shrapnel digging into his flesh. He tried to remove it, but it was too deep, and his fingers slipped, each effort only intensifying the pain. Sweat soaked his body as he focused on the bridge. *He wanted to sleep, end this agony, but he also wanted to live. "Focus, focus," he warned himself.* There were two soldiers lounging on the bridge and John considered surrender, even if it meant his death.

He knelt by the water and concentrated on defeating the pain. He would not give up like a beaten dog. Gritting his teeth, John slid into the stream and worked his way under the bridge. Gunfire erupted from the hills and the guards overhead shifted to the far side, where they could see the rifle flashes.

John floated for some moments, water lapping over his body and easing the pain in his chest. He heard a match striking and then heavy boots. Two soldiers with glowing cigarettes between their lips came to the edge of the trestle and looked down. John heard them boasting about their conquests, about sending the rebels packing into the hills. One of them described how a captured rebel had revealed the whereabouts of the arms cache at the queen's house, as well as the location of guns at Diamond Head. "He even told us where the conspiracy was being planned in Waikiki."

The water next to John's face sizzled as two cigarettes were tossed in. The soldiers continued to the far side of the bridge, allowing John time to ease from the shadow of the trestle. As gunfire and occasional bombs went off in the hills, he dove beneath the surface and emerged at a weeping willow tree. Moving under the protection of its drooping leaves, he inched himself onto the bank and made it to the road.

The minute he reached the gate of Malia's cottage, he fell to his knees. Bleeding heavily, he crawled past the fence, up the path, and onto the stairs. He collapsed against the door. John rapped it feebly.

"Who dat? What you want?" Malia said.

John scratched the wood until she opened the door. He fell onto the parlor floor and could not speak. As he lapsed into unconsciousness, he heard his Aunt's voice saying, "Come quick, John is hurt bad."

Warm water washed his body, a ghostly figure floated over him. Tears dripped onto his bare skin. John grappled with the mists shrouding his thoughts; somehow, he knew this apparition above him. He reached out to it and a trembling voice whispered, "Sleep, darling. Sleep, sweetheart." A wet cloth covered his face, its strong aroma filling his lungs. He touched a soft cheek. "Sleep baby, sleep." Moist lips kissed his forehead as his rising passions slipped away into darkness.

Sunlight pierced the bedroom, flooding its light onto the bed where John lay. His hand fumbled over his face as he tried to shut out the brightness. Muttering for water, he forced himself awake. At his bedside was a pitcher. He grasped it in both hands and lifted it to his mouth, slaking his thirst. Pain jolted his side as he drank. He sensed a stirring and, as his eyes came into focus, he saw the face that had for so long existed only in his dreams. Now, miraculously, she lay on his bed. A powerful yearning seized him, overcoming his dizziness and the aching of his body. With an effort, he reached to Leinani, caressing her hair. Annoyed by the combs that held it into a bun, he pulled them out and ebony cascaded over her back, around her waist. Sunlight shimmered against his hand and his body tingled. Particles of emotion coursed through him as long-denied feelings threatened to overcome reason and injury.

Fighting his pain, John moved to the edge of the bed and Leinani snuggled into him. He raised her face, saw that she was startled, eyes opened wide. He searched for her lips, tasting the salt of her tears as he probed her mouth with his tongue. She did not resist, instead responding eagerly, passionately. John fumbled with the fastenings of her dress, his passion seeking a fulfillment that had been denied for too many years. All pain and suffering were pushed aside. But it was Leinani who, moments before, had surrendered so willingly, and now pressed her palms against John's shoulders and separated them. He tried to reach for her, but the pain was too great, and he fell back onto the bed. He stared at this woman long loved, now huddled on the floor, hands over her eyes to stem the weeping. "No, John, stop. She moaned. "I won't do this."

"Why won't you? I've wanted you for so long. Why didn't you wait for me? Why did you choose a haole for a husband? Because he was rich, and I was a poor brown Hawaiian?"

Leinani looked at him, her eyes flashing angrily. "How can you be so cruel?" she snapped. "Do you think I care about your color or your lack of money? It is what you did that confused me. It made me doubt your love for me."

"Why did you doubt? I have always loved you. I love you now more than life itself." The pain from his stitched wound shot through him, taking his breath away. He gasped and fell back onto his pillow.

Leinani rose, her face wracked with emotion. Tears streamed down her cheeks. "If you loved me, why did you make love to Maria? My father said you raped her. I was told that there was a warrant for your arrest! I wrote you seeking the truth. You did not answer me. I did not know what to believe or to do. My father, step-mother, they said you were an evil man and that I should marry Kingsley. He said he loved me, offered marriage. I did not love him. But Malia told me what my mother would have wanted me to do."

She is so beautiful in her fury, John thought, as he watched her body trembling by his side. Her tears dampened his sheets. Her fists clenched as if to pound into him the horrible mistake that he had made. "You must know now that I never raped Maria. I admit that I made love to her. It was not the right thing to do. I did not love her. I have always loved you."

Leilani's body stiffened. She stopped her tears and said, "Before she left for France, Maria told me that you loved her! She gloated over your love making! You betrayed me!"

"What are you saying?" John whispered, unable to lift his head from the bed.

Leinani studied his face, as if trying to decide how far to take this. "I would not have married Kingsley if you had come to me and explained." Her voice faded into sobs, her body shook. She reached her hand to John. He took it, squeezed, and pulled Leinani to him. She did not resist as she bent over him.

Aunt Malia entered the room, a tray of food in her hands. "Eh, what you guys doing?" she demanded. "Good thing you not fooling around. Plenty angry if you bad." And then she laughed at her joke and placed the tray on the bed. "Something for John to eat."

Malia began to feed him and Leinani spoke about her family, about the life she shared with Kingsley, how their children had been educated at Punahou and were now at college on the mainland. She mentioned that her husband was away on Maui on sugar business. When it was John's turn, he told Leinani about Mahealani and JJ, and sat quietly while she cried. She was cheered when John described each of his grandchildren. Somewhere in that conversation, John looked at his hands, rough and calloused by hard work and he sighed. "Reverend Zachariah was a great teacher, but my education was limited. I wish my grandchildren could have as good an education as yours."

Leinani soothed John with the coolness of her hands. She stroked his hair, felt the throbbing pulse at his temples, and then drew his face toward her. "I promise you that the children of your body are my adopted children. They will have the finest education money can buy. You will never have to worry for the future of our family."

John's eyes blinked away tears. He took Leinani's hands in his, kissing them. Losing the battle for control, emotion overcame him, and tears streamed from his eyes. "That is the finest gift anyone has ever offered me," he said, his voice wavering. He looked up and saw that Malia was weeping as well. The emotions drained him, and he fell back onto the bed, his eyes closed, and his body succumbed to fatigue.

Leinani leaned into him, kissing his forehead. "I must go home, my darling, but I will be back in the morning."

CHAPTER 60

———

"Get up, lazy one, the sun is shining. Let me look at your wound," Leinani demanded as she pulled the bed sheet away from John's body. "It looks good. Stitches aren't angry. Now get out of bed, shave, bathe, and put on these new clothes. Breakfast is in twenty minutes."

By the time John was dressed, Leinani called him to the table. He moved slowly into the front room, smoothing his unruly hair with his palms. She picked up a plate of eggs, rice, and bacon from the kitchen counter and set it before him. "Drink some coffee," she said, pouring steaming black liquid into a cup.

Aunt Malia handed John some newspapers. "You can read them," Leinani said, "or I can tell you what's going on." Without a pause, she launched into a description of current events. "Martial law has been declared," she said lightly, handing him the cup of coffee. "More than a hundred arrests have been made and more are promised. Wilson is at large in the hills, and Liliuokalani's favorite supporter is up there with the other rebels. Let's see," she said, pausing for a moment. "Oh yes, the police found a bunch of Springfield rifles and bombs buried in the queen's garden and they seized her diary, where they found plans for a new government. She might be arrested and will probably be forced to abdicate the throne."

John listened, his anger growing. "Damn it, we really did have a traitor in our midst. He must have spilled everything. She knew nothing about the weapons in her garden."

Malia sat quietly, but Leinani was shaken by his admission. "When I worked on your wound, removing the metal from your side, I denied to myself that you were part of the rebellion. My father is in the hospital, seriously wounded. He was shot by his own men. In his delirium he talked of being attacked by a crazed Hawaiian." Leinani paused, looking at John, her eyes widening. "Was it you?"

John sighed and said, his voice faltering, "I admit that it was. I was in a rage, motivated by the losses I have suffered, my dead family, my lost land, all because of him. Yet when I saw his eyes, your eyes staring at me, I could not kill him. Forgive me."

Leinani drew breath in several times. She visibly fought with her emotions. Malia came to her side, stroked her hair, a great sadness in her eyes. John was puzzled, but remained silent, waiting. She finally spoke, "My father used me to save himself from bankruptcy. He suspected that I loved you. He claimed you raped Maria to drive me into marriage with Kingsley."

John rose from his seat and reached for the woman that he wanted so much. "And your father sent a man to kill me, so I would not meet you here, explain Maria to you, and tell you I have always loved you."

Malia shook her head and said, "All my fault. I tell John to let you marry Kingsley. Rich man is best than a poor Hawaiian. I promise Lei's mama; her child marry man of great power. But now when I see you two, when I see how much you love each other, maybe I wrong."

Leinani stood. They moved together. She placed a hand on his shoulder. Her hazel eyes brimmed with tears, her breath flowed sweet, mixing with his. Her lips parted, "It is not your fault that my father is near death. He was ruthless to you. He preyed on my emotions to get what he wanted, debt forgiveness from Kingsley. His twisting of the truth forced me into a marriage that was not what I would have chosen."

"I know you loved me once. Do you still love me?" John asked eagerly, as he felt a mounting tension rising within him, a desire to take her no matter the consequences.

Leilani glanced at Malia who rocked more rapidly in her chair, then said, "My husband loves me. He gives me everything I could want. I would be fool to choose any other. Yet ever since I felt your body pressed against mine in Shaw's cabin, the imprint of our melding has never left me. Despite your betrayal I can no longer deny the overwhelming love that I have for you."

John moved to take her, but her hand remained firm against his shoulder. The warmth that had filled the room only a moment ago was gone. "You must promise to give up this rebellion. I cannot bear to lose you again."

"The rebellion was a failure. What is there to worry about?"

"Don't you see, John, that everybody involved will be arrested? You'll be charged with treason, attempted murder, and tried by a military court. The penalty for rebellion is death by hanging," she cried, twisting her hands.

"But that can't happen to me, I didn't kill anyone."

Leinani stepped away and stared hard into his eyes. "Shots were fired in the night. Don't you know that government soldiers were wounded, one man died, my father was injured, he may die as well? They'll blame you and all the rebels." She pressed her hands against her face. "My mind is whirling with fear. Promise me that you will give up this rebellion. Do this for me, please, please." John nearly fell when she threw herself against him, wrapping her arms around his body, pulling him into her.

Aunt Malia stood. "I think I go outside, leave you two alone."

John stroked Leinani's hair, seeking to calm the fear that convulsed her. She lifted her face, tears glistening in her eyes. "Promise me," she repeated.

Her anguish quenched the fires that had fueled his revenge. He kissed her eyes, wiping away the tears. "Our revolt was over before it ever started. But yes, I promise to give up my hatred, end my rebellion."

Leinani kissed John with fierce desperation. "Thank you. I could not bear to lose you again." She rested her beautiful face against his shoulder and he stroked her body, unable to do more. She played her lips around his neck, his ears, his cheeks, smothering him with her passion. John knew that the chasm had closed, that Leinani belonged to him. He led her into his bedroom, Leinani clinging to him. The room crackled, charged with electricity, with their heat. Despite war and uncertainty and John Tana on the brink of being hanged as a traitor, Leinani fulfilled her love for him and John surrendered to his dream.

They made love for hours. They took brief moments to cool their passion before coming together again and again in wild excitement, their continued ecstasy filling a long-suppressed hunger. When it was time for Leinani to leave, she promised to return in the morning. "I love you so much."

John watched his woman ride away, the dust kicked up by her frisky mare blowing into the sky and then drifting away. When he stepped back into the cottage, Aunt Malia was rocking in her chair and staring at him. She pursed her lips, her forehead wrinkling. "John, you thinking only of yourself. You make love today, but what goin' happen tomorrow? You bring Leinani down. When you show your face you will hang. Your grandchildren will not get education. Everybody will lose." John mulled over those words, harsh, yet honest. He knew from his own life that an education for his grandchildren would open a new world of opportunities for them. Educated, they could escape menial jobs and compete in this new world that had been forced upon the Hawaiians. The more he thought, the more certain he was. He asked Malia for pen and paper and began to write.

Kuu Ipo
I know that I have made mistakes, but those mistakes have saved you from a
lifetime of privation and hard living with a landless Hawaiian. Your prom-
ise to educate our family fills my heart with love for you. Were I to remain
near you, our love would destroy us. Were I to remain, I would be arrested,
tried for treason, and hanged. I cannot humiliate you or our family by being
hanged for treason. It is better to be remembered as a good man than a dis-
graced Hawaiian.
Alohamepumehanakuuipo,
John

John completed the letter and wrote another, this one to Nani. In it, he explained his decision to go away, told her of Leinani's promises, and outlined what he wanted for his family. By the time he finished, night had come. He shared a light supper with Malia and asked her to wake him early in the morning.

Before dawn, John arose from an untroubled sleep. It was still dark outside and only the light of a lone kerosene lantern illuminated the kitchen. Malia had prepared a breakfast for him and packed a bag. "This will help you, wherever you may be going," she told him, her smile loving and encouraging.

When they stood together at the front door, she refused to say goodbye. "Dem soldiers, they will arrest a lonely Hawaiian, but if you helping grandma, they no stop you."

They walked together on the roadway that led to Diamond Head. Malia used her cane, stumbling often on the uneven road, yet held steady by John's firm hand. Sunlight peeked over the Koolau Mountains, driving away the blue shadows hanging over Waikiki and Mount Leahi.

John broke the silence between them, "Auntie, conniving sugar people have made your prediction come true, 'Hawaiian man got nothing'."

Malia paused and pointed her cane at Diamond Head. "I know you not happy with this new world that come Hawaii. But over there is old temple, Pua-ene-ene. People sacrificed there when I was a child. People sacrificed in temples all over the islands. Chiefs no care how many die. Took the Christians to stop that stuff, to finally end kapu, get rid of the kahuna."

When John visibly tensed, her eyes misted over, and her voice softened with love. "I tell you when I young, everybody but royalty have hard times. Now I think all the bad stuff is in the past. Christianity, the plantations good for us. Make money, people who smart living better. No run away? Stay."

John kissed the woman's cheek. "I respect your wisdom, Auntie, but you know that I have no chance. Hawaiians are treated without dignity or respect because we're brown and uneducated." Before she could argue, he rushed ahead. "That's not the reason I must disappear. If I stayed, Leinani would suffer and I would be caught and hanged."

Malia began to protest, but John placed his fingers to her lips.

"I know we are in a new world, with a new culture in control of our islands. But the methods of suppression are the same as the old. Instead of the kahuna we have the Christian ministers who screech from their pulpits no-no's, threatening hell and damnation to those that do not obey their commands. Yes, we no longer have chiefs, but instead we have lawyers conniving with judges, demanding that the law must be obeyed using this power to rob the poor and suppress the working man."

Removing his fingers from her lips, Malia nodded her head in understanding. "Maybe you right. Maybe few like me lucky in this new world. While others, they suffer."

"Can't you see Auntie, there is nothing for me in this Christian, capitalistic, sugar plantation world except slavery and death? There is no joy in it. No happiness in being alive. I cannot live, bowing my head to my oppressors, living like a man in a coffin. No, I want to live life a free man, finding my own way to survive

in the adversity that nature throws at you. That I can understand. I can cope
with what comes from the earth, sea, and sky. Our ancestors did it. I will do it."

John reached down and gathered his aunt into his arms, holding her ancient
body against his chest. After several minutes, he stepped away and began to walk,
leaving her there, on the road, leaning on her cane and smiling with understanding. They waved to each other one last time and then John disappeared around
a bend in the road.

As he walked toward the base of Diamond Head, he thought of his grandchildren and how he had taught them to survive. *They knew how to find the fresh
water shellfish under the rocks, the shrimp and gobey in the streams; the fruit and
berries to eat. They knew how to build a home from bamboo and pili grass. He smiled
as he recalled how intently they watched as he wove a mat from the leaves of a hala
tree, laughed aloud at the memory of how they paraded about in their hats that he
had fashioned for them from coconut fronds. And he nearly wept when he recalled
their awe when he introduced them to his aumakua, the tiger shark, its fins swimming around his legs and driving fish into his net.*

John strode into a small compound of Hawaiian huts at the base of Diamond
Head, his double canoe at anchor, bobbing on the water like an eager puppy. His
friends helped him with preparations.

*Everything accomplished, he thought of his grandchildren, felt the touch of
Leinani. Who would teach the children the legends of Hawaiian gods and goddesses?
Who would describe the whistling that whirled around their shack as an uhane came,
after being summoned to protect them from evil?* "Nani will do this," he said aloud.
"And the schools, they will teach them, too."

Toward evening, John loaded the last of his goods into the double canoe.
When all was ready, he pushed it into the sea, jumped inside, and began to paddle.
He paused for a moment and turned back for one last look at this place he so loved.

Clouds drifted lazily across the darkening sky, the evening was windless.
The crab sail hung limp against the center pole. *Which way to go? To the right was
Kauai, straight ahead were the South Seas. To the left, I will find Maui.*

For a long moment, John Tana rested, unsure of his direction, and then he
began to paddle. His craft rode easily over the tossing jet-black water, and from

the depths a great fin rose to meet him. Its triangle of tough skin knifed through the water, its great grey body nudging against his craft and pushing him out to sea.

The wind freshened as his sail unfurled and the shark moved ahead, its fin and body producing a wake that was easy to follow. When John was well beyond the breakers, he let his canoe float on the water. *He removed JJ's belt and took Mahealani's locket from his pouch. Holding them in his hands, he pressed them against his heart and then kissed these precious objects, extended his hand, and let them slip through his fingers and into the sea.*

The winds blew strong and the clouds broke away to reveal the bright sparkles of the heavens. The northern star beamed on his right shoulder. John Tana picked up his paddle and followed in the wake of his ancestors.

EPILOGUE

President Grover Cleveland could not persuade Congress nor the new Republic of Hawaii to restore Queen Liliuokalani's authority over the Hawaiian Islands. Royalists made one last attempt to place her back on the Hawaiian throne in January of 1895. This rebellion ended in disaster. More than a hundred revolutionaries were captured by the Republic's militia and, along with Liliuokalani, imprisoned. All faced a sentence of death for treason.

Persuaded by the threat of hanging the revolutionaries, Liliuokalani abdicated the throne of Hawaii. A hundred-year old monarchy ended. Worse events for Hawaiians would soon occur.

The Republic of Hawaii continued to pursue annexation to the United States. Thirty-nine-thousand Hawaiians protested annexation and sought restoration of the monarchy. But the Spanish-American War, as well as the opportunity for trade with Asia, persuaded the United States Congress to annex Hawaii in 1898. Transferred to America by the Republic were nearly one-million-nine-hundred-thousand acres of former Hawaiian monarchy lands. Native people received nothing from annexation.

Western contact proved disastrous for Hawaiians. Hundreds of thousands died from diseases introduced to the islands. The overthrow of the monarchy and confiscation of monarchy lands by the United States eliminated any chance pure Hawaiians had to rehabilitate themselves from poverty. Liliuokalani said: "The people of the Islands are relegated to the condition of the aborigines of the American continent." Along with these losses came the further indignity of the suppression of the Hawaiian language and culture.

In centuries past, Polynesians, when faced with disasters or oppression, had ventured out into the Pacific to find new islands to occupy and renew a life of freedom. By the time Cook landed in Hawaii all the unknown parts of the world had been discovered. There were no unoccupied lands to escape to.

John Tana's story reflects the difficulty Hawaiians had in coping with a new world of profit seekers. The nineteenth century was marked by what Liliuokalani called: "The Right of Conquest, under which robbers and marauders may establish themselves in possession of whatsoever they are strong enough to ravish from their fellows." This contrasts with the communal sharing society that John grew up in.

Where could a man like John go in this new world of *laissez-faire?* He had tried to cope with it, but lost his land, wife, and son. Revolution did not provide an answer. In his decision to follow in the "wake of his ancestors" he sought a place that continued to retain the communal and sharing value system that he understood. It would be a place where he could live a life free from profiteers. Could he find it? His aumakua, the tiger shark, will direct him to it.

BIBLIOGRAPHY

There are numerous resources for learning more about the 19th Century in the islands, especially the overthrow of the monarchy and efforts to restore it. The resources below are excellent, especially the *Lost Kingdom* book which is heavily researched and footnoted. There are many more.

Leprosy and the Board of Health determination to imprison thousands of Hawaiians, many without a true diagnosis, on a remote part of a small island where they would be hidden from Western business interests is a horrifying story. The Frazier book translates from Hawaiian the story of Kalalau Valley and the artillery attack on innocent, sick people. A friend pointed out the scars on the Valley cliffs to me more than fifty years later.

By this selection of books, I do not intend to slight any others for their excellent work.

Allen, Helena G. *The Betrayal of Liliuokalani*. Honolulu, Hawaii: Mutual Publishing, 1982.

Siler, Julia Flynn. *Lost Kingdom, Hawaii's Last Queen, the Sugar Kings, and America's First Imperial Adventure*. New York, New York: Atlantic Monthly Publishing, 2012.

Frances N. Frazier, Translator. *The True Story of Kaluaikoolau, As Told by His Wife, Piilani*. Honolulu, Hawaii: Distributed by the University of Hawaii Press, 2001.

John Traynor. *The Colony, The Harrowing True Story of the Exiles of Molokai*. New York, New York: Scribner, 2006.

ABOUT THE AUTHOR

William J. Fernandez, Judge, ret.
Santa Clara County Court, San Jose, CA

Half-native Hawaiian, Bill Fernandez graduated from Kamehameha Schools, and Stanford University and Law School. He practiced law in Sunnyvale, CA, before his appointment to a judgeship in Santa Clara County, CA. When he retired, he and his wife returned to the Kauai home that his mother bought with her cannery earnings and began writing. Bill serves on a social service agency board, Hale Opio, was appointed by the governor to the Juvenile Justice State Advisory Commission, served as president of the Kauai Historical Society, and is on the board of the Native Hawaiian Chamber of Commerce.

www.ingramcontent.com/pod-product-compliance
Lightning Source LLC
Chambersburg PA
CBHW020600030726
47497CB00007B/2027